My Love Won't Last Forever: Chaotic Bliss

Jahzara

Special Thanks

Thank you to Tekesha Firefly Martinez for allowing Nyree Chandler to utilize your poem, "I Waited On You."

Thank you to Dawn Desiree Banks for lending your poems "Kyra Speaks" and "Love Gone Wrong" in the first printing of Chaotic Bliss.

Thank you, Lacha' Mitchell for allowing use of your poem, "A Fool For You".

Special thanks to my readers for all of your support over the years.

**Xoxo
Jahzara**

A Word From The Author

To anyone who is going through something … God is able. I thank God for the gift of writing. Writing has gotten me out of several predicaments in my life. I was able to write my way to a passing grade in Genetics when I was in undergrad.

In 2024, when I was diagnosed with Renal Cell Carcinoma and then discovered tumors in another area in my body it was not a fun time. God told me He was bigger than the problem. I prayed, fasted, read my Bible and God allowed me to reconnect with my first love… writing to get me through that time.

In 2024, I republished my first book, Contradictions as well as My Love Won't Last Forever: Matrimony. I worked hard on rewriting My Love Won't Last Forever: Chaotic Bliss as well. Writing provided me with comfort while I fought a horrible disease.

Today, I am cancer free.

"With men this is impossible; but with God all things are possible."
Matthew 19:26

Jahzara
iamnicolebradley.com
www.nicolebradleycandles.com

Chaos
by Nyree Shaw-Chandler

This one individual
Is something like a smooth criminal
He stole my heart
From the start

I gave him my all and all
I'd check my caller ID a million times
To see if he had called

He pretended to be tough
Gave him my all but it was never enough…
Loved him more than life
Loved to hear him call me "wife"
Never wanted the drama
Didn't sign up for mess with a baby momma

We're like fire and ice
When he pisses me off it ain't nothing nice
Wish there were a drug
To flush him out my system
It doesn't exist
Chaos is bliss
Love him. Love him not. Love him. Love him not

Aris

Aris Smith's heart pounded so hard she thought it might explode right out her chest. Three days without food would do that to you, but the betrayal—that's what really had her body fucked up.

"Tyler, don't play me like I'm stupid!" Aris yelled into the phone, gripping the receiver so tight her knuckles bulged. Her breath came in ragged gasps as she tried to steady herself, but the pain in her chest refused to let up.The panoramic view of Lake Michigan from her office suite—normally her daily reminder of how far she'd come from Gary's concrete jungle—now just blurred into a haze.

Her voice echoed off the glass walls of her lakefront office. The framed diploma from Indiana University's Kelley School of Business seemed to mock her now. All that business acumen, yet here she was, being played by this low budget novice. This was the same no-having-game dude that used to pass her notes in Mrs. Jefferson's eighth grade science class.

She hadn't eaten in three days. Couldn't. Her stomach was a war zone, and her bathroom trips were endless. How was that even possible when she hadn't consumed a damn thing? Well, that wasn't exactly true. She stayed hydrated by guzzling Hennesy and lemon water.Her body was running on empty, but her mind was on overdrive. This was it. The end. She could feel it, like a dark cloud suffocating her.

The curse of abandonment that had followed Aris since birth felt like a physical presence in the room. Her father choosing a football scholarship over fatherhood. Her mother vanishing before Aris could even form memories of her face. And now Tyler—the one she'd believed would break the pattern.

Her whole life, all she wanted was love. Real, unconditional love. Sure, Aunt Trina held it down, but that nagging question always lingered: *What was so wrong with me? Why did everyone leave?*

Every relationship ended the same way: lies, cheating, betrayal. At age twenty-one, Sean had been the exception—or so she thought. He was supposed to be her happily ever after, the love of her life. That illusion crumbled, too, and when it did, Tyler swooped in, piecing her back together. He was always there, her rock, her safe space. But deep down, she couldn't shake the feeling that his exit was just a matter of time. Everyone left eventually. Why would he be any different?

"Why are you doing this, Tyler?" Aris snapped, her voice breaking. Her mind was racing. Did she have "FOOL" tatted on her forehead? If anyone should've known she wasn't the one to play with, it was him. Years of friendship, of him being her constant, and now this?

"You were supposed to be different," Aris whispered, her entrepreneur's composure cracking. "You watched Sean destroy me piece by piece, held me while I cried, then turned around and did the same damn thing."

Tyler's voice droned through the receiver—excuses about

"hanging with the fellas" and "losing track of time." Standard playbook. Aris knew it all too well.

"Nah, save that weak shit," Aris cut him off mid-excuse. "I got the whole rundown from Keisha. You wasn't losing track of time with no 'fellas.' You was at my own damn club, making it rain on Cinnamon like you ain't the one signing her checks!"

Half Past Eight—her other baby. The upscale gentlemen's club on Broadway that had the ballers from Chicago driving down Interstate 90 just to spend their paychecks. The spot that had put her on the map as more than just another pretty face with ambition. The same club she had trusted Tyler to manage while she built up Tranquil Moments.

She stared at the photograph on her desk—Jamaica, last summer. Now she saw what she'd been blind to then: Tyler's eyes, distant, focused somewhere beyond the camera. Beyond her. *Why is this my first time seeing this? I guess you see some things, and you don't see others. His body was there, but his mind was somewhere else,* Aris reflected to herself. "It ain't even about you being at the club," she said, sliding down in her leather chair. "It's about respect. I built this shit from nothing, T. Remember when US Steel laid off half of Gary. Indiana, and everybody said I was crazy for taking my severance check and investing in a day spa? When they said black folks in Gary wasn't spending money on cucumber facials and hot stone massages?"

She allowed herself to slouch down in her oversized leather chair as she viewed the lakefront from her office and clutched the picture to her heart. This property—her crown jewel. Six figures of her own money plus the loan she'd secured by herself. The ultimate security that no man could take away.

No, boo, it's not like that," Tyler's voice droned through the receiver. "You're going too far with this paranoid—"

Aris hurled the crystal paperweight across the room, watching it shatter against the wall like her trust. Maybe taking herself off the Prozac had been a mistake. Dr. Williams had warned her about stopping cold turkey, but Aris hated how the pills dulled her edge. And in '98 Gary, a black woman entrepreneur couldn't afford to lose her edge.

Tyler kept insisting that she had a crazy alter ego. "Aris and Eris," he called it—playing on her name like she was two different women. The calm, collected businesswoman and the raging fury who could cut a man with just her words.

"I'm going to have to let you go," she partially whispered, suddenly aware of someone clearing their throat at her door.

She spun around in her chair and found herself facing the most gorgeous man she'd laid eyes on since D'Angelo's "Brown Sugar" video. He had to be six-foot-three, two hundred pounds with about seventeen percent body fat, skin like burnished copper and a clean-shaven head that gleamed under the recessed lighting.

When she placed the phone onto the receiver, he smiled—a confident, knowing smile that revealed perfect teeth and deep dimples.

"Yeah, you need to let that go," the stranger said, running his cupped hand over his goatee. "Anything that has a queen like yourself screaming like that can't be good for your blood pressure.

Standing up behind the handmade oak desk that had been given to her as a gift from one of her clients, she looked at the man in his soft brown eyes and commented, "I don't take advice from strangers," she said in her harshest tone—the one that made the girls at Half Past Eight straighten up quick. "Who are you and how did you get past Erin?"

He opened his mouth to speak, and she dismissed him with the flicker of her wrist and pressed a button on her phone and called her assistant.

"Erin. Erin?" After moments with no response from Erin, she asked, "What do I pay her for?"

Solomon smiled again and said, "I had a one fifteen appointment with you. I'm Solomon James."

"I see. Unless my time piece is wrong," she said as she looked at her TAGHeur, "and I doubt that it is, you're fifteen minutes late."

He was not wearing a watch. Her Aunt Trina told her that a man who does not wear a watch cannot be trusted. That man has no sense of time and will do nothing but waste time and your time as well.

Aris frowned on gross tardiness. Most times, she was running five minutes late, but fifteen minutes late said to her that this person did not care about her, her time and what she had to do. One of Aris'pet peeves was waiting. She hated to wait for anyone or anything.

"Yeah, I know. I called, but did not get an answer."

She knew he was lying, but there was something magnetic about this Solomon that had her curious. She wondered if he had been named after King Solomon from the Bible. In all her twenty-eight years hustling in Gary, she had never met anyone named Solomon.

"Well, Solomon, I'm going to be up front with you. I don't have time for bullshit," she said, leaning forward on her desk. The scent of her Thierry Mugler perfume—another luxury she'd denied herself until success came—filled the space between them. "I'm looking for a business manager to help me out. Someone with strong management skills, organizational ability, and references that ain't their cousin or their baby mama. You got that?"

"Yes." He quickly responded.

"What you may not know is that I also own Half Past Eight, an upscale gentlemen's club over on Broadway. My business manager would handle affairs there too," she said, gauging his reaction. "Most men I interview start drooling at this point, thinking they'll be 'auditioning' the talent."

Aris looked him up and down, from his clean bald head to his polished shoes. They were Kenneth Cole—not top shelf, but not Payless either. A man who cared about appearances but wasn't flashy. *Interesting.*

"I bet you're like all the other men I've dealt with in this life," she continued, circling around her desk like a shark. "Put 'em in a strip club, and they lose their damn mind. It's crazy—I lost Sean because of a stripper, now Tyler. What makes you different?"

Solomon blinked three times in quick succession—a tell that she filed away for future reference. He was caught off guard, but recovered quickly.

"Mrs. Smith, I believe I can manage all your establishments with minimal... distractions," he said, voice steady despite the flicker of heat in his gaze. "Once hired, I'd like to review your financial statements and see where we can maximize profit. In this economy, with Gary struggling, you need someone who understands both the business and the streets."

"It's Ms. Smith," she emphasized, though he'd gotten it right. A test that he'd passed. "I like you already. However, my next step would be to present your qualifications to my board of directors. If they're impressed, we'll schedule a second interview."

He smiled again—that dangerous smile that reminded her of why she was taking a break from men. "I'm sure you'll like what you see... and what you've already seen."

Aris extended her hand to conclude their meeting, noticing how his large palm engulfed hers. *Warm. Solid. Dangerous.*

As she watched him walk out, she wondered if Solomon James might be the business solution she needed... or just another heartbreak waiting to happen. Gary, Indiana, had taught her one thing above all—trust was a luxury most couldn't afford, especially a black woman building an empire on the ashes of what US Steel had left behind.

"Erin!" she called to her assistant once Solomon was out of earshot. "Get me everything you can find on Solomon James. And call Darnell—tell him I want new locks on all the doors at Half Past Eight. Tyler's officially done."

She'd learned the hard way that in business and in love, sometimes you had to cut your losses before they bled you dry.

Solomon

Standing in the parking lot of Tranquil Moments Day Spa, Solomon "Money Man" James glared at his silver '86 Oldsmobile Ninety-Eight—his "Nine-Eight"—as if it had personally betrayed him. The hollow click when he turned the key had him seeing red. He slammed his palm against the hood, the metallic thud echoing across the lot.

"Mothaf—" he caught himself, swallowing the curse as frustration burned through him.

This was not how a man with his reputation should be looking. Back before everything went down, Solomon had been known throughout Gary as "The Money Man"—the brother with the golden touch when it came to business. That MBA from Howard wasn't just hanging on his mama's wall for decoration. Before Kyra's death, Solomon could walk into any boardroom in the Midwest and have executives hanging on his every word about investment strategies and market forecasts. Now look at him—struggling with a busted ride in some spa parking lot.

This heap had picked the worst possible moment to give up. After bombing that interview, his pride couldn't take walking back inside to beg for help. That woman, Aris, would probably curl those full lips into a smirk and dismiss him with an icy "Not my problem." The memory of how she'd barely paid attention during their conversation still stung. Every few minutes, a disinterested "Sure" while those cold eyes drifted elsewhere.

Solomon had caught the drama before they even sat down—Aris screaming into her phone at some unfortunate dude, her voice sharp enough to cut glass. When she'd hurled that paperweight across her office, Solomon had flinched, grateful the leather chair had intercepted what could've been aimed at his skull. Back in his prime, Solomon would've smoothly turned the situation, used his charm to get her focused on the interview. But that Solomon had died alongside Kyra on that July night in '97.

He checked his phone—no service. Typical Miller neighborhood bullshit. This section of Gary had always been like that—beautiful lake views, sand dunes, and money flowing through the streets, but you couldn't make a damn call to save your life.

"PIECE OF GARBAGE!" Solomon pounded the hood again, his knuckles aching. "Good for nothing son-of-a—"

"Watch yourself, Mr. James. My ears are delicate. Besides, that won't fix what's broken."

Solomon turned to find Aris approaching, her entire vibe transformed. Gone was the professional blouse and tight skirt from earlier. Now she rocked a pink and white tennis outfit that hugged curves he hadn't fully appreciated during the interview. Her shoulder-length hair was pulled back in a sleek ponytail, making her look even younger than he'd first thought—maybe twenty-six at most.

A flash of jealousy hit him as he calculated all she'd accomplished while still so young. His mother's voice echoed in his head: "Despise not a person's youth. To whom much is given, much is required."

What was required of him? Nearly thirty—the big 3-0 just a month away—and what did he have to show for it? An MBA that had once made him the talk of the financial district. That same degree that his high school economics teacher, Mr. Francis, never thought he'd earn. Dude had predicted Solomon would either be dead by twenty-five or unemployed and crashing with one of his baby mamas.

Francis had been halfway right. At twenty-nine and a half, Solomon was back living with his mother and his youngest, Madison. Five kids, four different women. His oldest, Solomon II, was twelve now; Nina and Simone, both ten; Malik, five; and his princess, Madison—"Madison Square Garden"—just turned two.

The irony wasn't lost on him. Once upon a time, bankers and investors had called him "The Money Man," fighting to get his financial wisdom. Back in '96, he'd turned a failing community credit union around in just six months, made it profitable enough to start issuing small business loans to folks in the neighborhood who'd been denied everywhere else. The Post Tribune had even run a profile: "Solomon James: The Financial Prophet of Gary." That man seemed like a distant memory now.

Every time he looked at Madison, he saw Kyra's face—the woman who should have been his wife, whose blood had stained their satin sheets that Fourth of July night in '97. Things had been good between them—he'd even put a ring on it, ready to make it official. No more shacking up. But Mona Lee, mother to Simone and Nina, couldn't stand that he was finally settling down with someone else. And honestly, she had every right to be bitter. Whenever Solomon found himself between relationships, he always seemed to find his way back to Mona's bed.

Solomon had cheated on Kyra once during their three-year relationship—just once, but it was enough to crack the foundation of trust they shared. During one of their brief breakups, he'd stumbled into Mona's bed, drunk off caramel apple martinis and regret. That night, he'd whispered all the right words into Mona's ear, promises he didn't even remember making.

"I'm going to marry you one day," he'd said, his lips brushing her neck. "You'll always have a place in my heart."

Mona had clung to those words like a lifeline, replaying them in her mind long after the sun rose and Solomon sobered up. When he laughed it off as drunken nonsense, Mona didn't laugh with him. Instead, she became a problem—a shadow. She'd show up uninvited, call his phone at all hours, and leave cryptic messages that made Kyra raise an eyebrow. Solomon had managed to keep her in the background, but Mona was like smoke—lingering and impossible to pin down.

The Fourth of July Ball at Marquette Park should've been a perfect night. Kyra looked radiant, her golden dress hugging her curves, her laugh lighting up the darkened beach as fireworks lit the sky. But Solomon couldn't shake the feeling that someone was watching them. His eyes darted across the crowd, but he saw no one.

"Stop being paranoid," Kyra teased, sipping her third glass of champagne. "Let's just enjoy tonight."

Solomon was not ready to leave the festivities. "You go ahead then," he told her. "I'm just going to stay a little longer."

Kyra pouted. She leaned in close, her lips brushing his ear. "Don't take too long. I'll be waiting for you... in bed."

Solomon stayed another hour, caught up in conversations and drinks with potential investors who wanted "The Money Man's" advice. By the time he returned to their beachfront condo, something felt off. The door was unlocked—a habit of Kyra's that always drove him crazy.

"Damn it, Kyra," he muttered under his breath, locking the door behind him.

As he stepped inside, a sweet, familiar fragrance filled his nostrils. It wasn't Kyra's perfume. No, this scent was bolder, headier—a fragrance he hadn't smelled in months. It clawed at his memory, sending a chill down his spine.

His mind flickered to Kyra's earlier words. "I'll be waiting in bed."

Excitement replaced unease. Stripping off his clothes as he tiptoed down the hallway, Solomon was ready to surprise her. But when he reached the bedroom door, he hesitated. It was closed.

Odd.

He pushed the door open, and his world shattered.

Kyra lay sprawled across their bed, still dressed in the shimmering gown she wore to the ball. Blood seeped into the satin sheets, pooling around her head. Her lifeless eyes stared into nothingness, and the gunshot wound at her temple told him everything he didn't want to know.

"Kyra!" he screamed, his voice raw and cracking.

His knees buckled as he staggered toward the bed. His hand trembled as he reached out to touch her face, her skin already growing cold beneath his fingers.

The perfume hit him again, sharp and unrelenting. His blood ran cold.

That scent... Mona.

The realization slammed into him like a freight train. His stomach churned as the weight of his mistakes bore down on him.

Who else would dare?

The game had changed, and Solomon was no longer a player—he was a pawn in a deadly game of revenge.

The only solace was that his daughter, Madison Square Garden, hadn't been present. He had never been able to forgive himself for Kyra's death; if he had not given in to his lustful desires, the true love of his life would still be alive.

After Kyra died, he sold the condominium they had shared and moved in with his mother. She looked after him and Madison while he fell apart. Solomon was not ashamed to admit it—after the death of Kyra, he suffered from depression and lost not just his job but his reputation as "The Money Man." Firms that once would have paid six figures for an hour of his financial wisdom now wouldn't even return his calls. His former clients whispered about how the murder scandal had tainted his name, wondering if he'd been involved. Word on the street was that Solomon James had set the whole thing up—hired Mona to take out Kyra for the insurance money. It wasn't true, but in the business world, perception was reality.

Kyra had even haunted him for a while. When he would try to lie down to get some sleep, it was the worst. He would hear Kyra's voice repeating what seemed like poetry over and over again, her accusatory words cutting deeper than any knife.

After nearly a year of being unproductive, his mother, Selena James, had insisted that Solomon get up and get back into the workforce to take care of his financial responsibilities. She'd reminded him that "The Money Man" needed to reclaim his throne.

Mayor Damien Carrington's call was right on time. The mayor had even tossed him a measly stack of crumpled bills – pocket change compared to what Solomon used to make in a day – with a tight-lipped warning to "take care of his shorties" and, more importantly, "keep that girl quiet." That girl was Shauna, mother of his son, Malik, and, Solomon couldn't forget, also mother to Damien's daughter, Taylor – a messy complication they all tried to ignore. Under normal circumstances, this whole situation would have twisted Solomon's gut into knots, violating every code he lived by. But his back was against the wall. He mumbled a silent prayer, a desperate plea for forgiveness, hoping Shauna would remain quiet about what she knew.

****

"Would you pop your hood for me? Hand me that stick right there," Aris pointed. When Solomon looked at her as if her tone were too harsh, Aris softened and continued, "Would you?" Once he handed her the stick off the ground, she used it to trigger something in the carburetor. Smiling because she seemed certain this maneuver would work, she lifted her head up and focused on Solomon. "Okay, now start the car."

He did as she instructed but doubted that the car would start. The Nine-Eight had been as reliable as his love life lately—unpredictable and prone to leaving him stranded.

When he heard the engine roar, he ran to her side and inquired, "What did you do?"

She smiled and nudged him gently in the ribs. "If I tell you, I'll have to kill you."

Solomon did not return the smile. After seeing his dead fiancée, who had been shot down in cold blood less than a year ago, he did not find statements like that funny. Mona used to joke with him that if she couldn't have him, then no one would. Now Mona Lee was sitting in a cell at Indiana Women's Prison, awaiting trial for first-degree murder, and those words didn't seem like jokes anymore.

Noticing the glare in Solomon's eyes, Aris offered an apology.

"I'm sorry, I was just joking. Have a good day," Aris said as she walked over to her Mercedes, which was parked in the next space. She muttered to herself, "He didn't even say thank you. Where is the gratitude?"

Solomon felt bad, as he could sense that he had angered Aris, and he needed this job. The Money Man needed to make a comeback, and this spa gig could be the first step. So, he walked up to her door and held it open as she put her key in the ignition.

"Thank you for getting my car started. I accept your apology. I know you were just joking. At least, I hope you were joking. Jokes like that are a sensitive issue for me. Last year, my fiancée was killed in cold blood. I was the one who found her." He shook his head, feeling his eyes start to mist up.

Quickly, he turned away and walked to his car, which was still running. *Breathe,* he found himself thinking. *BREATHE.*

This was no time to have an anxiety attack. Dr. Gia Black, his therapist, had told him moments like this would occur, and he should breathe and try to think calming thoughts.

He had found singing the lyrics to the opening theme song, 'Won't You Be My Neighbor,' from the Mister Rogers' Neighborhood television show calmed him down. Solomon had not had much interaction with the outside world since the death of Kyra, so reading social cues and gestures were problematic for him at times.

Feeling like the world's biggest jerk, Aris hopped out of the driver's seat and scurried over to Solomon before he could close the door. Now she remembered where she knew the name Solomon James. The Midwest Vein had covered that story for about two weeks. In fact, some of the ladies at the beauty salon her aunt owned, Intricate Style, thought that Solomon had something to do with the murder.

Aris spoke, "Mr. James, I am so sorry. I had no idea. Your name sounded familiar to me, but I didn't make the connection until you mentioned your fiancée. Wait—you're Solomon James? The Solomon James? The Money Man?"

Solomon winced at the nickname. Once it had been a badge of honor; now it felt like a cruel joke.

"That was another lifetime ago," he said quietly.

"I'm so sorry. Here I go again rambling on. I do that sometimes, please forgive me."

"No. No, it is not your fault. I don't know why I am even telling you all this. Look, I am interested in the position; please consider me for the job. I know I probably got off to a bad start. First, I was late, then you had to get my car started. I tell you about my relationship drama... Please, don't hold this against me. I'm just a man trying to do the right thing and provide for my family. I have great references. You'll see Mayor Carrington is one of them."

"That's it. Yeah, yeah, yeah," she snapped her finger. Proud that she was connecting the dots, she continued, "I know your name. Yes, Damien said he thought you would be a perfect fit for Tranquil Moments when I met with him the other day regarding a business venture. He mentioned you handled his investment portfolio before... everything happened. Said you made him more money in six months than his previous financial advisor did in three years. It's just been so much on my mind lately... Mr. James, maybe you could meet me for lunch tomorrow here in the café, and we can discuss business."

A spark of the old Solomon—The Money Man—flickered in his eyes. One year after losing everything, maybe this was his chance to rebuild.

"Sure. I hope my car will start."

"Don't worry about it. I can give you a call around ten o'clock in the morning and have a car sent over for you, say around eleven. If you are available," Aris said.

"That would be great. I better get going while the car is still running," Solomon said as he eased into the driver's seat.

His breathing was returning to normal. Maybe, just maybe,

The Money Man was about to make his comeback. He'd spent a year mourning what he'd lost—Kyra, his reputation, his career. Perhaps '98 would be the year he took it all back. First step: this job at Tranquil Moments. From there? The sky was the limit.

But first, he had to make it home without the Nine-Eight breaking down again.

Shauna

"If y'all kids don't sit y'all bad little asses down, y'all better. See, y'all think somebody playing with y'all. Y'all think fat meat ain't greasy, but I'm the one to show you," Shauna Buchanan yelled at her children, Malik and Taylor.

Nobody looking at this scene would believe this woman graduated top of her class at Valpo Law. That expensive-ass degree from Valparaiso University—the one she'd sacrificed sleep, sanity, and social life for—was now collecting dust under a mountain of junk in the guest room closet. In '98, that paper meant something, but right now, in this moment, them law books and legal theories couldn't help her handle these kids or this life.

Shauna wished like hell Malik had been feeling well enough for school today. The five-year-old was walking around looking pitiful, fever making his brown skin flush, thick green mucus running from his nose that he kept sniffing back up with a disgusting slurp. He'd come home from kindergarten yesterday warm to the touch, but Shauna hadn't paid it much mind—hadn't even bothered taking his temperature.

Truth was, she couldn't find the damn thermometer if her life depended on it. Last time she'd laid eyes on it, Taylor had been playing with it like a toy, and Shauna had been too blunted out on some potent chronic to give a damn. Better to let the baby have the thermometer than listen to her scream and kill that sweet high she'd been nursing.

Now her two-year-old daughter was stumbling around the apartment in nothing but a yellowed onesie and a diaper so saturated it hung like a water balloon between her legs, ready to drop any second from the weight. Shauna paced the carpet, each step grinding down her patience even further.

Damn, if it weren't for bad luck, I wouldn't have ANY, she thought as she pulled her hair. *Baby need diapers, Nipsco— light and gas bill is due. Cell phone bill is past due too; it's 'bout to be disconnected. I'm so sick of seeing that warning message on my screen. I could use a dime bag of that green, sticky, stuff and a grape blunt. God, if one more thing happens, I tell you, I don't know what I'm going to do.* She glanced at the clock: twelve noon already, and she hadn't even hit a blunt yet. By this time most days, she'd have at least found a roach to take the edge off.

Where the FUCK is Damien Carrington? she fumed, checking her pager again. She'd been blowing up his pager all damn morning with no response. Probably laid up at home playing family man with his wife. That thought made her blood pressure spike.

He craziery than a Betsy bug if he think I'm gonna be over here raising HIS daughter with no help. I don't care if he is married—shit, he knew damn well he was married when we was laying up making Taylor. I just didn't know it.

Shauna's daddy's insurance money had felt like a fortune when it hit her account after the funeral. Now it was trickling away faster than water down a drain. She hadn't even taken the Indiana BAR yet—another expense she couldn't swing right now. Each month that passed, that law degree became more like a cruel joke.

If he don't call me back by three o'clock, heads WILL roll, she promised herself, glaring at the silent pager, *and that's on EVERYTHING I love.*

Shauna ran her fingers through her brown curly hair. The tip of one of her acrylic nails got caught in a tough section of her hair. All she needed to do was wash, condition, and apply some styling gel to her hair, and her natural curly locks would reappear.

"When is the last time I washed my hair? It feels so dry and brittle," she spoke aloud.

She watched Malik wipe his nose with the back of his arm, as he stuck his head in the refrigerator.He just stood there and gazed.

"Malik, if you don't get your tail out my 'frigerator, you betta. Tired of yo' butt opening and closing that 'frigerator. You ain't put nothing in it, so stay out of it and go wash your hands and arms.Don't tough that 'frigerator again!" Shauna yelled at her son.

He looked up at her with his big, brown, saucer eyes and whined, "I'm hungry. I didn't eat breakfast or nothing."

Shauna looked down at her butter complexion feet, which looked white in some places. She was ashy.When was the last time that she had applied lotion to any part of her body, she began to wonder?*How about when was the last time I took a shower?* She questioned herself. Most days she was good about maintaining her personal care. However, on a day like today, when nothing seemed to be going her, way she became lax.

As she looked at her son's hand gripping the handle of the refrigerator door, she realized that she too was hungry, but there wasn't anything in the house that she wanted to eat.

Solomon was going to have to do better with Malik's child support; he had not given her anything for over three months now. His excuse was always that he was in between jobs. She knew that Kyra's senseless killing had been devastating to him. But why she should have to suffer was beyond her comprehension. Did anyone care when her daddy died five years ago due to a stroke? He was only fifty-three years old, but did anyone care? Did life stop for that? The answer was no. Bills still came in the mail, creditors continued to look for their payments, and Malik still cried. Shauna had come to learn life just continues to go on, despite your trials and tribulations.

And if anyone were to ask her philosophy on life, she would simply sum it up by saying, "If it ain't one thing then it ain't a thing at all."

Typically, one tragedy happened and then another happened; however, most often, for her, tragedy ended and then two more would occur simultaneously.

This is why she often commented, "Life sucks."

She shuffled over to the freezer and felt her extra weight jiggle as she pulled a frozen pizza out of mounds of packages that were covered with ice chips.

"One day I am going to clean this thing out," she mumbled, as she pulled the pizza pan from under the sink and tossed the pizza onto it.

Taylor stood at Shauna's side as she watched her mother place the pizza into the oven.

"I guess you hungry, too," Shauna said, after pushing the oven door closed.

With a quick sweep, she scooped the child up, placed the child on her hip and sashayed down the hall to Taylor's bedroom to change the toddler.

"Ooh, girl, you stank," she said, as she stared down at a pile of green fecal matter in the diaper. Holding her breath as she changed the diaper and wiped her child clean, Shauna reached for her last diaper. Now what was she going to do?

"Okay, you'se clean…now scoot girl," Shauna told the toddler.

Every time Shauna glanced at Malik and little Taylor, a fresh wave of shame washed over her, thick and suffocating. She was tired of this solo mission, this constant hustle with no backup.

Damn, she wished she could rewind time and snatch back every penny she'd pissed away from her daddy's will. Three years. Four hundred stacks. Practically gone, poof. All she had to show for it was this slightly run-down hundred-thousand-dollar house, the Beemer that was probably about to get repo'd, a closet full of designer clothes she couldn't even squeeze a toe into anymore, and a monkey on her back that wouldn't quit. She'd at least had the sense to throw fifty grand into each of the kids' college funds, a small flicker of responsibility in the raging dumpster fire of her life. But then there was Damien. Seventy-five thousand dollars – a straight-up donation, let's be real – to his mayoral campaign, money he'd promised to pay back, a promise as empty as her bank account now. She remembered how it all had gone when he asked for the money.

****

The sheets were still damp with sweat, tangled around their bodies like evidence of what just went down. Shauna's beach house—bought with daddy's money before the cash started running low—was quiet except for their breathing and the distant rhythm of Lake Michigan waves outside the window."Hey, Baby," Damien said, as he drew Shauna closer to him. "I was thinking…" he trailed as he ran his fingers through her tresses.

"Here we go. Damien, why do you have to always do that?" Shauna pulled away as she stared into his emotionaless brown eyes. This man was so handsome. His smooth brown sugar skin and soft full lips were her weakness.

"Do what, Shauna?" The sigh he let out, let her know that he was irritated.

"After we get through making love, now you want to ask me for something?" She wrapped the sheet tighter around her breasts, already building her defenses.

"What makes you think I'm going to ask you for something?"Damien's tongue slowly traced his bottom lip—a calculated move he knew drove her wild.

" How do you know that I wasn't going to say I want to take you on a get-a-way this weekend?" Damien licked his lips, a gesture that he knew would weaken Shauna.

Hope flickered across Shauna's face before suspicion crushed it. "So, where are we going? You know I have to find a sitter… It's

Thursday, why are you just saying something now..."

"Shauna, I was asking a hypothetical question. I didn't say we were going anywhere. Besides, you know I can't go anywhere now with the election, and Beverly is sick again. She had to take another chemo treatment yesterday. I can't go anywhere..."

The mention of his wife irritated her soul. "It's always something or somebody else before me. Damien, I'm sick of this. You said we were going to be a family, and you were going to leave Beverly."

"Shauna, we will be a family, but I can't just up and leave her now. I'm in the middle of an election, and the woman is dying. You want me to leave her on her dying bed."

Shauna wasn't certain about what she wanted.Shauna wasn't trying to play games. What she *was* sure of was that she wasn't about to let some dude play *her*. Damien was giving her major mixed signals, and she wasn't having it. The fact that they had a whole one-year-old between them – a screaming, diaper-wearing reality check – just cranked up her anxiety.

Yanking the comforter up to her neck, the cheap sheets clinging to her skin, she turned away from Damien's wandering hands. "Just spit it out, D. What you came here to say."

He smiled because he was finally going to get to the point of their rendezvous. Damien had concocted a story to get out of the house and was sure his Nokia, was probably vibrating on the expensive leather seats of his Lexus that was parked in Shauna's garage.

"So, like I was saying. I was thinking that you could be my campaign manager and oversee..."

"What happened to Brad? I thought he was your campaign manager," Shauna questioned.

"He was, but he doesn't really have the ability to do the job. His heart is in the right place, but he just doesn't have the skills that you do. I mean, you know how to get results. You were the driving force behind getting your father elected as a judge. And I need someone to help manage the funds, too. I think Brad has been stealing, but I'm not sure."

Shauna's law school brain kicked in. "What do you mean stealing? I doubt that your brother, upstanding, Officer Friendly, would steal from you."

"You don't know Brad like I do. He's my brother and all, but there has always been sibling rivalry. I just thought that he would be happy for me and want to see me accomplish this, but he's been trying to sabotage my campaign. I need you. This will open up the door for me. Taylor will be set for life, you and Malik, too."

Shauna beamed. *Damien still wants us to be a family. He's trying to make a good life for us.*

"Okay, I'll do it. So, how much do you have in your campaign fund?"

"I have about ten grand, but I know I need at least one-hundred grand just to continue. Shauna, I don't know where I am going to get that kind of money," he started. "Maybe, I should just give up on my dream. What was I thinking, undertaking such a task as this? I just need to focus on my law career," Damien stammered.

She took the bait. "I'll give you, no, loan you, seventy-five thousand dollars, so all you need to do is come up with fifteen thousand. You should know some generous people who can help you with that."

Damien's face lit up like Christmas. He showered her with kisses—face, neck, breasts—his gratitude as passionate as his lovemaking had been minutes earlier. "Thank you, baby. Thank you."

Her man was happy, and so was she. But somewhere in the back of her mind, a small voice wondered if she'd just been played… again.

****

The sharp crash of glass shattering against the floor jolted Shauna back to reality. She stared at the mess, her heart pounding. Damien hadn't repaid a single dime, and the ugly truth was glaring—she was dead broke.

"What am I going to do?" she muttered to the empty room, her eyes wandering to the Massage Therapy Certification hanging crookedly on the wall. It mocked her, a dusty reminder of another dream she'd let slip through her fingers.

I could open my own spa, she thought, her mind flickering to a vision of scented candles, plush robes, and steady clients. The idea had once been her lifeline. Now, it felt as out of reach as the stars. Sighing, she swept up the shards of her favorite glass, the sting of reality biting harder with each crunch under the broom.

Later, she collapsed onto the couch with a sad excuse for dinner—a $3 frozen pizza from the Key Market down in Miller. As she bit into the greasy slice, tomato sauce dribbled down her chin. She sucked it up, trying to salvage what little dignity she had left, but it was no use.

Her belly brushed against her thighs as she leaned forward, and tears stung her eyes. "I'm a fat, hot mess," she muttered, barely above a whisper. "Two hundred and twenty pounds of failure. When am I gonna lose this damn baby weight?"

As if on cue, a voice cut through her self-pity, sharp and clear: "When you get yourself together and stop this pity party."

Shauna froze mid-bite. Her eyes flicked to the bulky, wood-paneled entertainment center housing a large tube TV, the screen dark against the backdrop of the choppy blue water visible through the sliding glass doors. The spacious living room, with its slightly dated but expensive furnishings, was eerily silent save for the low hum of the central air. A shiver traced her spine as she subtly scanned the room – the plush, floral-patterned sofa set, the heavy glass coffee table holding a stack of home decor magazines, the framed watercolor landscape of the dunes hanging above the faux fireplace. The kids were finally out cold on the oversized, cushioned wicker chairs, their half-eaten plates of pizza rolls and apple slices resting on the matching wicker side table where they'd crashed after getting on her nerves all day..

"What the hell..." she whispered, her voice trembling.

She shook her head, trying to brush it off. "Man, I'm tripping. I must be having some kind of withdrawal or something. Maybe the weed man laced my stash. Yeah, that's it. Ain't no way I'm still tripping the *day after.* Damn, I gotta leave that stuff alone."

But before she could convince herself, the voice came again, calm yet commanding: "The day that you hear the voice of the

Lord, harden not your heart."

Shauna's breath hitched as the plate slipped from her hands and hit the carpet with a dull thud. Her chest tightened as she whipped her head around, her eyes scanning every shadow in the room.

"What?" she croaked, her voice barely audible.

The voice didn't waver. It came again, louder this time, cutting through the room like a knife: "The day that you hear the voice of the Lord, harden not your heart."

Panic overtook her. She bolted from the couch, her bare feet skidding across the floor as she ran to her bedroom. Throwing herself onto the bed, she yanked the covers over her head like a child hiding from a nightmare.

"This is crazy. I need some damn sleep," she mumbled, her voice muffled by the blanket. Her thoughts raced, each one more frantic than the last. "Does God even talk to sinners like me?"

The question hung heavy in the air as Shauna's eyes fluttered shut. Sleep claimed her, but her heart remained restless, the voice echoing in the depths of her mind.

Nyree

Margo Shaw stood in the doorway, her presence commanding the small hospital room like a queen surveying her court. Draped in a tailored Chanel blazer, its classic tweed shimmering subtly under the fluorescent lights, she paired it with a cream silk Hermès scarf tied delicately around her neck. Her sleek Valentino heels clicked against the tiled floor as she adjusted the strap of her quilted Saint Laurent bag resting elegantly on her shoulder.

"Well, dear, I'm going to be heading out now," she announced, her tone clipped but laced with just enough motherly concern to soften the edges. Her perfectly manicured hand gestured vaguely toward Nyree, who sat slumped in the chair by the hospital bed, her shoulders drooped in defeat.

"You need to get out of this dreadful place and try to enjoy your birthday. And for heaven's sake, sit up straight. You're no good to yourself or to India looking like that," Margo said, her sharp gaze sweeping over her daughter as though trying to will her into compliance.

Nyree barely stirred, her eyes fixed on the floor.

Margo's attention shifted to Malachi, standing stoically by the window. Her diamond bracelets caught the light as she placed a hand on her hip, her lips curving into a faint but pointed smile.

"Malachi, *please* talk some sense into her," Margo added, her tone carrying the weight of expectation. Without waiting for a response, she turned and strode out of the room, the soft swish of her designer trousers the only sound breaking the silence she left in her wake.

The faint scent of her Jo Malone perfume lingered in the air, a reminder of her polished, affluent presence—a stark contrast to the tension and despair weighing down the room.

Malachi pretended not to hear his ex wife's mother talking to him. Her visit had lasted thirty minutes, and these were the only words she had said to him. They both hated each other.

Nyree surmised that the hatred stemmed from the fact they were cut from the same cloth. Two years back, the family's perfect façade had shattered when they discovered Margo's secret past. Before becoming the respected psychiatrist of Gary, Indiana, Dr. Shaw had worked the pole in Tallahassee under stage lights, paying her way through college one dollar bill at a time. The "Love Doctor" hadn't just crossed professional lines —she'd obliterated them by fucking one of her therapy clients during marriage counseling.

When that man wound up dead, Tallahassee newspapers plastered Margo's face across their front pages. Though she beat the murder charge, she fled Florida faster than summer lightning, reinventing herself in the industrial shadows of Gary where nobody knew her name.

That was the clean version. The truth had teeth.

The secret might have stayed buried if Margo's father hadn't lost his mind in that nursing home where she'd stashed him. One bad day, one nurse who listened too closely, and suddenly Margo's carefully constructed life came crashing down.

In reality, he should have been praying for having the courage to say, "Later this year, two different women are going to give birth to my children, and they will be six weeks apart."

Nyree was glad that her mother was gone. They had never been close. Nyree always felt that her mother was more loving to her brother Kyle, while Kyle felt that their father was more loving to Nyree. Yep, her parents had favorites. Nothing Nyree ever did was good enough for Margo Shaw.

Throughout her marriage to Malachi, Margo often said, "Nyree, you've done some dumb things in your life but marrying that bum takes the cake."

Nyree and her mother both got divorced the same year.

When Margo learned of Nyree's pregnancy after the divorce to Malachi she said, "I don't believe in abortion, but I truly believe having a baby by that bum will be the biggest mistake you've made ever." Nyree could only muster up a generic response of "Wow," because what mother says this to her child.

Five minutes after Margo left, Nyree Shaw decided to straighten herself up in the chair. She had been bent over sobbing after hearing Dr. Bradley's intern, Dr. Herrera, tell her with his fancy medical jargon that there was no hope for her daughter, India. Dr. Herrera told her that her fourteen-month old daughter would probably not survive this ordeal, and even if she did survive, it was likely that there would be some neurological damage. There was a strong possibility that her child would suffer developmental delays.

India had contracted meningitis, and it was not looking good. *There is no way in the world that God would give me such a precious gift and then snatch it away from me, is it? Nope, that is negative thinking, and I refuse to entertain those negative thoughts. The devil is a liar.* The high fevers and seizures had not subsided, despite the fact that India was receiving medication. The last time India had a seizure, it seemed as if it would never end. Nyree had hollered and screamed for the nurses to do something as she watched her baby's body move uncontrollably. *This was a bad nightmare. When did things get like this?* Her life was out of control, *and there was nothing she could do about it. Nyree felt helpless as she continued to watch things spiral out of control.*

"Do something. Do something," Nyree had demanded of the nurse who just stood and watched in silence.

The woman,who looked as if she needed to retire, turned to Nyree and said, "There is nothing anyone can do. All you can do is wait for it to pass."

"Wait for it to pass?"

Nyree twisted her lips as she contemplated what to do. Something inside of her wanted to smack the woman wearing Winnie The Pooh scrubs so hard that her hand imprint would remain on the nurse's cheek for hours. Then she had a flash of her pulling the woman by her red curly locks and pounding her face into the wall. *Now, wait for that to pass, trick. Stank heifer just gonna sit there and watch my baby seize like it's a show. I should just go on ahead and smack her silly.* Nyree quickly dismissed that thought. An image of her being photographed for a mug shot and finger printed in the dirty, musty, dingy city jail located on 13th and Broadway raced through her mind. She got depressed every time she had to go in there and pay a ticket. She could just imagine how the people who worked there on a daily basis must feel. And the poor inmates who were lucky to get a bologna sandwich, Nyree quickly snapped her mind back to reality. She hated bologna, and if she ended up in that jail that would probably be the cuisine that was offered to her.

Nyree surmised that she would do what she had always heard Grandma Lula say and that was to speak to her mountains.

This mountain was her daughter's illness, and so she quietly whispered to her daughter, "India, come on. I need you to settle down and come back to Mommy. It is time for us to go home."

Dr. Bradley's colleague, a neurosurgeon, wanted to operate on India's brain, but Nyree had demanded a second opinion when hementioned the procedure. The word hopeless kept replaying itself in Nyree's head, like a broken record. Malachi's words echoed as well.

He stood up and looked the elderly gentleman in the eye and demanded to know, "Who gives you the final say? You're not God. I'm putting this is in God's hands."

Nyree sat in the hospital recliner rocking back and forward, holding herself tightly and in her mind and spirit saying, "I'm giving this to you, God. I'm putting this one in your hands."

Never in her life had she felt so helpless. All she could do was sit there and gaze at her baby hooked up to IV tubes. Nyree watched specialists and nurses come in and draw blood, perform one test after another, monitor blood pressure and temperature.

The lady from the cafeteria came in and said, "Can I get you something?"

Nyree sniffed and took her tissue that she had been holding for what seemed forever and dabbed her nose and responded,

"No, thank you."

The woman, who was short and wore her hair in a bun, offered a genuine smile and said, "Baby, you have got to eat. You have to maintain your strength for that pretty little girl. She's going to need you to be strong.That is the only way you will be able to care for her."

Nyree smiled. Other than Malachi, this was the only person who had given her a ray of hope. Let everyone else tell it, Nyree may as well have pulled out the black dress and been on the phone with the funeral home, Guy and Allen Funeral Home, making funeral preparations.

"The doctors have given up hope on my baby. They say it's not looking good, and if she pulls through this she may have some neurological damage. I'm not going to eat until she comes around."

The woman responded, "Your baby will make it. At least, let me bring you some juice and water to keep you hydrated." She persisted. "Dad, can I bring you something? Take care of your wife; she is going to need you more than ever in these coming days."

Malachi asked for some fruit. Nyree thanked the woman for caring, and while she wanted to let her know that Malachi had not been her husband for a long time, she could not bring herself to correct the woman.

For a hot second, her mind flickered back to when Malachi was solid, back when he actually looked out for her, made her feel like she wasn't carrying the whole damn world on her shoulders. But that flashback got cut short real quick, the reel rewinding to all the times he'd stepped out, the lies piling up so high she lost track of the score. This was the same dude who slid a ring on her finger knowing his other baby mama was about to pop, the kid dropping before their six-month anniversary. What the hell had she even seen in him back then? Must have been blinded by something, some smooth talk, hot sex or maybe just plain desperation.

There was nothing extraordinary about the lady from the cafeteria. When you looked at her, she was just average size, average looks, but when she opened her mouth and spoke, her words were gentle; yet she spoke with authority. She spoke like she knew somebody in high places, like she knew what she was talking about. Nyree wanted to be like that. Her grandmother, Lula, walked in this same manner.

Nyree looked at the lady and said, "My baby has been here for a week now, and I feel bad that I don't know your name. What is your name?" Nyree asked.

The lady smiled the most angelic smile you have ever seen and said, "My name is Mary Hampton. I will see you all later."

Nyree smiled back and said, "Thank you for all your kindness, Miss Mary."

As she left the room, Nyree turned and looked at Malachi, who smiled back at her.

"I'm really sorry that you have to spend your birthday here in the hospital," he said. "I feel like this is all my fault.Will you forgive me?"

"It's not your fault. At first, I was blaming you in my mind, but it's not your fault. I don't know how she got meningitis, but it can't be your fault unless you had some hoochie mommas all up in my baby's face," Nyree said jokingly.

"I haven't been seeing anybody. I guess you still dealing with ole boy, the work-out man," Malachi teased.

Nyree did not respond to Malachi's teasing.

She began thinking about their child, and her smile faded quickly as she said, "Malachi, they want to take our baby to surgery. Do you think that I am wrong for wanting all these second opinions? I don't want anyone cutting on my baby."

She began to sob, and Malachi stood up and held her tightly. It felt like old times being in his arms again. She forgot how loving he could be. The embrace was interrupted by the sound of a man clearing his throat.

As they pulled apart from each other in slow motion, they observed Colin Jordan standing in the doorway in yellow protective suit apparel provided by the hospital.

Nyree's gaze locked onto the hazmat suit, a slow burn igniting in her chest. Hospital policy, yeah, she knew the drill. Protective gear for visitors. But seeing it draped over folks coming to check on India always felt like a slap in the face. And seeing *Colin* in it? That was a whole different level of disrespect. Colin, who'd been rock-solid for both of them, her and India. They'd never thrown shade his way, never intentionally caused him pain. Didn't he get it? India wouldn't hurt a fly, let alone him. So why the hell was he rocking that janky yellow getup like he was walking into a biohazard zone?

"How dare you come here! You have no reason to be here," Nyree shouted at Colin, as he began walking further into the room toward her.

"Been blowing up your phone, Ree! What you expect me to do when you ghost me like that?" Colin's voice was tight, laced with hurt and a simmering anger. "Then I roll up here, and you all cozy with... *him*? Same damn vibe as that day I pulled up on you at the bookstore." His nostrils flared, each breath sharp and ragged.

"Hold up, fam," a low voice rumbled. Malachi stepped forward, his eyes narrowed on Colin. "You don't know me, blood. And trust, you don't want this smoke. You got beef with Ree, keep it between y'all. Don't come at me sideways. I ain't the one you wanna test." He locked eyes with Colin, a silent threat hanging heavy in the sterile air. "Ree, I'ma bounce for a sec, give y'all some space before I catch a case up in here."

Colin's face was a mask of pure venom. If looks could straight-up delete a man from existence, Colin would've been dust.

Nyree grabbed Malachi by the arms and turned him towards her and said, "You don't have to leave. We are going to step outside. I'm going to have a word with Colin, and I'll be right back," Nyree said, as she walked swiftly past Colin and indicated for him to follow her into the hallway, "Colin. Let's go. Now."

Colin wobbled out of the room in his protective gear. "Yo, just so that we're clear," he spat, his voice low and dangerous, "if there wasn't a damn camera in there – and bet your ass it's recording sound – that dude would be picking his teeth up off the floor right now. The only reason I hold my tongue is because of you."

Once the door completely shut, Nyree approached Colin with

arms folded and asked, "Why are you here? We are over, remember? You were the one who could not deal with me and all my drama. My relationships are toxic. Those were your words."

Colin dropped his head and focused on the hospital floor. He noticed that the freshly waxed white tile had specks of powder blue, brown, and pink in it. As he focused on the design of the tile, he found himself wishing that he had never uttered those words to his fiancé.

"It's funny how your words will come back to haunt you. What can I say now? I mean, I did say that. I spoke those words out of anger at the time. I was tired of the drama, but that was when you were going through drama with Malachi and him writing his book. But this is about India, I love her. I would never leave you, Nyree, in the midst of this, but you're shutting me out. What am I to do?" Colin asked.

Nyree said nothing.

"Nyree, I know what I said, and I'm sorry. I can't be without you. I love you, and I love India like she's my own..."

Nyree began walking back to the hospital room and said, "Goodbye, Colin."

Nyree did a quick 180, like a switch had flipped in her head. Suddenly, her fingers were all over the ring on her left ring finger, twisting it back and forth. It was tight, a symbol of something that was clearly about to break. After a little wrestling, she finally yanked it off and held it out to Colin. His jaw muscles flexed, tight as piano wire. He just shook his head, a silent "nah, Babe" that cut deep. Nyree was *the* one. The first woman he'd ever dropped an engagement ring on. And now? She was trying to give it back like it was some unwanted mixtape.

He started backing away from her, trying to keep his face from showing the earthquake happening inside. Dude was strong, for real. Could throw up three plates on the bench without breaking a sweat. But the weight crushing his chest right now? That was a whole different kind of heavy. He'd tossed around "I love you" like it was a casual greeting back in the day, but Nyree? She was the real deal. His first, his only.

Nyree watched him disappear down the hallway, then pushed open the door to India's room. *Welp. Guess this is how it ends,* she thought, slipping the one-carat heart-shaped pink diamond into the pocket of her oversized hoodie. She took a couple of steps into the room, then abruptly spun around and marched straight to the bathroom door, slamming it shut behind her.

"Is everything okay?" Malachi called to her.

He was glad that he was not the one that had caused her to slam the bathroom door. Although Nyree was short and petite, Malachi had found out a long time ago, that size was relative. When Nyree became angry or upset, she possessed the strength of a man.

Malachi remembered the time that Nyree had jumped on his back and tackled him to the ground and punched him in the face like a man. He could laugh about it now, but when he was experiencing that torture all he could do was pray not to respond violently toward her. Deep down in his soul, he wanted to hit Nyree back. He remembered feeling less than a man for wanting to hit Nyree and for enduring such a beating. Malachi tried to get her off of him, but it seemed as if she had the strength of three women her size, and he could not move her.

"Yes," she yelled out over the running water, as she washed her face.

Nyree stayed in that cramped hospital bathroom until the red rimming her eyes finally receded and she felt like she could face the world without her composure cracking. She wasn't about to give Malachi any new tea to spill, no fresh dirt for his gossip column. Dude had gone from straight-up broke, couldn't afford a toilet to piss in , let alone a place to toss the evidence, to living that "movin' on up" life like the Jeffersons. His whole come-up was fueled by that scandalous tell-all he dropped about their marriage and her family's dirty laundry. That joint sold a million copies in three months flat, catapulting him from nobody to rubbing elbows with late-night hosts and soaking up daytime TV spotlight. Nyree wouldn't be surprised if he was secretly relishing her pain right now. That was their messed-up cycle, their twisted give-and-take. When he was shining, she was in the shadows, and when she was down, you could bet he was somewhere celebrating. They both seemed to thrive on the other's downfall, a toxic game they played way too well.

****

Dr. Bradley entered the room, smiling and holding her clipboard in hand. This was the first time since India had been in the hospital that Nyree had ever noticed the young woman smile. Yasmine Bradley was the best pediatric doctor in the Midwest, which was why Nyree contacted her immediately when Malachi called her in the middle of the night stating that India was going to be hospitalized.

Initially, Yasmine Bradley had rejected the assignment as she had planned to go on a much needed vacation during the first week of March. After hearing the desperateness and pleading in Nyree's voice, she decided that her vacation could be prolonged until India Chandler recovered. Nyree told her that India had been perfectly healthy until going to Malachi's home for the court ordered weekend visitation. Malachi's call made it sound as if India were on the brink of death.

Yasmine stood before them, and in a soft voice that commanded their attention, said, "Mr. Chandler and Ms. Shaw-Chandler, I have some good news for you. We examined the cerebral fluid that was taken from the cerebral tap. It seems that the medication is working, and if India continues to progress she could be leaving in the next three or four days. I consulted with several neurologists and reviewed the CAT scan, and we have concurred that surgery will not be necessary. Of course, in three months, I will want you to follow up with Dr. Sherwood, as a routine precautionary measure, and if things go well at that visit you should not have to see a neurologist again."

Nyree jumped for joy and embraced Malachi so hard that he thought she would crush his ribs.

"Hallelujah," she screamed, as tears of joy ran down her face as she embraced Malachi with a bear-hug and held him tightly.

Malachi held her just as tight, a relieved grin spreading across his face. "What about the seizures, Doc?" he asked, his voice still tinged with worry. "Will those keep happening?"

Dr. Bradley walked over to him, placing a reassuring hand on his forearm. "Medically speaking, I can't give you a hundred percent guarantee." She paused, her gaze steady. "But I'm also a woman of faith, and while that's not exactly water cooler talk in my field..." She smiled gently. "Based on what I've seen God do in your daughter's life in this short time, I honestly don't think you have anything to worry about. When I first saw India, things were... bleak. I wasn't even sure how we were going to proceed. It looked bad."

"Thank you," Malachi interrupted, his voice thick with emotion. "Thank you for everything."

Dr. Bradley shook her head, a playful wag of her finger. "No, Mr. Chandler. This isn't my doing. This is the work of God. He just used me as a vessel. Honestly, I was at a loss. I cracked open every textbook, but it was divine guidance that led the way." She moved over to India's crib, her professional demeanor softening as she watched the little girl let out a tiny yawn, followed by a sweet smile and a soft giggle.

Nyree finally pulled back from Malachi, her face radiant as she saw her baby smile for the first time in what felt like forever. Dr. Bradley began checking India's vitals, her touch gentle and practiced.

When she was done, she turned to Nyree, her expression bright. "If she keeps this up, you should be able to take her home on Thursday. We'll arrange for a visiting nurse to come by three times a week for three weeks to keep an eye on her, and of course, there will be an office visit. But don't worry, we'll go over all the discharge details."

Nyree couldn't stop the grin plastered across her face. This news was a shot of pure joy straight to her soul.

Malachi looked just as relieved, the tension finally easing from his shoulders. He reached out, taking Nyree's hand in his. "Look," he said, his eyes meeting hers, "this is no way to spend your birthday. Let me take you out to dinner."

Nyree looked shocked. She was surprised that he remembered, let alone even cared about her birthday.

Placing her hand on his face, Nyree responded, "It is truly a sweet gesture, but I am going to stay here and ..."

Suddenly, she was embarrassed about her display of emotion toward him. She hoped that she hadn't given him the wrong idea.

"Nyree, we have been posted here day in and day out for almost two weeks. We have got to get out of here and get some air. She's doing better. I think that we have taken a hard hit. You look like you have lost twenty pounds since this ordeal began."

"Boy, shut-up," she said, as she jabbed him in the ribs and he stumbled.

"Dang girl, you're going to kill me with that sharp ass elbow. First, you try to hug the life out of me, and now, you're going to break my ribs. If I continue to stay around you I am going to have to get checked into the hospital. Speaking of ribs, I could go for some Ribs on the Run, and you know they have the best dressing in Gary, next to your grandma's. By the way, how is Miss Lula?"

"She's fine. She still asks about you. Just because we're not together, doesn't mean you can't go by and see her. As much as I hate to say it, she loves her some Malachi Chandler." Nyree rolled her eyes.

She hadn't meant to say all of that. It just came out, and she couldn't take it back.

"Oh, I got all off the subject. What were we talking about? Oh yeah, Ribs on the Run is closed now.Boy, where have you been? There is another restaurant, Season's, that has great food. They treat you like family. I eat there all the time.If you like my granny's cooking you will love their southern food. I will gain these twenty pounds back in no time. Okay, you convinced me, but I need to go home and take a shower. Where do you want to meet?"

"Why don't you come over to my place, and we can leave from there? What's that look for? I want to show you around my new house.I want you to see what your interior decorator did," Malachi said sincerely.

"I guess. I'll stop by once I'm dressed. Where are we going?" Nyree asked.

"Wherever the birthday girl wants to go," Malachi said with a mischievous grin and putting emphasis on the word go.

She twisted her lips and gave him her famous, "I know you didn't just say that" look and sashayed out of the door, swaying her hips because she knew he was watching.

"Season's," he called behind her. "Listen, the way you just described the food there, I'd be a fool not to take you there," Malachi said.

Malachi

"Hey," Malachi said boyishly, as he opened the door to his fifty-five hundred square foot home, which called Lake Michigan its backyard.

Following him into the living room area, Nyree couldn't hide her smile as she sank into the plush suede sectional in the living room he referred to as *'The Spot.'* The space exuded a masculine sophistication, a far cry from the days when Malachi was crashing on an air mattress in his mother's cramped two-bedroom apartment. She had to admit, he had come a long way. It wasn't a Shaw Enterprise mansion like she was used to, but her subtle nod gave him her unspoken seal of approval.

Rumors had been swirling around Gary, Indiana, about Malachi's so-called "palace"—a nine-room masterpiece built from the ground up and paid for in full. Now, Nyree had the chance to judge for herself.

Her eyes wandered over the towering nine-foot cathedral ceilings, accented with intricate crown molding that gave the room an almost regal air. The walls were painted in deep slate gray, their bold hue offset by sleek black-and-white photography framed in brushed steel. Below her feet, the rich espresso-stained hardwood floors gleamed under halogen track lighting that bathed the space in a warm glow.

Her gaze landed on the living room's centerpiece: a cherry wood mantle over the fireplace, carved with clean, modern lines that framed a sleek gas fire. Above it hung a flat-screen TV, flanked by built-in shelves that housed leather-bound books and vintage vinyl records. It was the perfect blend of sophistication and bachelor swag.

After a tour of the nine-room house—including four bathrooms, a fully equipped recording studio, a state-of-the-art movie theater with reclining leather seats, and a three-car garage with his meticulously polished Range Rover, Escalade, and Ducati parked inside—Nyree raised an arched brow and smirked at him.

"You have a very nice home," she said, the faintest edge of teasing in her voice. "I like *'The Spot,'* as you call it. It's very... *bacheloresque.* I love it."

Malachi let out a deep, intoxicating laugh, the kind that had always made Nyree's stomach flip. He raised an eyebrow at her, a playful challenge glinting in his eyes.

"Bacheloresque? Now, I don't have the most extensive vocabulary, but is that even a word, or did you just make it up?" he teased. "I like it, though. I like it a lot," he added, licking his lips in that signature LL Cool J way that sent a jolt through her.

Nyree's knees buckled, and Malachi's reflexes were quick. He grabbed her gently by the elbow, his touch firm but tender, and guided her to the sofa.

"Don't tell me you've been drinking without me? You know you've never been one to hold your liquor," he said, smirking.

"No," she said, settling herself on the couch. "Actually, I don't drink often. I guess I just lost my balance."

Malachi saw right through her. He knew the effect he still had on her, and truth be told, she had the same effect on him. They were supposed to be over each other. *Supposed to be.*

But the fire that had once burned between them refused to fully extinguish. It was like one of those trick candles you put on a child's birthday cake—the flame kept reappearing no matter how many times they tried to blow it out.

He wasn't buying her story about her losing her balance and he told her so.

"Yeah, right. I think I have that effect on women," he said, flashing his signature smile that was known to make her feel butterflies.

"Still an arrogant bastard," Nyree mumbled. Nyree quickly changed the subject and asked, "So where are we going? I'm really kind of tired, you know?"

Malachi could tell that she was tired, but he yearned to be in her company and did not want to let her off the hook for dinner. He figured that he just might have a chance to reconcile things with her. After all, she was spending her birthday with him and not What's-His-Name, so that had to count for something.

"I went grocery shopping, and I can go in the kitchen and make us a gourmet meal if you'd like?" Malachi suggested sincerely, as he looked at her.

She looked like an angel with her pink sweater and black linen slacks on. He could tell that she had washed and styled her hair.

"I hate to be a party pooper, but I am really tired. That would be great if you don't mind and I will owe you dinner at Seasons on our next date," Nyree said.

"No, I don't mind," he paused and realized what she said. Unable to contain his smile, he continued, "Our next date, I like the way that sounds and I'm going to hold you to that. It's cool but I do have one request…"

"Nope," she said, throwing her hands up in protest. "I saw that dishwasher in your kitchen, so don't even think that I am going to do dishes," Nyree finished and allowed her hands to rest on her hips.

"I wouldn't ask you to do dishes. Besides, I have a lady that is coming to clean tomorrow…"

"A lady?" Nyree gasped. Now it was her turn to smile. " Oh, so that's how you keep your crib so clean," Nyree teased.

"Oh, don't trip. You know I don't keep a nasty house. I cleaned our place many a day…" he trailed and watched her roll her eyes.

How I miss that, to see her roll her eyes and wiggle her nose. Man, I miss that. What I wouldn't do to have her back, to hear her call herself going off on me. I miss all of that. Never thought I'd hear myself saying I miss a woman going off on me. Never thought I would be heart broken over a woman. As the fellas would say, 'she's got me sprung' he thought to himself.

"No, but what I was going to say was can you keep me company in the kitchen?" He continued and was surprised by how sensitive he sounded. He had to protect his manhood so he hastily said, "You know, I just want to show you how I throw down in the kitchen. I might be able to teach you a thing or two," he teased.

Nyree smiled, because she had heard the gentleness in his voice.

She followed him into the kitchen and said, "Yeah, I'll keep you company, but I doubt that you can teach me anything," she said provocatively.

Ooh, she just doesn't know how long it's been since I've been with a woman. She can't be making statements like that. He envisioned himself in the hot tub with her, and the two of them sipping on some chilled champagne and eating grapes. In his vision, he heard her say, *"I have missed you so much, Malachi."*

As he opened the door to the refrigerator, she pulled him by the arm gently and turned him towards her and looked into his alluring eyes and said, "You know, you don't have to play Mr. Tough Guy with me. I know that deep down under that hard core exterior that you try to personify that you have a heart."

He gently stroked her cheek and nodded his head and then reached in the refrigerator for the ingredients that he needed and mumbled to himself, "Yeah, but that didn't keep you from divorcing me."

"What did you say?" Nyree asked.

"Nothing," he chuckled to himself. He did not want to let her know that he still grieved for his marriage and what they had shared.

"I was talking to myself. I'm going to make a fine dinner for you. You'll be singing ooh-lah-lah-lah, I love you baby," he ended in a song.

"Boy, do I miss your singing. Remember how you used to sing Jodeci's *"Forever My Lady"* to me?"

Malachi laughed as he reminisced.She must have requested that he sing that song over a million times. Each time she requested, he would smile and oblige her. He loved to sing, but never thought of himself as a singer. It was Nyree who always encouraged him to sing and told him that he should be a singer.

"Yeah, I do remember that. That seems like many moons ago. You were so young and innocent then," Malachi told her and then began to croon a couple of bars of the song.

Nyree smiled and rocked to the beat of the song. She found herself having a delayed laughing reaction to his description of her being innocent as she sat and watched him work magic on the stainless steel stove top.

She said, "I don't know what you're talking about when I was so young. I'm still young. I'm only twenty-five."

"Yeah, right. More like twenty-eight, but you look good. You can still pass for twenty- five," he said with a smile.

She returned the smile. That was Malachi. He always knew what to say to her. Malachi could charm the socks off of anybody. He had charisma. He knew as a woman that Nyree appreciated being told that she looked younger than her age. It was a compliment that she accepted without hesitation. Malachi always knew what to say.

"Something in my soul is telling me to beware of you, Malachi. You're so full of it. It was your smooth words that caused me to end up in that Titanic marriage with you. If I'm honest with myself the marriage was a sinking ship from day one. I only realized it when I began floating in waist-high water. Don't look at me like that. I'm just telling the truth. Enough of that, I don't want to spoil my birthday by thinking about times past. Our daughter is on the road to recovery," Nyree said with a partial smile.

"Wow, you said a mouth full, but like you said, let's not rehash the past. Tonight is about you, and so we should celebrate you!" Malachi exclaimed, trying not to focus on the hurtful words Nyree had spoken.

He was laying it on thick, all apologies and regrets. If he could rewind the clock, erase all the BS he'd put her through, he probably would. Maybe.

"Malachi, that dinner was on point," Nyree said, staring down at her spotless plate. "I was expecting some basic chicken and peas or something, but you came through with that grilled salmon, that special sauce you do, over wild rice. And that wine, the Marea Nero d'Avola? Chef's kiss. It really brought out the flavor. Seriously, thank you. Let me help you with these dishes."

"Nah, no way. You're the birthday girl, my guest. I got this. You save room for dessert?"

"Dessert? You serious? I'm stuffed," Nyree said, rubbing her stomach. As she made that little circle, Colin's face flashed in her mind – Mr. No Dessert, who thought Jell-O with Cool Whip was pushing the boundaries.

"Too bad, 'cause I got your favorite. Or at least, what *used* to be your favorite... Key Lime Pie."

"No freakin' way!" Nyree said, a genuine smile finally breaking through the tension, and she giggled, sounding like some high school girl crushing on the captain of the football team.

"Yes way," Malachi said, returning the smile. He was tempting her and he liked it.

Nyree was still the same woman he had fallen in love with. It did not take much to please her. Something as simple as him having her favorite dessert brought a smile to her face. That brought him pleasure.

"Oh, you are so bad. I am going to gain a thousand pounds dealing with you," Nyree teased.

"You worry too much about your weight. You looked good when you were pregnant, and you look good now."

"Malachi, you are such a liar. I gained sixty pounds when I was pregnant. My feet were so swollen I couldn't even wear shoes. In the dead of winter, I was wearing flip flops," Nyree said pouting, remembering how pregnancy had changed her life.

"And you looked great," Malachi said, remembering how sexy he found her to be during that special time.

"You always knew what to say." Malachi's phone began to ring, snapping him back into reality.

"Aren't you going to answer your phone? Don't mind me. I'll just go to your restroom. It must be important because that's about the fourth time she's called you today, and you keep ignoring it," Nyree said, trying not to sound jealous.

Malachi continued to serve Nyree a slice of Key Lime Pie and then himself.

Ignoring the call again, Malachi looked down at the floor with embarrassment and laughed nervously. Finally he explained,"It's not what you think."

Nyree waved her hand and said, "Oh, you don't owe me an explanation. I just didn't want you to miss out on whomever has been calling you all day, because of me."

"Nyree, it's not like that. It's my manager, Antigone, and I know that she is going to want to know if I've found… oh, my goodness. Oh my goodness," he said laughing and then jumping up and down while squeezing Nyree's hand.

"What?" She asked quizzically, not sure what to make of his hysteria.

And who in the world would name their child Antigone? Somebody must have read a little bit too much of Oedipus Rex.

"I think I've found her. I mean you. That is, if you would agree to it. I know I have no right to ask you for a favor, but I need you. Say yes. Please."

Malachi's upscale kitchen, all stainless steel and granite countertops under the track lighting, felt way too sterile for this conversation. Nyree leaned back against the cool island, arms crossed. "Okay, Malachi. Look, I don't know what kind of trip you're on, but you gotta speak English. Lay it out for me, slow and easy, 'cause somewhere between your jibberish and whatever planet you're on, I'm lost. I have no damn clue what you're talking about."

"Alright, alright. You know I wrote that book, *Confessions of a Playa,* right? Went number one on the New York Times bestseller list. Things have been… really good for me."

"Yeah, I know you made a real come-up, alright. By airing out our dirty laundry and spilling tea about my family for all of America to read. You're lucky I haven't slapped you with a libel suit."

"Come on, Nyree. My book was good for your business too.

You guys got tons of exposure. Look, I'm sorry if I hurt you. All I knew was that the woman I loved bounced, and I was hurting. I wanted the world to know I was a victim in all this too..."

"A Man Scorned is what you should've called that mess. I never saw you as some victim. All I saw was you selling out to Rayna Summers at that rag they call a newspaper, *The Midwest Vein*. You know that whore's been thirsty for you for years. And you know I don't go around calling women names, so if I call her a whore, she's earned it. Does anyone even *read* that trash newspaper she works for? Seriously, if I was out of Charmin, I wouldn't even use that rag to wipe my behind. Anyway, next thing I know, you got a book deal and you're all over these talk shows," Nyree said, shaking her head in disbelief.

"I told my story, Nyree. What was I supposed to do? No real high school diploma, no job, another kid on the way. I messed up, okay? I even faked my diploma to get into the Navy. I thought about disappearing, going off the grid somewhere, but then I figured, when the going gets tough..."

"Yeah, yeah, I know the saying. So, back to your 'idea'." Nyree's voice was flat, her expression unreadable.

"Right. So, I just finished my first rap album. It's also called *Confessions of a Playa...*"

"Congratulations, Malachi. I know that is something that you always wanted to do. I'm happy for you. You're doing what you love. "

"Right. So, I am supposed to be doing a video for it soon and working out the logistics. I need a leading lady, which I had told Antigone that I wanted to choose; but because India's been sick I have yet to do it. But the time is almost at hand, and well, would you do it?"

"Me? Nah, Malachi, I don't think so. I'm not exactly the music video type."

"You'd be perfect, Nyree. We already know each other, so we wouldn't have to fake the chemistry, and..."

"Malachi, I don't know... Maybe you should ask my dad's wife, Amber? She's a model and all that."

"Nah, I don't want her. I want you. So, how's that even going? I mean, you're older than your stepmom. That gotta be awkward, right?" Malachi asked, totally derailing the conversation.

Nyree let out a deep breath and sighed, "Tell you the truth, at first, it was hard for me to adjust, but we're all cool. If you thought Kyle and my dad's relationship was weird before, it's even worse now that my dad has married her. Oh, I shouldn't be talking to you about my family stuff. You might decide to publish another book.

It's common knowledge that my dad hired an investigator to investigate my mom. Amber was the investigator who uncovered all the dirt on my mom. She and my father worked closely together documenting her findings to support the divorce. I knew they had gotten close, but I guess I just never figured he would actually marry her. I was okay to some degree with them being a couple, having a stepmother younger than me is awkward; if my dad is happy then so be it. Why am I running off at the mouth like this? I can give you Amber's phone number, and she can..."

Malachi reached over the table and placed his hands on Nyree's hands and looked her in the eye and said, "I don't want Amber. I want you.What will it take to get you to do it? How much? I have a pretty nice budget," he said with a smile.

Nyree gave Malachi a tight smile, almost laughed. He'd come a long way from crashing on his mama's floor to this lakefront crib and a music video budget that probably rivaled her annual marketing spend. She knew, with the way his book had blown up, he could back up that offer with serious cash. But for Nyree, it wasn't about the money. It was about stepping way outside her comfort zone, diving headfirst into some unknown ish. She was a businesswoman. She knew about boardrooms and bottom lines, not about modeling or being on blast on MTV. Still, she had to admit, the idea did a little something for her ego, even if she wasn't ready to admit it out loud.

"Look, Malachi, this ain't my world. Why don't you have your lawyer draw up a contract and send it over to my attorney, Nicole Rouse? You know Nicole, right? She handles all my legal stuff. Once she goes over it, we can sit down and talk, see where it goes from there."

"Alright! Let me get Antigone on the phone right now." He practically vibrated with excitement. "I can't believe you said yes! I gotta call her before you change your mind."

He snatched up his cordless phone, punching in numbers fast. "Yo, Antigone? Yeah, yeah, I know. Good news, found the girl. Nyree... Yeah, there's only one Nyree I know. Look, I need you to get a contract drafted up ASAP, send it over to her lawyer, Nicole Rouse. Once they've reviewed it, Nyree'll let me know if it's a go or a no-go. So, make it good, alright? 'Cause I want her. Peace."

"So..." Nyree prompted him after he hung up with his agent.

"The contract will speak for itself. But trust...this is a done deal, and you're gonna be happy with the terms. Your boy–the workout dude, he gonna be jealous as hell. You know every guy in America is gonna be hitting you up once they see you in this video. If you think you're famous now, you're about to be mad famous after this."

Nyree shook her head, a small, disbelieving smile playing on her lips. It was almost impossible to imagine being even more in the spotlight than she already was. It was bad enough she could barely step out without some paparazzi dude flashing cameras in her face.

"Yeah, I know. Did you see how all the photographers were snapping pictures when we came out of the hospital together?" Nyree asked.

"Yeah," he said dully, "I didn't like that. That shi--, I mean, that ish wasn't cool. See, I've even cleaned my language up. But on the real, Ma, I'm at the hospital because my daughter was fighting for her life, and they are camped out trying to get a story to sell their magazines or newspapers or whatever. That's not cool."

"I know. That's not cool at all," Nyree chimed in, as she stifled a yawn and noticed that she had an incoming call on her cell phone.

"Excuse me," she said to Malachi, as she answered the call. "Hi Daddy. Thank you. Thank you. I feel good. Yes, she may be coming home Thursday, so Malachi and I left for the evening. Yes. Yes. Daddy, don't go there. Daddy, mind your business. Tell

Amber I heard that, and I'm going to… Daddy, you're crazy. Love you, too. I'll talk to you tomorrow. What's that? I'll stop by the office tomorrow and check on it and let you know. Everything is on hold with that. You know what, Daddy; I'm not worried about that. We sent Aris certified letters about the matter. She did not respond, and well, she'll see that we mean business when we no longer finance that operation. I don't even know why Grandma got involved in that mess. It's okay. She's on her own with those raggedy businesses. She is no match for me. I know her and her skill set is no match for mine. Enough said."

Nyree sighed and took a breath. She was not getting through to her father.

"Daddy, I mean, if you want to keep giving her chance after chance and babying her you can. I don't get you," Nyree said through clenched teeth, not wanting Malachi to hear her.

"When Kyle betrayed you, you wrote him out of your will. You disowned him and everything. She's not a blood relation, and you're willing to bend over backwards for her. I think you could extend the same courtesy to your son. Look, we can talk business tomorrow. I just want to enjoy the last few hours of my birthday. Yes, with Malachi. I'm hanging up now, Daddy. Goodbye," Nyree told her father.

Just as she was getting ready to disconnect the call she heard a question that caused her to put the phone back to her ear and continue their conversation. She knew Malachi was listening, but at this point did not try to whisper.

"No. I will not have my name associated with that type of operation. She was not up front and forth right, and there was a clause in the contract that spoke to that issue. *Was*, Daddy, **was,** that is the key word. Daddy, I'm being rude. I will talk to you tomorrow. Thanks again. Love you," Nyree said, as she hung up the phone with her dad.

Malachi watched Nyree, noticing the shift in her mood, the way her usual spark had dimmed. He wanted this night to be special, for her to actually enjoy herself for once.

"Everything alright?" he asked, his voice low.

"Yeah, sorry. That was my dad. You probably figured that out, though. Just some work stuff I gotta deal with. Well, it's getting late, I should probably get going," she told him, already edging towards the door.

"Why don't you just crash here?" Malachi blurted out, the words escaping before he could overthink them. *Too late to take it back now.*

Nyree looked surprised, maybe even a little thrown. She told him she thought it was best if she headed home. All she really wanted was to crawl into her own bed and decompress, you know?

"Thanks for the offer, but I can make it. Besides, I can't even remember the last time I slept in my own bed," she yawned, a wide, genuine yawn, then politely excused herself.

"Yo, Ree," Malachi said, closing the distance between them, his voice dropping a little. "I ain't gonna play games or front. Imma just lay it all out, right here, right now. Might look like a straight-up clown later for this, but I can't be sitting around playing the 'what if' game so I'm just going to put my cards on the table. I don't want you to leave."

He walked her to her whip after she curved his offer again, polite but firm. "Aight, look, just hit me when you get back to your crib, let me know you good. Dead serious, don't forget, 'cause I'ma be waiting on that ring. And if my phone stays silent? Best believe I might just have to slide through." Malachi shut the door to her silver Benz SLK, the click of her locking her doors echoing in the night air.

She'd said she'd call, but a knot of dread tightened in his gut. He had a bad feeling his Motorola flip phone was gonna stay dark tonight. He stood in the middle of his circular driveway for a minute, hands deep in his pockets, watching the empty street where her taillights had vanished. He was stuck wondering if he could ever even begin to untangle the mess he'd made. He'd sworn to himself, the day he got a chance to make things right with Nyree, to win her back, he wouldn't fumble the ball. His little angel, India, had brought them back into each other's orbit, even if it was just for a hot second. Now, it was on him to make it last. But deep down, a nagging voice whispered that he might just be incapable.

Aris

Sitting on her Italian leather sofa, Aris sipped warm Bailey's Irish coffee from her blue and white ceramic sorority mug. She cuddled up in a hand crafted blanket that had been made in India. This blanket was as close as she had come to India. Tyler had purchased it from a boutique on the lakefront. All the lights were off in the house. Sean Parker had picked up their one year old son for the weekend, and the house was still. Aris hated to admit that she still harbored ill feelings toward Sean; the nerve of him threatening to sue for custody of Matthew.

Aris held the letter she received from Sean's attorney in her hand with a tight grip. Evidently, Sean felt that Aris' ownership of a strip club made her an unfit mother. Just today, she read in *The Midwest Vein* that there had been allegations of prostitution and other illegal activity being linked to her club.

That's just icing on the cake for Sean. I bet he really loves this. That bastard is the cause of everything that's wrong in my life. I wish he would just fall dead and then maybe my life would get better, Aris thought.

It was almost eerie how quiet it was. The phone had not rung all day, and while under different circumstances she would have been happy, it was almost depressing. It felt as if no one even cared about her or remembered her.

It had been two months since Aris had given Tyler his walking papers, and when she did he didn't even protest or blink. He left with a smile on his face.

When she questioned him about not taking his belongings, other than his clothing, he simply laughed and said, "Keep it. Have a rummage sale. I don't care."

It infuriated her that he had been so nonchalant about the matter.He just left and had not called once. At least, when she had broken up with Sean he had called, he had demanded to see her, but with Tyler... nothing. When she tried to add fuel to the fire and tell him that he was fired he didn't flinch one of those chiseled muscles.

He just responded with, "That's fine."

Aris wanted to ruffle some feathers, but Tyler had remained cooler than a cucumber.

It was a quiet Saturday night, and her mind continued to focus on all the things that had gone wrong in her life. For a brief period, she thought of her mother, Kila Smith, who had abandoned her as a baby. *Maybe, I have abandonment issues*, she thought. *My mother left me on my aunt's doorstep when I was an infant. I never knew my father. My aunt loved me and took care of me, but maybe that was out of obligation, not love. All my life I have been tossed to the side. Never a real true connection, I thought things were going to be different with Tyler*, she thought to herself.

Tyler. The name alone was a trigger, sending Aris back to the day when she left Sean–the memory still fresh like an open wound refusing to scab over. Maybe that was her whole damn problem; never letting injuries heal before picking at them again.She'd jumped into things with Sean after catching Kevin, her man at the time, all up on some other chick. And yeah, Kevin was Sean's day-one. Then, plot twist, Sean pulled the same BS, leaving Aris straight in Tyler's comforting arms, her bestie holding her down. You'd think the drama would clock out there, right? Wrong. The drama should have ended there, for real. But now? A baby. And the gut-wrenching uncertainty of whether it carried Sean's or Tyler's blood. Her auntie's words echoed in her head, a harsh truth: she'd messed around and found out with that whole double-dipping situation.

I got enough drama here for a soap opera or a best seller. Maybe I should do a "Malachi Chandler "and write about my story and become a self-made millionaire. Talk about a rags-to-riches story; I bet he'll hold onto those riches now that he's got them. Nyree used to be my best friend, but after the stunt she pulled, I'm glad Malachi exposed her and her family.

I was set to partner with Beach Body Gym and Colin Jordan. In every one of his gyms there was going to be a Tranquil Moments Day Spa. That was going to be huge for me. After the heated verbal exchange I had with Miss Lula, her grandmother,I find out from Colin that my day spa wasn't quite what his facilities would be needing. It was funny to hear him say that because at our initial meeting he was head over hills in love with the idea. He went on to say that after careful consideration and consulting with Nyree, they just didn't see it being a lucrative venture. I've tried to venture out and partner with other businesses in Gary, and it seems like my name may as well be mud. I have a premiere day spa, but Nyree has blackballed me.

I am the only sad old maid in the house on a Saturday night, Aris began to think.

Pouting, she asked to no one in particular. "How did I end up like this?"

When had her life gotten this crazy and out of hand, she wondered and then pinpointed it to the day she left Sean.That was it.The day she left Sean had started it all. Well, no, that was not exactly true, but it put things in gear.

Aris poured more of the Irish coffee into her mug and recalled the day that she left Sean. That year roller coaster with him had been just that... a roller coaster. She recalled the day as if it were yesterday and figured now was as good of time as any to deal with that emotional turmoil in her life. She feared that if she did not deal with the mistakes of the past now it would end up haunting her future and causing her to resent her son, Matthew.

Aris sloshed the last of the liquid around in her cup.There were more bottles waiting on her. *Sean was where it began, but my problems didn't end there. Nope, I should have never gotten involved with Tyler. He was my best friend, and I should have kept things like they were. But nope, I didn't. I had never had a man to taste every inch of my body like he did. He hooked me with the sex, and the fact that we were already friends just made it that much easier. And when he took me back after I got pregnant by Sean, I put him on a pedestal. You would have thought that he was a saint the way I carried on about him. Saint Tyler could do no wrong. I made him ruler over my business affairs. STUPID! STUPID! STUPID! I should have kept sex and business separate. I thought he was tipping out with the strippers at the club, but baby, when he came to pick up the last of his stuff with my hairdresser, Akim, I could have snatched out every strand of that two-hundred fifty dollar invisible weave. I can still hear Akim's voice in my head.*

Solomon

The last two months had been a whirlwind, but Solomon was finally finding his rhythm. Life was starting to feel normal again —at least, as normal as it could. He leaned back in his sleek leather office chair at Tranquil Moments, the polished oak desk in front of him gleaming under the soft LED lights. His eyes landed on the framed photo of Madison sitting prominently on the desk. His daughter's smile radiated through the picture, bright and full of life, and for a brief moment, it calmed the storm brewing in his mind. Her happiness was his anchor, and on a day like today, he needed that reminder more than ever.

With a sigh, Solomon turned his attention back to the financial reports spread across his desk. The glossy printouts and spreadsheets told a story he didn't want to read. Expenses weren't adding up, and the incoming revenue streams seemed to be drying up in places they shouldn't. A cold knot twisted in his stomach as he tapped through the bank statements on his dual monitors, each click confirming what he feared: someone had been playing fast and loose with the company's money.

"How the hell am I supposed to explain this?" Solomon muttered, running a hand over his smooth, peanut butter complexion. His sharp navy-blue shirt clung to his broad shoulders, the suspenders stretching taut as he popped them against his chest—a nervous tic that left a faint sting but helped him focus.

He was only ten weeks into his new position, and already the cracks were showing. The previous accountant had kept things running smoothly—until the final months before Solomon stepped in. Now, there was a ten-thousand-dollar hole in the finances, creditors breathing down their necks, and Solomon on the brink of having to deliver bad news to the boss he'd confidently told he could "turn the company around."

The weight of his promise hung heavy. Solomon wasn't one to back down from a challenge, but this was more than he'd bargained for. As he loosened his tie and leaned forward, his fingers flying across the keyboard in a desperate search for answers, one thought echoed in his mind: *This can't be the thing that takes me down.*

Lord, you got to help me. I don't know where the problem is. You got to show me what to do. Solomon prayed silently then rubbed his bald-head and shut his eyes.

They had some investors that provided them with funds each quarter. Solomon decided to check the accounts to see what monies had been received, and if payments were pending. Every investor had followed through with his/her pledge except Shaw Enterprises. This was a sore spot for Tranquil Moments; Solomon immediately picked up the telephone and called Nyree.

"Ms. Shaw, this is Solomon James with Tranquil Moments."

"Yes, Mr. James. How are you? I am not familiar with you. I usually speak with Tyler Woods. Where is Mr. Woods? Did he have you to call me in regards to my correspondence?"

"No, Ms. Shaw. Mr. Woods is no longer affiliated with Tranquil Moments. I am the new Director of Operations and was calling in regards to Shaw Enterprises Partnership with Tranquil Moments."

"I see. What exactly is your question? I thought the correspondence that we mailed sufficiently explained that we are, as you so eloquently put it, 'no longer affiliated with Tranquil Moments'. Go ahead and ask your question."

"Well, that answers part of my question. I noticed that we had not received funding from you this quarter and was calling to inquire about that. I do not have the correspondence that you made reference to. May I ask why Shaw Enterprise has terminated the relationship?"

"Look...Mr. James is it?" Nyree huffed impatient and continued, "I do not know what kind of filing system you all use over there at Tranquil Moments, but my attorney sent the documents to you in Q1, and it is May. It seems to me that Mr. Woods would have communicated this information to you. Nevertheless, we terminated our partnership with Tranquil Moments due to breach of agreement by Ms. Smith. There are certain terms in the agreement, and one was in regards to the type of establishments that she would be operating. We had no problem with the day spa nor the fitness club. However, we take exception to strip clubs and establishments of ill repute; she was not forthcoming about that information. As partners and investors we should have been made aware of this, as the strip club operates under the umbrella of Tranquil Moments. She is lucky that all I did was pull my money and name out of this venture. I could sue if I had a mind to do so. Any other questions?"

"No, ma'am," Solomon said, feeling like a child.

Why hadn't Aris made me aware of this? He felt like a fool. Surely, Aris had to know that one day the Shaws were going to find out about the strip club.

"Well, you have a nice day, Mr. James," Nyree said, as she hung up the phone, leaving nothing but the dial tone in his ear.

Another one of his pet peeves was people hanging up the telephone without saying goodbye. He had heard that Nyree Shaw was a shrewd business woman, and today, he was finding that to be true. It seemed a bit odd to him that these two women, who had a history of being friends, were not communicating with one another. And this Tyler Woods, it seems as if he had dropped the ball, and now, it was affecting the company. Solomon did not like having to go behind a grown man and clean up his mess.

Standing at Aris' office door, Solomon could tell by the way she was staring at a blank wall that his boss was emerged in deep thought.

"Knock. Knock," Solomon said, trying to get Aris' attention.

He prayed for the right words to say to her. She had become cold toward him when he informed her that he was not looking for a woman. Solomon liked his position and desperately needed it, so they were going to have to move past that incident and take care of business if Tranquil Moments Day Spa was going to have to survive.

"Hey Solomon," Aris said without much enthusiasm."What you got there?" She asked, as she noticed that he had a stack of papers.

Aris had enough problems to deal with and was hoping that

Solomon's stack of papers would not be more bad news.

Solomon stepped into Aris's office, an elegant blend of modern and edgy sophistication. The sleek glass desk, with its chrome accents, was impeccably organized, save for a single steaming cup of coffee. Framed abstract art in bold black and gold tones hung on the walls, adding a touch of luxury, while the plush gray velvet chairs on either side of the desk gave the space an inviting yet professional vibe. It was a room that screamed power, style, and just the right amount of warmth.

Seated at the desk, Aris looked as if she hadn't slept in days. Her caramel complexion appeared slightly dull under the harsh glow of the office lighting. Her hair was pulled back into a no-nonsense ponytail, with minimal makeup enhancing her sharp cheekbones and full lips. Dressed in tailored black slacks, a crisp white blouse, and low nude heels, she exuded a polished, no-frills vibe, despite the exhaustion etched into her face.

Solomon cleared his throat, his fingers reflexively running over his bald head as if searching for the courage to deliver bad news. His navy suit complemented his deep complexion, and his pearly, straight teeth flashed briefly as he gave Aris a tense smile. Though they hadn't worked together long, she'd already picked up on his tells. The strained look in his eyes and the way he toyed with his head confirmed what she suspected: whatever he had to say wasn't good.

"Alright, give it to me straight—no chaser," Aris said, her voice calm but firm. She leaned back in her chair, crossing her legs and gesturing for him to sit. There was no patience today for sugarcoated nonsense.

Solomon exhaled and dove in. "We're in the red. Ten thousand dollars. And Nyree Shaw is no longer an investor. She informed us through her attorney back in March that Shaw Enterprises would no longer partner with Tranquil Moments. Apparently, Tyler knew about it but didn't share it, and there's no letter in the file to back it up."

"What?!" Aris's tone sharpened, her exhaustion replaced by indignation. "When did we supposedly receive this information?"

"Ms. Shaw says it was sent months ago and claims Tyler knew. But her reasoning for pulling out? She says you weren't forthcoming about the strip club."

"Gentlemen's club," Aris corrected, narrowing her eyes.

"Strip club," Solomon repeated flatly, folding his hands. "Let's not play. Ms. Shaw said her company had a strict agreement on what it would fund, and she's upset her money was tied to a strip club. She's not planning to sue for breach, but she's done with us. Now, we need to figure out how to fix this mess. My suggestion? Sell the club and save this business."

Aris flicked her hand dismissively. The bluntness of his words stung, but she had asked for the truth. It wasn't often someone stood up to her, let alone told her exactly what she didn't want to hear. While irritation simmered beneath her calm exterior, she knew Solomon wasn't wrong. Still, the realization of how deep this issue ran made her blood boil.

"I'll handle it," she said curtly, her voice a mix of defiance and determination. This was her business, her empire, and no one— not even Solomon—was going to tell her how to run it. But as she sat back, letting his words sink in, she couldn't deny the nagging thought in the back of her mind: *Maybe selling the club is the only way to stay afloat.*

Shauna

"Come on Shauna. Get up off the bench. Just sitting there staring isn't going to make something happen. The real movers and shakers get up and move and shake," Jeremiah Hawkins told Shauna, as she sat on the bench in the indoor track of the gym holding her flabby oblique's muscles.

"Alright...alright, man, I hear you. I'm tired," she panted, as she took a swig of her lemon, cucumber, and mint sprig water from her water bottle. There was an X20 packet which was a sachet with over 70 trace minerals in it. Jeremiah had introduced her to Xooma, the company that sold it and she had become a representative. She was proud of her website www.xoomaworldwide.com/lovemyh20 .

He just doesn't get it. If I had his body, I would be moving and shaking all the time. He could at least cut me some slack.I mean, I did lose twenty pounds in a month, since he's been my trainer, but he just dismissed that as water weight.

"Look Jeremiah..."

He interrupted her and said, "Listen Shauna, if you don't want to put in the effort then let me know, and we can end this session."

Shauna became angry and said, "What do you want from me? I just did ten minnutes on the elliptical machine, ran on the treadmill and worked out for an hour. I don't have anything else left. I'm trying, but excuse me for being a human being with limitations. Everybody can't be like you," she yelled and ran off the track to the dressing room.

I hate him. He's Mr. Perfect with the Perfect Life. I don't even know why I listened to Solomon about joining this gym. I'm grateful that he hooked me up with a massage therapist job at Tranquil Moments Day Spa, the premiere spa in Northwest Indiana.Because of that, I get free membership at the health club, but hiring this coach was a mistake. He's arrogant and obnoxious, and I hate him.

Shauna checked her reflection one final time in the polished chrome mirror of the exclusive staff locker room at Tranquil Bliss Day Spa. Her cocoa-butter skin glowed from her post-workout shower, and she'd traded her form-fitting gym wear for a crisp white uniform that hugged her curves just enough to be professional yet noticeable. The emerald spa logo shimmered on her breast pocket—a reminder that she'd worked her ass off to earn the reputation of the spa's most requested massage therapists.

With a confident toss of her honey-highlighted braids, she flung open the locker room door and slammed straight into six-foot-two of pure muscle.

"Excuse me," she gasped, flustered as her keys clattered to the Italian marble floor. "I had no idea you were standing there." The scent of his expensive cologne—something with sandalwood and bergamot that probably cost more than her car payment—invaded her space.

Jeremiah bent down, reaching for her keys at the same moment she did, their fingers brushing. "No, I apologize," he said, his deep voice carrying that hint of arrogance she'd come to both despise and secretly respect. "You certainly weren't expecting to see me standing here."

"No, I wasn't." Shauna snatched her keys back, standing to her full height—which still left her looking up at him. Her voice had an edge sharper than the diamond studs in her ears. "There isn't anyone else in there if you're expecting a client."

"Shauna, wait." Something in his tone made her pause despite herself. "Can I talk to you? Do you have an appointment now?" His usual drill sergeant demeanor had softened, catching her off guard. "I really would like, if you have time, to sit down in the café area and have a smoothie, sundae, or something..."

Shauna rolled her eyes dramatically as she strutted across the gleaming floor to the reception desk where Erin—the spa coordinator with her perfect blonde bob and too-bright smile—sat behind a curved marble counter.

"Any messages?" Shauna asked, ignoring the fact that Jeremiah was hovering nearby like an expensive shadow.

Erin tapped perfectly manicured nails on her keyboard. "No messages. Your four-thirty appointment rescheduled for next week."

"Thanks," Shauna said, calculating quickly. The appointment would have been her last of the day—which meant unexpected free time. She turned toward Jeremiah, who was watching her with an intensity that made her skin warm.

"I have a little time for a sundae, I guess," she conceded, adjusting her designer purse over her shoulder. "Since my day is over, I need to get my kids and spend some quality time with them." The mention of her children was deliberate—a boundary line drawn in invisible ink.

"Okay," Jeremiah nodded as they walked past the waterfall wall and through the aromatherapy corridor to the spa's café. The space was designed to feel like an oasis—with live palm trees, plush seating in cream and turquoise, and floor-to-ceiling windows overlooking the spa's private garden. Not the usual place Shauna would choose to confront her personal trainer, but nothing about this day was going according to plan.

They settled into a secluded booth near the back, where the wealthy clientele couldn't overhear them. A server in a crisp uniform immediately appeared with infused water and menus embossed with the spa's emerald logo.

"Look, Shauna," Jeremiah began after they'd ordered, leaning forward with his muscled forearms on the table. The sleeves of his designer polo stretched tight across his biceps—the result of the same ruthless regimen he put his clients through. "I'm sorry if I was too rough on you today. I like you a lot, I mean, as a person, you know, and I think you have a lot of potential, but you're not... Look, this is not coming out right."

Shauna gave him a blank stare, perfected from years of dealing with entitled clients who thought money bought them the right to her time, her emotional labor, her very being. The look that said: I'm listening, but I'm not impressed.

"Stop looking at me like that and hear me out," he said, his voice dropping to a near whisper. "I like working with you. You've made a lot of progress, and I know I don't say it all the time. I'm proud of you, and I think you could go far with this if you wanted to. You could eventually be in competitions. Don't quit on me."

The sincerity in his voice caught her off guard. For a moment, she saw past the chiseled jaw and perfectly sculpted body to something vulnerable.

"I'm not quitting," she fired back, leaning in. "I'm not a quitter, Jeremiah. I know my limitations, and you're not going to just talk to me any kind of way." Her voice was quiet but intense —the voice she used when her kids had pushed her too far. "You're not going to talk to me like I'm a slacker because I'm not. I'm in here four to five times a week, sometimes twice a day. I work out at the beginning of my day and the end unless I have a late appointment. Then I work out and shower before that appointment." She paused, letting her words sink in. "I just think we have a personality clash. You're Mr. Perfect, and I'm not perfect, and that bothers you..."

The sundae arrived between them—a mountain of premium vanilla bean ice cream, drizzled with caramel made in-house, topped with candied pecans and a single gold-dusted chocolate curl. Excess at its finest.

"Shauna, I'm not perfect," Jeremiah said, his eyes never leaving hers even as the server departed. "I don't think I'm perfect. I don't think you're a slacker, and if I came off like that, I'm sorry." He reached across the table, his large hand covering hers. The warmth of his touch sent an electric current up her arm that she wasn't prepared for. "I just see your potential, and I'm trying to get you there. I push you harder than you can go sometimes, but I believe in you. I believe you can handle it. I admire your strength, your dedication, your commitment."

Shauna quickly turned her head, breaking eye contact as

something shifted between them. For the first time since he'd become her trainer months ago, she saw Jeremiah as a man with compassion instead of a dictator barking out demands of "give me two more" while she struggled through another set of weighted squats.

She dabbed at some ice cream from the corner of her mouth with the linen napkin. "Well, I guess I better get going."

He sighed, a sound of genuine disappointment. "You haven't finished your sundae."

"Yeah, I know," she said, reaching for her purse. "I don't need it anyway."

"You deserve it," Jeremiah insisted, his voice gentle. "You've worked hard this past month."

What am I doing? Shauna thought, suddenly aware of how this might look to others. Her heart skipped as she spotted a familiar figure approaching their table. Here comes Solomon. What will he think?

"Hello," Solomon said smoothly, sliding up to their table in his tailored suit that screamed old money and power moves. He bent down to give Shauna a friendly hug, but his eyes took in the scene with calculated precision.

"Hey Sol," Shauna replied, hoping her voice sounded normal. "I'm getting ready to go get the kids from day care. We have 'kids' night' tonight. They'll love that," she added, glancing from Solomon to Jeremiah and back again, suddenly feeling caught between two powerful men.

"Uh, yeah, that's what I was coming to talk to you about," Solomon said, his deep voice casual but his eyes sharp. "I'm glad I caught you before you left and started running errands. I wanted to know if I could pick up Malik and Taylor for the weekend. I know it's not my weekend, but I really wanted to spend some time with them and..."

"Jeremiah, will you excuse me and Solomon for a moment?" Shauna cut in, standing abruptly. She led Solomon to another part of the café where they found a table secluded behind a decorative bamboo screen.

It was her practice not to discuss personal business in front of others—especially not at Tranquil Bliss. Solomon had pulled strings to get her this job at the spa, making it abundantly clear that he wouldn't tolerate any drama. No matter how heated things got between them as co-parents, they had an agreement: never bring those issues to work.

As she settled across from her ex, Shauna couldn't help glancing back at Jeremiah, who was now staring pensively at her half-eaten sundae, looking for all the world like a man who'd just realized he wanted something he couldn't have. Shauna's mind drifted back to the day Solomon told her about Tranquil Moments Day Spa.

****

When Solomon rolled up to Shauna's home on the lake – that sprawling house her daddy's paper had bought – it wasn't for a casual drop-in. He he wasn't just flexing his new title as Director of Operations at Tranquil Moments Day Spa. He came with something heavier on his mind. Stepping into her marble-floored foyer, Solomon kept it one hundred. "I'm stepping up for Malik. For real this time." The Motorola StarTAC on his hip buzzed, but he ignored it, locking eyes with Shauna instead. "And before you get in your feelings—I'm not judging you. But let's be real... you're too damn gorgeous and got too much talent to be trapped in the crib waiting by that cordless phone."

The truth stung, but Shauna wasn't about to let Solomon—or any man—think he had her figured out. Her Fendi slides clicked against the hardwood as she positioned herself on the Italian leather sectional, TLC's "No Scrubs" playing softly from her entertainment system.

"Sol, please," she laughed, rearranging her messy bun atop her head. "You don't know what you're talking about. Where is all this coming from anyway? Like what VH1 special did you watch that got you feeling like you're a life coach now?" She adjusted her Baby Phat tank top, not wanting to give his words power.

Solomon settled into the sofa beside her, the scent of his Issey Miyake cologne filling the space between them. His brown eyes softened, but his resolve didn't. "Shauna, I don't know what I'm talking about?" He let the question hang, deliberately ignoring her deflection.

"Listen. I know your daddy left you with mad paper—enough that you shouldn't want for nothing. But I also see you sitting in this fly crib day after day, watching BET, waiting for that married man to show up in his Benz with empty promises." He leaned forward, his FUBU jersey shifting with the movement. "That happily ever after you're chasing? It's not coming, Shauna. This is the real world."

Shauna stood center stage in her lavish beachfront living

room, the Lake Michigan waves crashing outside her floor-to-ceiling windows. Her caramel complexion was flushed with heat, her thick curves trembling beneath her Baby Phat loungewear as she fought to keep her composure. That auburn mane—the one she'd just dropped three bills on at Essence Hair Studio—was twisted into a messy bun, with spirals escaping to frame a face that had launched a thousand ships but now hosted mascara-stained tears and wounded pride.

"Look, So, I don't need your damn lectures, not today. I'm not waiting on any man," she choked out, hot tears betraying her as they slid down her face. She covered her face with hands sporting fresh acrylics—French tips she'd had done just yesterday, planning to impress a man who'd already moved on.Solomon stepped closer and gently pulled her into his broad chest. For a moment, she let herself collapse into his embrace, but just as quickly, she pushed him away.

"I know how pathetic I must seem to you," she continued, her voice cracking like a scratched bootleg CD. "But I *loved* Damien. Have you ever loved someone with your whole soul, only to have them treat you like you don't even exist? He promised me everything—said he'd leave her and take care of me and the kids. I *funded* his campaign, Solomon. Funded it," she clapped out the syllables on her hand for emphasis. "And he promised to pay me back. But it's been excuse after excuse, and last night, he had the nerve to call me from his Motorola and say he doesn't want to be with me anymore. He played me for three years. Three years! So nah, today is not the day for you to roll up in here preaching to me. I know I was dumb. I know I'm trash for messing with a married man. I don't need you to say it."

"Shauna, stop," Solomon interrupted, his voice steady but full of concern. The gold Cuban link chain around his neck caught the afternoon light as he reached out and tilted her chin up with one finger, forcing her to meet his gaze. "You're not dumb. You're one of the most creative, ambitious women I know. You've got so much fire in you, Shauna. You made a mistake. We all have. Trust me, I've made plenty. Remember crazy Mona?"

He gave a small laugh. "I know what it's like to give someone everything, to love them with every fiber of your being, and then lose them. I still blame myself for Kyra not being here. If I'd been smarter, kept my pants zipped, she'd still be alive."

Shauna wiped her tears with the back of her hand, smudging her MAC lip gloss, a tiny laugh escaping her lips despite the pain crushing her chest. "It's been a while since I had a massage," Solomon said, steering the conversation in a lighter direction, his eyes taking in the Pier 1 decor and the half-empty bottle of Moët on the glass coffee table.

Shauna laughed again, tossing her head back, the gold hoops in her ears catching the light streaming through her bay windows. "You don't want me giving you a massage right now. My energy is all the way off, and that's no joke."

Solomon's forehead creased with confusion, his fitted FUBU jersey shifting as he leaned forward.

"I never work on nobody when my energy is stale like this," Shauna explained, her freshly done nails tapping against her thigh. "I refuse to transfer that negative shit. You know what they taught us in massage school—energy isn't created or destroyed, it's transferred. That's science, baby." She snapped her fingers for emphasis, the tennis bracelet on her wrist glinting.

Solomon's expression softened, his eyes taking her in. "Damn, you went all scientific on a brother. Look, I'm the Director of Operations at Tranquil Moments now, and we're desperate for a massage therapist with your skills. You need a fresh start after that snake Damien, and this could be exactly it." He leaned closer, voice dropping confidentially. "Plus, there's free daycare for employees. Top-notch too—none of that bootleg babysitting. All I need you to do is show up and be the Shauna I know and love—the one who used to light up every room before that politician got in your head."

Shauna raised a perfectly arched eyebrow, her lips curving into a playful smirk despite herself. "Hold up—you love me and you're offering me a job? Where's the real Solomon 'It's-All-About-Me' James? What's the catch? You tryna get back with me or something?" She adjusted her Baby Phat tank top, eyeing him suspiciously.

"No catch," he replied, his tone shifting to serious as he held her gaze. "Things didn't work out between us romantically, but I'll always care about you. That's real. You're a great mom to Malik, and I want you to have this chance. The spa's blowing up —we just signed a deal with that new casino downtown. What do you say? Your skills are wasted sitting in this house waiting on phone calls."

Shauna looked at him, tears welling up again, but this time they weren't from sadness or anger. "I say God is good. This is exactly what I needed to hear today of all days." She dabbed at her eyes. "And you're *sure* about the free daycare? 'Cause Little Momma is a handful these days with all that Rugrats attitude she's picked up."

"Positive," Solomon confirmed with a smile, reaching out to squeeze her hand. "Kiki who runs it used to work at that fancy preschool in Oak Park. Taylor will be straight."

"Then I'm in. Little Momma needs to be around other kids anyway. Thank you, Sol. For real. I won't let you down." She pulled him into a quick hug, the scent of her Curve perfume lingering between them.

For the first time since Damien's last empty promise, Shauna felt a spark of hope flickering to life in her chest. Maybe, just maybe, her comeback story was about to begin.

****

Tranquil Moments Day Spa hummed with activity, the scent of essential oils floating through the air of the mini café where the elite of Miller Beach came to gossip over cucumber water and organic green tea. Solomon leaned across the marble-topped table, decked out in his tailored suit, waving his hand dramatically in front of Shauna's face.

"Earth to Shauna. Hello," he said, sarcasm dripping from his voice like honey. "The shuttle to reality is now boarding."

Shauna snapped back from her daydream, her freshly done box braids swinging as she shook her head.

"My fault. I was just thinking about something. Oh, yeah." She sipped her herbal tea, Solomon ordered while she was going back down memory lane. Raising a perfectly arched eyebrow. "Solomon, I have no problem with that, but what's really going on?"

"Shauna, I just wanted them to come over, and Madison's been asking about them. That's all." His gold watch caught the light as he reached into his breast pocket. "I also have a check for you..."

"Now, this is too good to be true." Shauna's eyes narrowed, skepticism written all over her face. "What's really going on?" The R&B playing softly in the background couldn't mask the tension between them.

"You, that's what's going on." Solomon's voice dropped low, serious now. "I've seen you really turn your life around here lately, and it had me thinking about myself, my shortcomings and what I need to do as a father." His eyes—those same eyes that used to make her weak—locked with hers. "I just want to make it right; will you let me do that?"

He pressed a folded piece of paper into her palm, his touch lingering just a second too long. "I can get them from the daycare now, if that's okay with you."

"That's fine, Solomon." Shauna tucked the check into her pocket without looking at it, pride keeping her from counting his money in front of him. "What are you going to do about clothes? Are you sure you want to take Taylor? Can you manage three children all by yourself, or will you be by yourself?" The question hung in the air, loaded with what she wasn't asking directly.

"Don't worry about clothes. They have clothes at my place." Solomon's voice stayed smooth, confidence radiating from him as he leaned back in his chair. "Yes, I want to take Taylor. I know I'm not Taylor's father, but I never want her to feel left out. That happened to me as a child."

His expression darkened briefly with old pain. "I know how it feels to see your siblings going with their family members, and you're left standing in the front door waving bye to them as the car pulls away. Besides, Taylor is adorable, and you can't help but love her."

A mischievous grin spread across his face as he caught the real question behind her words. "So, were you asking me if I have a girlfriend that is going to be at the house with me?"

Shauna's light hued complexion flushed with heat, her hand automatically going to the nameplate necklace at her throat. She'd been caught. "Uh, no. I wasn't asking if you had a girlfriend. It just seems like that is quite a big charge you have signed up for." She stumbled over the words, trying to save face.

"Shauna, you little liar, you." Solomon's laugh was rich and knowing. "You want to know, and so, I will tell you the answer. No, there is no one." His eyes flicked over her shoulder toward the juice bar where Jeremiah, the spa's star personal trainer, was pretending not to watch them. "Looks like Mr. Jeremiah is interested in you though."

Shauna hit Solomon on the arm—not a playful tap, but hard enough to make him grab his bicep with theatrical pain. "Whatever. He's just my trainer, that's all. I don't have time for a boyfriend." Her voice was firm, but the blush hadn't faded.

"Well, I'm going to get out of here and let you get back to your *trainer*," Solomon teased, rising from his seat with the smooth confidence of a man who knew exactly the effect he had. He strolled away, nodding at the receptionist who nearly dropped her Nokia trying to speak to him.

Shauna watched him go for just a beat too long before making her way back to the table where Jeremiah waited, his muscled frame positioned to catch her every move as she approached.

Was that a hint of jealousy? Shauna wondered.

So, I'm back," Shauna announced, sliding into her seat.Her ice cream sundae had surrendered to the heat, melting into a swirl of caramel and chocolate that matched her conflicted feelings. The spa's signature waterfall trickled in the background, masking the awkward silence between them.

She fidgeted with her silver anklet, struggling for words. This was uncharted territory—Jeremiah had always been just "two more reps" and "feel the burn," never this... whatever this was.

"Now that your children are gone for the weekend," Jeremiah leaned in, his 24-inch pythons flexing beneath his fitted uniform polo, "I was wondering if you would consider having dinner with me?" His cologne—Acqua Di Gio, no doubt—hit her senses like a physical touch.

The question blindsided Shauna worse than any of his killer ab workouts. Her mind raced faster than the latest Aaliyah track as she watched him waiting, those hazel eyes locked on hers.

"Um, I don't know. I think I am going to go home and heat up some left-overs." She stirred what remained of her sundae with the plastic spoon, avoiding eye contact. The last thing she needed was this brother catching her slipping.

Truth was, Shauna wasn't looking for a man or a relationship. Not anymore. She was finally getting her life right after years of wrong turns. Just last month, she'd walked down the aisle at

New Hope Baptist Church, giving her life to the Lord with tears streaming down her face while the choir sang "Stand."

Living righteous was already a daily struggle. She'd hidden her Black & Milds from herself, thrown out her stash of chronic, and was still fighting the urge to cuss out rude clients who showed up late for their deep tissue appointments. Adding a man—especially one built like Jeremiah—would be like throwing gasoline on an already complicated fire.

Pastor's wife, Lady Marie, had warned her during their Wednesday night new believers' class: "Baby girl, getting saved doesn't mean temptation stops knocking—it just means you got the strength not to answer the door."

"Amen to that, Lady Marie," Shauna had replied, nodding like she had it all under control.

But she'd kept quiet about how sometimes, after a long day of kneading knots out of entitled backs, marijuana called her name louder than her Bible. Or how her body still remembered what it felt like to be touched, held, wanted—memories that visited her late at night when her 2Pac CD played low and the kids were finally asleep.

Shauna looked across the table at Jeremiah—at the smooth chocolate skin pulled taut over sculpted muscles, at the full lips curved into a patient smile—and had to mentally rebuke the thoughts that had no business in her newly sanctified mind. *Lord, forgive me, but you didn't have to make the man look THIS good.*

Jeremiah could practically hear the dial-up modem of Shauna's brain connecting to the "dinner options" network. He offered a low-key proposition. "Hey, look. It's just dinner. Think of it as a totally casual hang. My treat, no expectations of, you know… anything. You were probably gonna microwave some popcorn anyway. Let's just grab something to eat. Like I said, it will be my treat. You know you want to…" He smiled.

Shauna shrugged, a tiny crack appearing in her cool exterior. *Okay, chillax. Not every dude's trying to play you like a Sega Genesis.* He *said* just dinner. Maybe he wasn't trying to be all that. *If it's totally bogus, I can always page Brenda with a fake emergency. Gotta have an escape route. Just dinner, right?* She replayed the thought in her head.

Nyree

Nyree's Motorola StarTAC vibrated against her nightstand, the blue glow cutting through the darkness of her bedroom. She had just kicked off her Steve Maddens and peeled herself out of the little black dress she'd worn for her evening in Chicago with Malachi. The carriage ride and deep dish at Gino's East had left her floating, but now reality was calling—literally.

Annoyed, Nyree snapped, "Hello," irritation dripping from her voice like honey. "This better be good, whoever you are..." She adjusted her silk Donna Karan slip, sinking back against the Egyptian cotton sheets of her king-sized bed.

"Hey, Boo. I couldn't sleep and decided to call you and see if you wanted to go to the beach," Malachi whispered, his voice a familiar warmth in her ear.

Nyree sat up straight, clutching her phone tighter. She hadn't felt this electricity since those early days when he'd been pursuing her, showing up at her doorstep with lilies and Waiting to Exhale on VHS. Glancing at her Movado watch on the nightstand, she realized she'd only been asleep for thirty minutes—but damn if it hadn't been the best thirty minutes of shut-eye she'd had in weeks.

"Are you crazy? It's one o'clock in the morning." She tried to keep her voice stern, but something in her tone betrayed her—a softness she couldn't quite suppress.

"So?" Malachi challenged, confidence coating his words.

"So, I'm sleep, and I have a big meeting in the morning," Nyree countered, hoping he'd buy the excuse she was selling.

"Yeah, I know all about your meeting with Colin," he replied, jealousy seeping through his attempt at casual conversation.

"Yes, Colin and I have a meeting to go over some—Wait a minute, why am I explaining myself to you?" Her voice rose with each word. "I don't owe you an explanation. We're not a couple or anything. I'm super sexy and very much single and—"

Malachi always could bring out the raw, unfiltered Nyree—the one who didn't care about sounding proper or put-together.

"Whoa, settle down. I didn't say you owed me an explanation," Malachi interrupted. "So, if we're not a couple then what are we?" He crossed his fingers on his free hand, praying she wouldn't shut him down completely.

The past couple of months had been everything to him. They'd spent weekends browsing at the SouthLake Mall, nights watching Martin reruns, and mornings with him sneaking out before India woke up. If you didn't know better, you'd think they were back together—but they weren't. Not officially. And that was killing him slowly.

If Malachi thought turning flips in the middle of the mall food court would get Nyree back, he'd do it in a heartbeat. He missed everything about her—her smile that lit up rooms, waking up to her wild curls spread across his chest, her ice-cold feet searching for warmth against his legs in wintertime, her dramatic pouting, and yes, even her cursing him out when he deserved it. He was in love with her. Always had been. The divorce papers he'd signed had his signature, but never his heart.

"Malachi, do we have to do this?" Nyree sighed, twisting a lock of her hair. "We have—or at least I have—been having a good time. Let's not put any labels on it. Let's just see what happens."

"Look, I know you're not going to want to hear this, but yes, I need to know what this is." His voice dropped an octave. "I need a label. I lost you before to Colin, and I'm not willing to do it again. I took it because that's what you wanted. I didn't fight. Even when I found out you were carrying my baby, I just sat back and let you have your way."

He paused, gathering his courage.

"Not this time though. I love you. I need you, and I can't keep doing this. Please, tell me you are not playing with my emotions. Although you would have every right to after all the torment I put you through, but please..." His voice cracked, emotion breaking through his carefully constructed walls.

Nyree felt her heart hammering against her chest. This wasn't part of the plan—falling back in love with her ex husband while trying to rebuild her life.

"Malachi, I'm not playing with your emotions," she admitted, surprising herself with her honesty. "I mean, I can be a 'b' at times, but that's just taking 'b' to another dimension." She laughed softly.

"You didn't lose me to Colin. You lost me because you weren't real with me. Colin was real, and he was there, but..." She stopped herself. "No, I'm not going to talk about me and Colin and what was. I respect Colin, but I cannot be in a relationship with him. He's a wonderful guy, but there is something that is missing. I kept thinking that I could fill in the blank, ya know? But I couldn't, and I didn't want to waste his time."

She took a deep breath before continuing.

"You, oh my, I don't know what it is. I should probably walk away from you now before I get in too deep and get hurt again, but..." Her voice trailed off.

She couldn't believe she was being this vulnerable with Malachi—the same man who had shattered her heart into a million pieces when she found those text messages from Tamar two years ago. Opening herself up like this was something she'd vowed never to do again after spending nights crying into her pillow while carrying his child. She had been hurt too many times, but something about the way he'd been showing up lately made her willing to risk it all again.

"I love you. I would die for you. I mean that," Malachi declared, his voice thick with emotion. "I would die for you and India. I wouldn't think twice about it. I'm not going to hurt you. I promise you that. I put that on everything I love. Please, let me spend the rest of my life showing you."

A tear slid down his cheek in the darkness of his home—the first tear he'd shed in front of her since signing their divorce papers at the courthouse.

"Malachi, I don't know. I don't know. What are you saying?" Nyree whispered, her defenses crumbling.

"Let me come over and tell you."

"No. This is not going to be a two o'clock in the morning booty call," she replied firmly, though part of her wanted to say yes.

"You think I want sex?" He laughed softly. "I mean, I ain't gonna lie, a brother is hurtin', but this is not about sex. This is about my love for you. I have been abstinent for so long."

He caught himself, realizing how that sounded.

"Look, that doesn't even matter. Just allow me a few minutes to come over and talk to you. You don't even have to open the door. You can just talk to me through the door. I just wanna see you. I just wanna be in your presence. I don't care. Please, just give me five minutes. Every minute that I'm without you..."

"Goodnight, Malachi," Nyree interrupted, her heart racing.

"What about tomorrow after your meeting?" he pleaded, refusing to give up.

"Malachi, I said goodnight." Her tone was firm but not cold.

"Come on now, Nyree, you can't do a brother like that after he pours his heart out to you," he protested.

"Tomorrow was just going to be me and India. I wanted to spend some quality time with her before leaving for New York in two days," she explained. "You'll have me all to yourself then."

"I wanted to spend time with India, too. Maybe it could be all three of us," he suggested hopefully. "Nyree, stop teasing me. We'll be doing the video shoot, and you'll probably get out there and see some movie star. Yep, you'll see Michael Ealy and forget all about me and—"

"You know, I love me some Michael Ealy," she sighed dreamily. "I heard he's married. Go to sleep!" she yelled playfully into the phone. "Call me tomorrow evening and maybe I'll let you take me and India to dinner. Love to you."

She hung up before he could respond, before she could change her mind and invite him over.

Nyree rolled over and hugged her mink teddy bear—Boo-Bear—tightly against her chest. It still smelled of her signature fragrance, Chaotic Bliss, created by her college roommate turned celebrity perfumer, Jahzara Bradley. She laughed at herself for clutching the stuffed animal so desperately and hopped out of bed to check on India.

She tip-toed down the hallway of her lakefront home, the plush carpet silent beneath her manicured feet. Nyree didn't want to wake her baby girl—not when she needed to be sharp for tomorrow's meeting with Colin. Peering into the nursery, she found her precious child sleeping peacefully in her white crib, surrounded by the designer baby bedding Malachi had insisted on buying.

Leaning over the rail, she bent down and pressed her lips against India's velvet cheek and whispered, "I love you. Sleep well."

Nyree smiled and held her breath when she saw a smile spread across India's face in her sleep. Please, don't wake up now, she thought. I have to get some sleep so that I will be prepared for this meeting with Colin tomorrow morning.

But as she crept back to her bedroom, her thoughts weren't on fabrics or design specs—they were on Malachi's words, echoing through her mind like a song she couldn't stop playing.

****

"Ms. Nyree," called Claudia through the closed door.

"Yes," Nyree mumbled, as she placed the pillow over her eyes to block the morning sun.

It can't be six o'clock yet. I just went to bed five minutes ago.

"There is a telephone call for you," Claudia stated.

"What? I didn't hear the phone ring. What time is it?" Nyree whined.

"I think your ringer is off. It's five forty-five," Maria called through the door.

"Okay. Who in their right mind could be calling this early? Hello," Nyree answered the phone snappily.

"And good morning, to you," Colin replied, his voice infuriatingly cheerful. She could practically hear the smirk through the phone line..

"Yes?" Nyree kept her response clipped, unwilling to give him the satisfaction of pleasant conversation.

"I was calling to see if you were up and ready for our meeting this morning," he said, the professional veneer barely concealing something more personal underneath.

"I remembered the meeting. You didn't have to call to remind me," Nyree fired back, her fingers tightening around the cordless phone.

"Actually, I was calling to tell you that the venue has been changed," Colin announced, a hint of satisfaction coloring his words.

"What are you talking about?" Nyree demanded, her free hand instinctively reaching for the coffee mug on her nightstand. *The venue has changed? What the heck? It's not like we're going to trial.*

"The meeting place," he clarified unnecessarily. "We're going to have it at La Dolce Vita," he announced, pride evident in his voice.

"Why are we having our meeting at a *restaurant*?" Nyree emphasized the word, unable to keep the suspicion from her voice. "Who chose that *place*?"

"I did," he said curtly, the cheerfulness abruptly replaced with something harder.

I know he doesn't think I'm going to go to his favorite hang-out. The thought burned in her mind as images flashed of the society page photos she'd seen just last week—Colin with his arm draped possessively around his latest conquest, champagne flutes glittering in the restaurant's signature dim lighting.

"Figures," she said, infusing every syllable with sarcasm. "You know what? Why don't you all fax me a copy of the minutes? I don't have time to be lolly-gagging around. I'm leaving town tomorrow and have something to do—"

"Not possible," Colin interrupted, his tone suddenly all Shaw Enterprises business. "You need to be there. The client specifically requested that you be in on every phase of the project, and—"

"Colin, I'm sure you could cover this one time," Nyree softened her approach, falling back on tactics that used to work when they were together. "Tell him I had an emergency or something." She let a hint of vulnerability seep into her voice.

"So, you want me to lie for you." The flatness in his response told her the old methods wouldn't work anymore. "I've covered for you a lot these past couple of months. It was no problem when India was sick, but because you and Malachi are hanging out until the wee hours of the morning and—"

"You know what, Colin, forget it," Nyree cut him off, her voice rising with each word. "I'll be there. Don't act like I didn't land us some major deals and do a lot of work. I work hard. Sometimes I just work from other places besides the office." She was nearly shouting now, years of complicated history spilling over. "Don't ever get it twisted. As for me and Malachi—it's business. We do have a child together, remember? The same child that you couldn't deal with!"

"Nyree, you know I love India," Colin's voice lowered, genuine emotion breaking through his professional façade. "I never had a problem with India. My problem was with her father and all the drama. But seems like you can't get enough—"

The satisfying slam as Nyree hung up was replaced by the digital era's anticlimactic button press, leaving only the harsh dial tone ringing in Colin's ear. She tossed the phone onto the bed, already mentally cycling through her wardrobe for something that would make her look both devastatingly professional and completely over him.

Malachi

"I'm glad you decided to do the video," Malachi tolNyree, as they walked down 59 th Street between 7th and 8th Avenue in New York.

He motioned for her to remain where she was standing while he hurried to one of the flower vendors.

"Let me get three dozen of the purple roses," he told the woman standing at the cart.

The woman smiled at Nyree as she whipped the floral arrangement together.

"Are these for the pretty lady over there?" tThe short, elderly lady whispered to Malachi.

"Yes." He smiled.

"Trying to win her heart?"

"Trying to win her back. I broke her heart a while ago. I'm trying to make it right now,." Malachi said, more to himself than anyone else.

"Ah. Purple roses are an excellent choice. Purple roses symbolize desire,

enchantment, and that the pursuer is proceeding with caution. Good luck this time around. This time you treat her well."

"I will. How much do I owe you?"

Malachi pulled his wallet out.

"Nothing. I'm a sucker for love," she smiled a wide grin at Malachi.

He pulled out a one hundred dollar bill and placed it in her hand.

"This is for you. Stay blessed and stay well."

Malachi walked back to where Nyree was waiting for him. She looked angelic and peaceful. For once, she wasn't on her cell phone or in a hurry. Nyree was just standing in one spot waiting. Malachi hurried to her side and placed the roses in her hands. A horse drawn carriage trotted down the street in their direction. This was perfect. He flagged down a horse carriage.

"Come on, let's take a ride," he said to Nyree, as the carriage slowed down.

There was hesitancy on her part. Malachi sensed it. The driver smiled and looked at the couple with interest.

"Come on, Bae," Malachi coaxed Nyree. Flashing his million-dollar smile, he said, "You know you want to."

Seeing the tenderness and gentleness Malachi extended to Nyree, reminded the driver of his days of dating and brought a smile to his face.

"I don't know. Maybe we shouldn't. I feel guilty," Nyree said with her head hung down.

"Look, we'll take this ride and then we'll check in on India. You're a great mother, but you're no good to her or anyone if you're worn out and tired. Let me just show you a wonderful time and..."

"Okay. Okay. After this, we stop and check on India. Deal," she said, as she sat in the carriage and watched Malachi get in.

He nodded and drew her in close to him.

Aris

The sun was rising, and Aris had not moved from the sofa. Bottles of liquor littered the floor. Her drinking binges had become a nightly ritual. This was a time of healing for her. Had things worked out with Sean, she would have never been with Tyler, and her business would be okay. As Aris continued to lounge on the sofa, she thought of ways to acquire money for her failing business. Soon, her mind drifted to Sean. She continued to relive the past, as she thought about the catalyst of her problems.

Summer of 1996 is when things began to unravel.

Now, as Aris faced reality, she realized that she had lost her best friend, Tyler, and knew that the friendship could never be repaired. *I have got to be the biggest fool on earth. Everybody and their momma knew this man was gay but me. It's a wonder that Indiana University doesn't call me up and ask for the degree back. Hell, I should've went to The Ringling Brothers and Barnum & Bailey Clown College. What is it that Danny Dilworth with Dilworth Detective Agency always says? Oh, yeah, "Common sense just ain't that common." Wonder if he had me in mind when he said that.*

As much as she hated to admit it her aunt had been right about Tyler. The conversation played out in her head.

"Aris, I don't know. I just don't think that friends should become lovers. I mean, what happens if you break up? All those years of friendship down the drain," Aunt Trina had tried to warn Aris one day as they dined at the Bakery Restaurant, an upscale restaurant, specializing in French Cuisine in the Miller section of Gary.

Aris taking a long pull of the medium priced Chardonnay, let out a sigh and said, "That's not going to happen to us. We'll be fine."

After all what does Aunt Trina know about love, she still waiting for a married man to make her a wife? That's that old school foolishness.

The real foolishness hit when Tyler came by to pick up his CD collection- Biggie, Pac, Mary J.- and his clothing. But what really knocked the wind out of her was seeing Akim, her stylist, trailing behind him.

Their eyes locked, and Akim, always dramatic, stepped back, hand on his hip, attitude already thick in the air. "Hold up, Miss Thang? Is that *you*?"

Aris blinked hard, like she was seeing a ghost. Ain't no way Akim was in her living room. "Akim? What the hell you doing here?"

"Uh, Ms. Thang, this *is* you? Tyler, uh... what in the holy hell is going on?" Akim's voice was laced with the same confusion swirling in Aris's head. He kept it moving, though, his eyes darting between them. "I came... I'm here to help my boo, uh... Tyler, get his things."

Aris's laughter was short and bitter. "Wait a damn minute. *You* and Tyler? Nah, son. Akim, you been sleeping with my man this whole damn time? And I been pouring my heart out to you, telling you all the drama?"

She shook her head, remembering Aunt Trina's constant warnings: *Watch who you let get close, Chile. Snakes in the grass be wearing the prettiest smiles.* Never in a million years would she have clocked Akim as the other player in her messed-up love life.

"Sweetie," Akim said, his voice softening a fraction, "it ain't like that. I ain't never know that when you was talking 'bout your man, it was *my* man. Besides, you said he was cheatin' with some stripper."

Aris's eyes snapped to Tyler, who was standing there looking like a deer caught in headlights. "Tyler? What the hell is going on? You just gonna walk in here and not say a damn word? Talk to me!" She stepped close, her anger radiating off her like heat.

"Aris, get up outta my face. You wanted me gone, remember? So, I'm gettin' my stuff and leavin'." His voice was cold, dismissive.

"So why you bring *him* with you?"

"Look, Akim's just helping me move into my new spot. Let's go," Tyler said, shoving a box towards Akim.

"Akim," Aris said, her voice dangerously low, "this is the sorry excuse for a man I been telling you about. And *this* is your new boo, the one got you sprung?" She tossed her head, giving Tyler a look that could curdle milk.

"Come on, Akim, let's bounce. I ain't got time for this drama," Tyler mumbled, already halfway out the door.

"Nah, we gonna hash this out right here, right now," Akim shot back, surprising both of them. "You said you wasn't in no committed relationship, and you damn sure didn't say nothin' 'bout being into dudes."

Tyler sighed, running a hand over his freshly faded Caesar cut. "Okay. Y'all wanna hear it? Here it goes. I'm bi. Used to be all about the ladies, and I still dig 'em, but... that was 'til I met you, Akim. Back then, I couldn't help myself with Aris. But now... it's all about you." He licked his lips, giving Akim a look that was pure lust.

Aris felt like the floor had dropped out from under her. Her man – *ex*-man – with her *hairdresser*? The thought sent a wave of nausea crashing over her. Before she could stop herself, she lunged forward, the half-digested burrito and fried rice she'd scarfed down earlier exploding onto Tyler's pink Izod polo and crispy new jeans.

"Get the *hell* out of my house. Both of you!" she spat, wiping her mouth with a tissue she snagged from her FUBU jogging pants.

"I'm so sorry, Ms. Thang. I-I didn't know," Akim stammered, his usually smooth demeanor completely shattered as Aris slammed the door in his face.

Aris stared at the closed door long after they were gone, the silence in the apartment heavy and suffocating. Losing your man to another woman was bad enough. Losing him to some fly girl from the club – one of her own dancers – would have been a whole other level of betrayal. But losing him to another *man*, and her damn hairdresser at that? That was beyond devastating. It felt like a death sentence. How was she supposed to face the streets of Gary now? It was a small town; everybody knew everybody's business. She could already see the headlines in the

Midwest Vein: "Spa Owner and Strip Club Boss Loses Baby Daddy to Male Lover." And Sean's words echoed in her head, that low, knowing chuckle: *"Man always did have a way with the fellas, Aris. You just ain't see it."*

***

Aris curled deeper into the throw pillows on the sofa, the last of the Irish coffee burning a weak trail down her throat. "Damn," she muttered, staring into the empty mug. "Used to make this stuff stronger back in the day."

Solomon

Solomon woke up to the scent of barbecue smoke curling through his open window, mingling with the distant pops of firecrackers.

"July 4, 1998," he muttered, tugging at his Gucci silk sheets—luxury he had indulged in after hearing Lil' Kim rap about them. They felt cool against his bare skin. Sleeping naked was a rare indulgence, but with Madison spending the night at Shauna's, he had taken full advantage of the solitude.

Not that it mattered. Solitude had been his life since Kyra died. It had been a year now, and yet the ache still sat heavy in his chest. Sex had been his greatest addiction, his Achilles' heel, and his ultimate downfall. He used to chase that high, that moment of ecstasy—but what had it given him? Five kids he could barely provide for. A grave with Kyra's name on it. An oath of celibacy seemed like his only shot at redemption.

From his bedroom window, Lake Michigan stretched out before him, endless and indifferent. It didn't care about his regrets, his guilt, his past mistakes. The world kept moving, fireworks bursting in the sky, families gathering, lovers embracing. Meanwhile, his home sat frozen in time, a shrine to Kyra, her pictures watching him from every corner, reminding him of what he had lost.

It was hard for him to believe that it had been a year since

Kyra died. Something in him wanted to scream, cry, grieve, mourn, but he couldn't. He had spent too much time on the long, dead end road called Regret Boulevard. Nothing he could do would bring her back. He had played the "what if" game so many times, and still nothing could bring Kyra back. His home was filled with pictures of her so that the memory of her would be ever present for Madison.

Although he was home alone, he couldn't help but feel that he was not alone. As he brushed his teeth, there was a heavy presence. It almost felt as if someone were in the room with him. He had heard people talk about ghosts, but he never believed in that supernatural type of stuff. This was the day that Kyra died one year ago. Had her spirit come back to haunt him? Did she blame him for her death? These were just a few questions that bombarded him as he stepped into the shower. The warm water massaged his brown-sugar complexion. He closed his eyes and lathered up with the soap. As he inhaled deeply, his heart skipped a beat. When he opened his eyes he could have sworn that he saw a figure through the shower curtain.

"That's absurd," he said aloud, feeling embarrassed for talking to himself.

He continued washing himself, and when the soap fell onto the shower floor he was certain that he had heard more than soap fall.

"I'm losing my damn mind. The one day I have the house to myself, I start cracking up."

He shook his head in disbelief.

Was this the Post-Traumatic Stress Disorder Syndrome stuff

he had heard people talk about? *Nah, couldn't be. I mean…if I was going to go crazy it would have happened before now. A year to the date of Kyra's death, and I'm going to start freaking out. I don't think so. It's somebody in this house. I ain't crazy. I activated the alarm last night before I went to bed, didn't I? I didn't put the motion sensors on for upstairs though. Even still, how could a person by-pass the downstairs motion sensors?*

Solomon tip-toed out of the bathroom with a bath towel wrapped tightly around his waist. He eased around corners, looking back and forth, but he saw nothing. When he made it back to his room, he gently sat on his king-sized bed and sighed. There was that feeling again. He felt as if someone were watching him. His closet door was slight ajar. Solomon didn't remember leaving it open. *Should I open it? There's really no need. My clothes that I want to wear are in the chest of drawers.*

Solomon pulled his blue cotton briefs out of the top chest of drawers, along with a white tank top.

He walked over to the double doors of his closet and placed his hand on the door that was slight ajar and mumbled, "I'm not going to be held hostage in my own house. What is that smell?"

He inhaled a familiar floral fragrance but was having difficulty identifying the possible source.

Ah, he thought, *Shauna decided to surprise me. That makes sense. She has the code to my alarm system. Or mama, but no, she wouldn't go through all this trouble.*

"Shauna," he called, as he walked into the closet and observed mounds of clothing on the floor. Agitated he said, "Girl, what are you doing? Look, come on out, this ain't funny."

His eyes were locked on the silhouette standing in his bedroom doorway—a ghost he'd prayed never to see again.

"I know it ain't funny, Trick," Mona answered.

Solomon swallowed uneasily as the barrel of a gun touched his temple.

M...M...Mona," he stuttered, his throat suddenly dry as sandpaper. "What are you doing here?"

"What do it look like? I'm getting ready to hold you hostage," she said, pressing the cold steel deeper into his temple. Her smile was predatory, calculated. "Take your freedom away, like you took mine away for the past year."

Mona wasn't playing. Not today. Not on the anniversary.

"Mona, can we just talk? I mean, put the gun down and let's talk," Solomon coaxed, backing up until his calves hit the edge of his California king. The same bed where he'd once made promises to her he never intended to keep.

She guided him down with the barrel of the gun, watching him sink into the Egyptian cotton sheets that cost more than her mother's rent. Solomon felt exposed, vulnerable. For a man who had the gift of gab, who had always commanded respect in every room, he now felt like nothing. His swagger, his charm, his million-dollar mouth—all useless against cold steel and a woman scorned.

"Now he wants to talk," Mona laughed, but there was no humor in it. She took her time to blow a bubble with the stale bubblegum in her mouth. *Back in the day you get longer lasting flavor from bubblegum. Damn. They don't make nothing lije they used to. Focus.* "See, this could have all been avoided if he had done right by me." She backed toward the crème chaise lounge near the panoramic windows that showcased the Lake Michigan shoreline.

Mona placed the gun on the nightstand—close enough to grab if needed, but far enough to make a statement. "I don't want to kill you, but you know I will," she gigled. "You know what I'm capable of. You saw first hand what I can do with this handy steel," she blew another bubble. "I want to torture you like you've tortured me." Her voice cracked. "You played with my mind for years, Solomon. YEARS! All those promises while you kept me as your side piece, your rebound whenever your main chick wasn't acting right."

Solomon watched her, truly seeing her for perhaps the first time. Even in the state-issued orange jumpsuit with the faded DOC number stamped across the back, Mona Lee had something that made men stop and stare. Not the conventional beauty of the models and socialites Solomon typically chased, but something magnetic. Something real. It had been enough to keep him coming back to her bed for years, enough to father twins with her, even while maintaining relationships with other women.

"You wanna talk now?" Mona asked, wiping her face with the back of her hand. "It's really too late for that. Why didn't you want to talk when I called from prison? Why didn't you bring my babies to see their mama? My twins don't even know my face no more."

She stood up suddenly, pacing the luxurious bedroom that screamed of wealth. "Our kids are being raised by your mama while you out here living like a king in this lakefront condo, throwing parties for the Fourth like everything's all good." Her voice rose with each word. "Meanwhile, my family has disowned me, and when they catch me, I'll never see daylight again."

"How did you get out?" Solomon asked, feeling slightly bolder now that the gun wasn't against his head. The last time he'd seen Mona had been at her sentencing—twenty-five to life for shooting Kyra at point-blank range. The image of her lifeless, blood saturated body in their bedroom still haunted his dreams.

Looking at Mona now, Solomon saw how prison had hardened her. The soft curves of her face had sharpened, her once flowing hair now in tight cornrows with intricate zig-zag parts. Her cinnamon skin had lost its glow, grown ashen under fluorescent prison lights. Yet her eyes—those same amber eyes that had once looked at him with adoration—now burned with something between hatred and heartbreak.

"What's up with you? Why you over there crying?" Mona asked, noticing the tears Solomon didn't realize were falling. "You still have your life. You still have your freedom. You choose when to get up, what to wear, what to eat. Me? I'm property of the State of Indiana, and the state makes those decisions for me. Or they did, until I decided differently."

"I'm so sorry, Mona," Solomon whispered, the weight of his actions finally crashing down on him. "This is my fault. I'm the cause of you being where you are today."

"That's what I've been saying for over a year. See—"

"Let me finish," Solomon interrupted, his voice stronger now. "I took advantage of your vulnerability. I knew you loved me more than I loved you, and I used that. But you chose to kill. I didn't make you do that."

He shook his head, the reality of his selfishness dawning on him. "I always looked at it like Madison's mom was taken away from her. I never thought about our twins and what they were going through without their mother."

Solomon couldn't believe his own blindness. He had two beautiful ten-year-olds—Nina and Simone—who asked about their mama every night, and he'd given them nothing but lies. If Mona pulled that trigger right now, it wouldn't be anyone's fault but his own.

Solomon saw something shift in Mona's expression—something like resolve.

"Mona Lee! Mona Lee! Put your hands in the air. Do not move!" The shouts came simultaneously with the crash of his bedroom door being kicked open. A flood of tactical officers poured in, their weapons trained on Mona.

"Down on your knees! Down on your knees!" the lead officer demanded.

Solomon remained frozen, watching what seemed like an army of law enforcement filling his bedroom and spilling out into the hallway. Red and blue lights from the vehicles below now competed with the fireworks, painting his cream walls in alternating colors of emergency.

Exactly one year ago to the date, he'd watched Kyra's lifeless body being taken out of his condo.. He couldn't bear to witness another tragedy. With eyes squeezed shut, he prayed silently that Mona wouldn't reach for that gun. That his children wouldn't lose their mother permanently.

"Mr. James," a female officer called out once the situation was contained.

"Yes," he responded, voice barely audible as he opened his eyes to see Mona being handcuffed and led away. Her eyes never left his face—not accusing now, just sad. Resigned.

"On behalf of the Indiana Department of Corrections, you have my deepest apologies for this incident," the officer continued, extending her hand. "We've been tracking Inmate Lee since her escape during the prison transport three days ago."

Solomon mechanically shook her hand, then watched the procession of officers escorting Mona down his spiral staircase. The female officer paused at his front door.

"Mr. James, please be advised that the inmate will be transported to Pendleton Maximum Security Correctional Facility. Given the circumstances, I would recommend you consider filing for a protective order."

Solomon stood at the top of the staircase, watching as they took Mona away. The last thing he saw before the door closed was Mona looking back at him over her shoulder, her eyes carrying a message he couldn't decipher. Was it hatred? Forgiveness? A promise to return?

As the door clicked shut, Solomon sank to his knees, the weight of the afternoon crushing him. Outside, the fireworks sounded off, the sky a dull gray. In his heart, he knew there would always be a connection between him and Mona—one forged in passion, twisted by betrayal, and now stained with blood. Their sins would follow them both, no matter how fancy the address or how high the security.

Shauna

"Hey, is everything okay over there? You are the talk of every damn television station. Reporters and police are swarming your crib like roaches!" Shauna exclaimed into the phone, her eyes glued to the breaking news flashing across her 32-inch Sony. The afternoon sun sliced through her venetian blinds, casting jail-bar shadows across her living room.

"Yeah, I'm cool, I guess," Solomon said with his voice saturated in exhaustion. "I thought you were going to come over here, and we were going to have a cook-out? I got steaks and chicken marinating" Solomon asked.

Shauna twisted the pink phone cord around her finger, glancing at the patio where she'd already set up water guns for the kids. The summer heat was oppressive, making the air conditioning work overtime.

"I was, but under the circumstances, I don't think it's a good idea. The kids may not be able to handle all of that. Malik just asked me why is Daddy on Channel 7 news." Shauna told him.

"You're right. I guess I'm a hostage in my own house."He sighed heavily, and Shauna could picture him running his hand over his freshly cut fade—a nervous habit she'd noticed back when they were together.

"Why don't you pack a bag and come over here with us? Bring some of Madison's things and we can celebrate over here, at least until things settle down." Shauna paused, rethinking what she was saying, "I mean, unless you were going to go somewhere else. You know what, forget it..."

"Shauna, calm down. If you're thinking I'm seeing someone, I'm not. Haven't had time between my job and Madison." His voice softened. "I would love to take you up on your offer. It's just... I don't know how to say this without seeming vulnerable."

"Just say it," Shauna said, her heart thumping against her chest as she adjusted her tank top in the July heat.

"I'm feeling something for you, and I don't want to be the one to get hurt if you and Jeremiah get serious."

Shauna nearly choked on her sweet tea. "Oh, you're real funny. So you're a comedian now like Martin Lawrence. Ha Ha.That dude tolerates me, but he can't stand me, and I can't stand his bougie ass. Always talking 'bout my 'form' and shit."

"It didn't seem like that when I saw you all in the café together. You guys seemed real cozy sharing dessert and then when I came to the table he killed a thousand times with his eyes."

"He's my trainer, that's it, but what's it to you? I'm not trying to see anyone. My life is such a mess. I gotta get Shauna together."

"Last time I looked, Shauna was looking well put together," Solomon said, his voice dropping an octave. "Real well put together."

The heat in her cheeks had nothing to do with the July temperature"Really? Look, you ain't gotta gas my head up. I said it's cool for you to stay over here if you need a place to crash."

"You know me well enough to know when I'm blowing smoke, and that ain't smoke. I'll see you in a few minutes," he said before hanging up.

I'm glad he finally hung up. Did I hear him right? He's digging me. Oh, snap. I'm digging him too, but I can't get hurt by him again. Once bitten. Twice shy.

The ringing of her cell phone drew her out of her trance. City of Gary came across the caller ID. *Damien, calling to wish me a Happy Fourth of July. I'm surprised he's at City Hall today. But I guess holidays and Saturdays don't stop nothing in his world. Call me and tell me about some child support. Call me and tell me when you're gonna pay me the money you owe me, punk. I could give less than a damn about a holiday. Independence Day. I could be a whole lot more independent if I had my money. I should let it ring and go to voicemail, but I wanna hear what this sorry bastard has to say for himself.*

"Hello," Shauna answered unenthusiastically. Who would dare interupt her quiet, solitude?The burst of firecrackers outside reminded her that the neighborhood kids had been celebrating since the crack of dawn.

"Yes, is this Shauna Buchanan, the daughter of the late Judge Buchanan?" The woman on the other end of the telephone asked. *Welp, it's not Damien.* "Who is this?" Shauna demanded.

"This is Marisol Waters. I clerked at your father's office years ago. I am the personal assistant to First Lady Carrington."

Shauna had to hold back laughter, nearly spitting out her

tea. This was the first time she had ever heard anyone refer to Beverly Carrington like that. She had some adjectives that she would like to put in front of Beverly's name, but none would be appropriate in front of her kids, who were now running through the house with sparklers their grandmother had snuck them.

"Um-hum," Shauna said unimpressed, rolling her eyes.

"Well, First Lady Carrington wanted me to call you and see if you could meet with her on Monday," Marisol said.

"Regarding what?" Shauna asked, grabbing a pen and her day planner from her purse.

"Well, several things. One, she wanted to talk with you about the loan you made to Mayor Carrington's campaign, and two, she is planning on running for senate and is looking for a campaign manager."

Money and power. That's all that family ever thinks about. "Great, how about a breakfast meeting at Jonathan's Pancake House at nine a.m.?" Shauna suggested, knowing the public location would keep Beverly in check.

"That will work out fine," Marisol answered, sounding relieved the conversation was going smoothly.

"I'll see her then." Shauna confirmed, already planning her outfit—something professional but with enough edge to remind Beverly who she was dealing with.

"Okay. Thank you and have a Happy Fourth of July. By the way, how is your mother?" Marisol asked.

"She's wonderful. Have a great holiday," Shauna said and hung up the phone. Outside, the sound of bottle rockets and kids' laughter filled the air, but inside, a cold silence settled over

Shauna.

The thought of her mother hadn't crossed her mind until Marisol mentioned her.

Shauna had so much anger and bitterness toward Loretta Buchanan. How could she feel the way she did toward the woman who nearly lost her life to bring her into the world? Maybe it was because her mother acted like a moron over her father's will. Even though they had been married for twenty years, they had been divorced for over ten, and Shauna was named beneficiary. Her father felt like he had been the biggest loser in the divorce, so he didn't leave her much of anything, and Shauna's little sister didn't receive anything. That raised eyebrows. More eyebrows were raised when Loretta had to explain to Paris that the man whom she had called dad all her life was not her dad. Why was this Shauna's fault? Why should her mother be angry at her? Shauna knew that death brought the worst out in some people, so she tried to contain her composure for as long as she could. One day, her mother made a snide remark about the money, and Shauna let her have it.

"Look Loretta, I don't owe you nothing, and my daddy didn't owe you anything either. You got the house and the restaurant, what else do you want? You hate that I have a future, and I didn't have to lay on my back to get it," Shauna shouted and felt sorry after the words came out but refused to take them back.

"Mark my words, from this day forth, your days will be hard and difficult, since you want to disrespect your mother. You just sealed your fate with those words. Easy come. Easy go, you'll see," her mother spat.

No truer words had ever been spoken. Her mother cursed her that day. She may as well have spewed venom in Shauna's face. Shauna laughed at the conversation.

"It's changing as I speak, Loretta. Your words no longer have power over me, you witch," Shauna mumbled.

"Shauna, are you okay?" Solomon asked.

"AHHHH!!!!" Shauna screamed, nearly jumping out of her skin. "You scared the hell outta me! I thought I was in here alone," Shauna said, pressing her hand against her pounding heart. Solomon looked good—too good—in his white linen shirt and khaki shorts, a small overnight bag slung over his shoulder.

"I didn't mean to scare you. I thought you heard me when I came in. Who were you talking to?"

"I was thinking out loud about something Loretta said to me awhile ago." Shauna waved dismissively, trying to shake off the dark mood. "How are you? Sit down. Can I get you something? A beer? Some barbecue chips? I got your favorite—salt and vinegar."

"Yeah, you can get me a fat one," Solomon said with a sly grin, referring to the blunts they used to share back in the day.

"Boy, shut up." Shauna laughed, swatting his arm. "You don't know nothing about that. You know I don't do that anymore."

"Just checking to see where your head was," Solomon told Shauna. He smiled as he thought about how much progress she had made, from the wild party girl to responsible mother of three.

"Hey, I see you got the charcoal, grill, and lighter fluid out. Is that a hint?" He nodded toward the supplies on the patio, visible through the sliding glass door.

"Yep, if you feel up to it, you can do your chef thing," Shauna smiled, remembering how Solomon used to brag about his grilling skills at every cookout.

"Momma, hey Dad, can we get in the pool?" Malik asked, as he peeked in the room, his swim trunks already on and a towel draped around his shoulders like a cape.

"Yep, but you gotta wait for me to get on my swim wear. What's the rule?" Shauna asked, giving him the mom eye.

"An adult always has to be in the pool with us, 'cause you ain't trying to be on the front page of *The Midwest Vein* being called a negligen momma," Malik recited, bouncing on his toes with excitement.

"Negligent momma," Shauna corrected him, smoothing his hair. "I'm not trying to be on the front page of that rag being called a negligent momma. Where are your sisters? It's about time to put some little ones on the toilet," Shauna stopped and paused.

Smiling, she continued, "You know Solomon, Madison is doing good with being potty-trained. Taylor is just about there. She has her lazy moments. Okay Malik, do you remember what I did with the swimming training pants?" Shauna asked.

"They are in the linen closet by the toilet paper," Malik replied, eager to get to the pool in their backyard.

"Solomon, if you would tell Madison and Taylor to go potty, I can change and will be out in a minute to help them get ready for

POOL TIME!"

Malik ran off excited and singing, "Pool time! It's pool time!"

Solomon remained fixed in place, his eyes traveling over Shauna in a way that made her feel nineteen again.

"What?" Shauna asked, pretending not to notice the heat in his gaze.

"Why I gotta leave? I can't stay and watch," Solomon flirted, leaning against the doorframe with a confidence that came from knowing exactly what he wanted.

"Out. OUT!" Shauna smiled, as she closed her bedroom door behind Solomon, her heart racing like she'd just run a mile in the July heat.

Through the window, fireworks began to light up the darkening sky, and Shauna had a feeling this Fourth of July would be about more than just America's independence.

Nyree

"Everything is fine with India." Nyree reported after speaking with Claudia, India's nanny, on her two-way pager. "Whew, I'm tired."

Nyree couldn't help staring at Malachi as he checked his email on his expensive laptop. She was catching the side view of him —fresh fade, diamond studs catching the light, muscular frame draped in designer gear—and it was more than quite sexy. They had experienced another great video shoot yesterday for the lead single off his platinum album, and today had been their day to sightsee. This was their second trip to New York City and Nyree was becoming pretty fond of the Big Apple.

Nyree ignored her cell phone ringing for the milloneth time today. It was Colin calling for the millionth time. Malachi let out a sigh that said he was annoyed, the platinum Rolex on his wrist glinting as he shifted in his chair. Nyree thought she had put her phone on vibrate earlier, but now, she quickly switched the lever to the vibrate side.

"Talk to dude would you? If you still want to be with him its cool. I would just like to know something," Malachi said, as he looked at Nyree holding her phone.

He could see that she was debating on taking Colin's call. He didn't want her to take the call, but he wanted to seem like he was unaffected just like the character he had portrayed himself as in *Confessions of a Playa.*

"Okay, Malachi, let's get this out the way," she said, as she sat on the bed in his hotel room. "I'm with who I want to be, and I'm where I want to be, right here in your bed," Nyree said a little more seductively than she had intended.

Nyree turned her phone off and stretched out. *What the hell? I can't believe I just said that. If that was true why did I insist on us having separate rooms? Too bad you can't suck your words in like you do your gut. There's no taking that back.*

Malachi shut down his MacBook and walked across the plush carpet of the penthouse suite at the Plaza Hotel. The New York skyline glittered through the floor-to-ceiling windows, the city that never sleeps living up to its reputation even at this hour. He nudged Nyree as her back was to him, her Versace silk pajamas catching the soft glow from the bedside lamp. She wouldn't budge. He turned her over onto her back and was now leaning over her, the diamond pendant on his platinum chain dangling between them.

"Say it to my face."

"Say what?" Her voice was husky but her eyes were alert.

"Oh, so now it's, 'say what'," Malachi teased her, his platinum Rolex glinting as he shifted his weight on the thousand-thread-count Egyptian cotton sheets.

Nyree stared into his alluring eyes, took a deep breath and said, "Look, ain't nobody scared of you. Just 'cause you on top of me don't give you no advantage. I'm not running from you anymore. I said I'm with who I want to be with, and I'm where I want to be."

Her heart was beating fast. She could not believe the words

that came out of her mouth. Outside, the sounds of Manhattan traffic created a distant urban symphony, seventeen floors below their luxury suite—a suite she could have secured through Shaw Enterprises connections, but she'd let Malachi handle it instead.

The look on his face suggested Malachi couldn't believe his ears. He had been waiting for what seemed like an eternity to hear those words come out of Nyree's mouth. After his triple-platinum album dropped a few month ago, and with his new single climbing the Billboard charts, he finally had the courage to reach out to her again. Now, his fate depended on how he reacted. He leaned closer and let his lips gently brush her lips. Then his tongue slipped into her mouth, and she allowed herself to relax and enjoy the heated kiss. She caught her breath and began to think about what could happen and where this was going.

Gently she pushed Malachi back and said, "I...I don't know about this. I'm sorry. I'm definitely feeling you, but...I need to go to my room and take a hot bath."

"What? Hot bath? That's the best you can come up with, Baby Girl? Umm, yeah, maybe we can go watch some fireworks later on?" Malachi asked, adjusting the diamond stud in his ear.

She knew he was calling her Baby Girl to get under her skin and force her to say what was really on her mind.

"Nobody calls me Baby Girl, but Grandma Lula. You know that, knucklehead. Yes, I'm going to take a hot bath. You got me all hot and bothered, and I need to think straight. Maybe you can order some food and come over in about an hour or so. Yeah, fireworks that would be nice," Nyree said, as she walked toward the door that joined their rooms, her custom Jimmy Choo slippers whispering against the carpet.

Malachi caught her by her arms and turned her toward him. He drew her in close and encircled his arms around her waist. He held her snugly but not too tight. He stood a whole foot over her, his six-foot-three frame towering over her petite figure. The scent of his Issey Miyake cologne mixed with her Chanel No. 5, creating an intoxicating blend. She looked down at the ground, past his FUBU jeans that hung perfectly on his athletic frame. Nyree refused to let her eyes meet his. She was afraid that if her eyes met his that they would dance, and she would feel those feelings she had just felt moments ago.

As if he could read her mind and knew she was avoiding eye contact with him, Malachi said, "Look at me, Nyree."

He tilted her chin up so that they could look at one another in the eye, his thumb grazing her flawless skin, reminding him of why she'd been on the cover of Essence twice in the last year.

"Malachi, come on, let's not do this," Nyree protested.

"Nyree, I want you to know that every time we're close you don't have to be afraid. You don't have to run from me. I am not going to hurt you. I promise you that. What do I have to do to prove it to you? I love you," he said. The pager on his belt vibrated —probably his manager calling to see how the video shoot had gone—but he ignored it.

"Malachi, it's been a long day. I'm not running away from you. We've been together all day, and... I just think right now that emotions are running high, and if we calm down we'll think more rationally."

"Nyree, you know good and damn well what I mean when I say running. I'm sorry for cussing. But look, what a brother got to do to prove to you that he loves you? I was wrong in the past. I'm sorry, Nyree, for all the shit, I mean stuff, I put you through, but I'm not going to let you just run off. This may sound cheesy and corny, but I don't care. I love you, and I want you to be my boo again. What is there to think about? I'm clear on what I want. There's nothing to think about," he said boldly, his voice carrying the same confidence that had women screaming at his shows across the country.

Nyree was running short on air. He had said everything that she had wanted to hear a year and a half ago when they signed the divorce papers in her attorney's Midtown office. Now, she didn't know what she wanted. Through the window, she could see one of the Shaw Enterprises buildings in the distance, the family logo illuminated against the night sky—a constant reminder of the empire her father had built and that she now helped run as Vice President of Acquisitions.

"Look, Chi, I'm going to go take a bath," Nyree said, fingering the tennis bracelet he'd given her earlier today—just a "small gift" he'd called it, though it probably cost more than most people's cars.

"Whoa! So, a brother just says he loves you, and all you can say is you're going to take a bath. Okay..." Malachi trailed, as he watched the door that separated their rooms close in his face. His cell phone rang in his pocket, but he let it go to voicemail.

Once inside her room, Nyree stripped down and put on her Couture Insanity robe with the matching slippers, the exclusive designer label that had become her signature since she started making appearances at Shaw Enterprises' high-profile real estate closings. She started her bath and brushed her hair into a ponytail, the diamond earrings he'd bought her for their last anniversary catching the light. A knock at the door put her on full alert. It was probably Malachi, but she decided to ask who was at the door. You could never be too careful, even in the most exclusive hotel in Manhattan.

"Guest services," a man called through the door.

She stood on her tip toes and could see he was holding a box. She felt a little silly for thinking that it would be Malachi knocking at the front door. Why would he do that when he could just very well knock on the adjoining door? Tugging her robe tightly, she opened the door and took the box from the man and closed the door, tipping him with a crisp fifty-dollar bill from her Fendi purse on the side table.

There was no return address, but it was addressed to her. She found that odd because no one except Kyle, her brother, knew where she was staying. *Why would Kyle send me a box without a return address? Oh my goodness, tell me he's not in trouble again. Now that she thought about it, he had called her earlier in the day on her new Nokia cell phone, and she ignored his call. I'm not going to worry about it now either. Kyle is going to have to stand on his own two feet one of these days. He can live a few days without me. I deserve a break, right? He was probably just calling to say Happy Fourth of July. I feel a little guilty for not being home for the holiday. However, sometimes I need time to do what I need to do.*

Nyree began tearing the paper away from the box, and the aroma hit her in the face. Immediately, she knew what the box contained and who sent it. It was a box of her favorite bath and body products from Nicole Bradley Candle Co. There was a note enclosed, written on monogrammed stationery with Malachi's platinum-selling record label logo embossed at the top.

Baby Girl,

I wanted to surprise you with some of your favorite goodies. Hope you enjoy. Know that I appreciate all that you've done for me and all that you do for our daughter. I love you to the end of eternity.

XOXO,

Malachi

Nyree read the note over and over again. It was as if she were trying to etch the words into her memory. Malachi could be so sweet at times, and other times, he could be asinine. She had mentioned her favorite fragrance line from the Nicole Bradley Candle Co Collection was Forbidden Fruit and he remembered.

Nyree folded the note and held it close to her heart. What was she doing? She couldn't go back, could she? His words were lovely, but how many times could she do that dance? One of them was off beat, and she knew it was her. She didn't even know if she wanted to follow his lead or dance to his beat. He possessed all the qualities that she wanted in a man, but had he truly changed? In the back of her mind, she couldn't help but wonder if it was all a game to him.

In one of his interviews with The Source magazine, he remarked, "I didn't ever lie to Nyree. She knew who I was and what she was getting when she got involved with me."

That wasn't true when they first got together, but now, yes, she knew exactly who he was or at least who he had been. If she got back with him, knowing what she knew, that would make her a stone cold fool in her mind. If he were to break her heart again, then, that would be her fault. Her father had warned her about dating entertainers, saying they'd never understand the responsibilities that came with being a Shaw. Maybe he was right. But then again, her dad had never approved of any man in her life. She was Daddy's little girl—the favorite who had followed in his footsteps while Kyle, her brother, had walked away from the family business, creating the rift that her mother still tried to mend at every holiday gathering. Smelling the fragrances from the box, she decided to forget about Malachi and enjoy a bath in the marble Jacuzzi tub that dominated her bathroom.

****

Nyree walked out of the bathroom with her towel barely closed around her naked body, when Malachi came through the door she had closed earlier. He startled her and Nyree screamed, dropped the towel and took a step back. The Notorious B.I.G.'s "Mo Money Mo Problems" played softly from the Bang & Olufsen sound system he must have turned on. Malachi's eyes surveyed Nyree's body, as she scrambled to pick up the towel to cover her naked form, the diamond belly button ring he'd bought her in Paris glinting in the low light.

"You don't have to do that. I've seen you naked before, and I'm liking what I see now," Malachi told Nyree, his voice deep with desire.

Nyree ignored him and continued to try to cover her naked body. The towel covered most of her body, yet, it barely covered her behind and lower extremities.

"I told you that wasn't necessary," Malachi smiled, leaning against the doorframe in a pose reminiscent of his latest album cover.

"Since when do I listen to you?" Nyree pouted. She was annoyed, but couldn't help but notice how good he looked in his designer clothes.

"Why did you scream, and where were you going?" Malachi laughed. He continued, "You know if you were in a scary movie you would have been done for, right? Like one of them Scream joints that just came out."

Nyree was so cute to him. As hardcore as she tried to be, wearing her success as VP at Shaw Enterprises like armor, it was times like this when her vulnerability showed, and he liked it.

"You think it's funny?" Nyree asked.

She tried to be mad but had to laugh at herself. She knew full well if she were in a scary movie she would be one of the first characters to die. Nyree could not run and in times of chaos, she panicked all the time. He was right. Where was she getting ready to run to? She clearly had seen it was Malachi so why had she screamed? Nyree had no answers for any of those questions.

"I guess I have that effect on you. I walk into the room and you come out of your clothes," he said, his platinum grill flashing as he smiled.

"Why are you here?" Nyree asked, as she clutched the towel even tighter.

She noticed he had changed into black Armani slacks, with a white silk shirt unbuttoned just enough to pique her curiosity.

His custom Timberlands had been swapped for Italian loafers. He had been working out, and his body was looking good to her—probably from all those dance rehearsals for his sold-out tour that would start after they wrapped the video.

"Dinner. We have a dinner date remember," he said, gesturing to the Cristal champagne he'd brought with him.

"Chi, oh shit!"

Whatever it was must have been serious because he rarely heard Nyree curse. That was one thing that turned him on about her. She was the coolest woman he knew, and her language was clean ninety-five percent of the time, even in the cutthroat world of real estate she now dominated back home in Gary, Indiana.

"What? What's up, Baby Girl?" he asked, concern crossing his handsome face.

"How many times have I told you about that Baby Girl stuff?" she asked, as she walked up to him and hit him in the chest.

He pulled her close to him and looked into her eyes. Before she could turn her head to avoid eye contact, he caught her by the chin and held it in position and asked, "What's up, Baby Girl?"

"I'm tired, for real. Would you be mad if we ordered in?" Nyree asked, as she puckered her lips and batted her long eyelashes. Outside, fireworks began to explode over the East River, visible from their window.

"C'mon, Nyree, not the face?" Malachi asked.

He was a sucker for that face. She could literally have whatever she wanted from him when she made that face, and she knew it.

She laid it on extra thick now and said, "Well?"

"Nyree, come on. You know we're leaving in two days after we wrap the video, and you're going to want to shop all day tomorrow at Saks and Barneys and will be too tired to do dinner tomorrow night. Is this your way of saying you don't want to have dinner with me? Just tell me. Don't string a brother on," Malachi said half-jokingly, his Cartier watch catching the light as he gestured.

"We can stay an extra day if that happens, and I'll pay to have the tickets changed. I got my own money now, remember?" Nyree said with pride, thinking of her upper six-figure salary and executive bonus from the Miller Beach Front redevelopment project she'd just closed for Shaw Enterprises. Her father had made sure his favorite child was well-compensated, even as he refused to have anything to do with Kyle, her brother who'd walked away from the family legacy.

"Okay, I'mma hold you to that," he replied, his eyes holding a promise.

"You're already holding me."

"I know, and I don't intend on letting you go. Come on, let me rub you down," he said, his voice dropping an octave.

"Ooh, you nasty."

"That's you, girl. I mean, you just got out the tub. I want to massage some of this Orgasm Body Butter that Nicole Bradley sent over for you," he said, flashing that to-die-for-smile that had graced the cover of Vibe magazine last month.

Nyree returned the smile and said, "Okay, but since I'm naked, you got to lose some of your clothing, too. Let the shirt and pants go."

Malachi came out of his shirt and pants before she could change her mind, revealing the physique that had earned him a spot in People magazine's "50 Most Beautiful People." He decided to make her wait awhile for her massage and ordered room service on the cordless phone and lit the Forbidden Fruit candle that was on the nightstand and dimmed the lights. The New York City skyline provided the perfect backdrop through the panoramic windows, making their suite feel like the center of the universe.

Nyree took a deep breath and allowed his hands to massage her skin. She felt a little squeamish, so she called his name.

"Yes, Beautiful."

"Thank you for the beautiful basket and everything. I've never felt so special in my life."

"You should feel special everyday. I'm sorry for all the hurt that I've brought you. I want to spend the rest of my life making it up to you," Malachi said, feeling her body tighten up. He whispered into her ear as he massaged the right side of her back, "Relax. I swear I won't hurt you. I'm not that same dude who was immature and too stupid to realize I had everything I needed at home. With everything I got going on now, it don't mean nothing without you."

Nyree took a deep breath and tried to let her body relax, but it was difficult. She'd given him one hundred percent of her before, and the story didn't end well. Now, she was vulnerable. Her father had nearly disowned her when she'd left the family business temporarily to follow Malachi on tour. That bridge had taken months to rebuild. Only her mother's quiet intervention had helped her get back into her father's good graces—the same mother who always took Kyle's side in every family dispute.

"Nyree, relax would you," Malachi said, moving her hair to the side so he could massage her occipital bone, in the back and lower part of her cranium.

A knock at the door interrupted everything, and she was glad for the diversion. Malachi slipped his slacks on and went to the door. It was room service. Malachi paid the bill with a hundred-dollar bill and gave the gentleman a large tip, telling him to keep the change. The server's eyes widened at the generosity before he wheeled in the covered silver platters.

Nyree scrambled to put on her Couture Insanity robe, the silk fabric cool against her warm skin.

Malachi laughed and asked, "Why are you so nervous for me to see you naked? I've seen you in the nude a million times. Don't you know I was checking you out from head to toe while I was massaging that body butter into your skin?" Malachi laughed, "You are so cute. As much as you give me a hard time and try to come off hardcore with your business meetings and closing million-dollar real estate deals, underneath it all, you really are just Baby Girl."

Rolling her eyes, Nyree said nothing. Malachi smiled to himself. This was one of the rare times when he had been able to get away with calling her Baby Girl, and she said nothing. He opened her tray and cut her filet mignon into bite size pieces and poured steak sauce over each piece and then fixed her baked potato just like she liked it with butter first, then sour cream, and a sprinkle of salt and pepper.

Then he fed her a piece of steak and asked, "So how is it, my lady?"

"Perfect. Reminds me of the old days," Nyree said, remembering how this used to be their ritual when he made dinner for her.

This was a night that rekindled a lot of moments from times past. As the fireworks continued to burst over the Manhattan skyline, casting colorful reflections across their skin, Nyree wondered if maybe—just maybe—they could create a new future together, one where his music and her real estate empire could coexist with their love. Maybe this time, she could balance her role as Daddy's favorite corporate princess with being the woman behind the music mogul. She reached for her phone, thinking she should probably call Kyle back—he may be her mother's favorite, but he was still her brother and the only one who'd supported her relationship with Malachi from the beginning.

Malachi

Malachi and Nyree had shared an evening of passionate lovemaking in the penthouse suite of the Plaza Hotel, overlooking a New York City still echoing with the previous night's Independence Day celebrations. Nyree had fallen asleep shortly after their third encounter, her breathing now soft and rhythmic against the silk sheets. Secretly, Malachi was relieved —he wasn't sure he had the stamina to match her insatiable appetite once more.

He watched her sleep for a while, the city lights casting gentle shadows across her face. Then, following his routine, he called to check on India. Satisfied that both women in his life were safe and sound, he allowed himself to drift off to sleep.

The harsh vibration of his phone against the marble nightstand jolted him awake at three in the morning.

"Who in the hell is calling me at three o'clock in the damn morning?" he muttered, rolling onto his side to check the screen. A 219 area code—Northwest Indiana. He didn't recognize the number. It had to be a wrong number; everyone he wanted to have his number was saved in his contacts. Before he could set it back down, the phone vibrated again—same number.

"Hello," Malachi whispered, stepping toward the bathroom to avoid waking Nyree. If it was a female caller, he definitely didn't want Nyree hearing that conversation.

"What now—" he began, but was cut off by the voice on the other end. "Say that again." Sweat was beading his forehead.

"Damn," he huffed, listening intently. He nodded several times before responding. "She's right here. She's asleep. You want me to do what?" His voice cracked slightly. "I mean... Damn. I'm so sorry. You alright? Okay. I will."

Malachi ended the call and turned toward the bed, watching Nyree stir slightly in her sleep. In the dim light filtering through the half-drawn curtains, she looked peaceful, unaware of how her world was about to shatter. He dressed quickly, calling the airline to book the earliest flight to Chicago Midway. He phoned the front desk to check out, then gathered Nyree's belongings before retrieving his own from his room.

Standing at the foot of the bed, Malachi wished he'd stayed in his own room last night. Their rekindled passion now felt like terrible timing—he would have given anything not to be the one delivering this news.

He sat gently on the edge of the bed and touched her shoulder. "Nyree. Nyree," he called softly.

She rubbed her eyes and smiled when she saw him, but her expression quickly changed as she registered his fully dressed state, the serious look on his face, and the lights blazing throughout the suite.

"You okay?" Nyree asked, sitting up.

Malachi held her Couture Insanity robe in his hands, silently helping her into it, his movements deliberate and careful.

"I got something to tell you, and I don't know how to say it."

"Did I hear you on the phone earlier?" Nyree asked, the last vestiges of sleep leaving her eyes.

"Yes," he said quietly.

"Is it about the phone call?"

"Yeah," he said sadly.

"Is it India?" she asked, her voice rising with immediate concern.

"No. No, she's fine."

Nyree sighed with relief. Whatever it was, she could handle it now that she knew her daughter was safe.

"So, was that one of your women? What, somebody else is pregnant?" Nyree's voice escalated to a scream. "This is so you, Malachi! I can't believe this crap!"

"It's not that," he said firmly. "I told you I wouldn't hurt you anymore. But what I have to tell you is the hardest thing I've ever had to do." His voice cracked as tears formed in his eyes. "Baby, believe me, I don't want to have to do this. I'm so sorry. I'm so sorry."

Tears streamed down his face, and Nyree realized the last time she'd seen him this distraught was when his cousin Frank had died. A chill ran through her body despite the July heat.

She locked her eyes on his, wiped his tears with her thumb, and said, "What is it? Tell me. Hold my hands and just tell me. I'm a big girl. Whatever it is, I can handle it."

"Nyree, I love you. I truly love you, and I told Kyle I would do this, but..."

"Kyle? Kyle called you?" Her brow furrowed. "He and Colin

have been calling me all day on yesterday, but I didn't want to answer. Malachi, tell me straight, no chaser."

"Nyree," Malachi squeezed her hands tightly and locked eyes with her. The smell of last night's champagne still lingered in the air between them. "Edwin had a stroke yesterday, on the Fourth... and he died an hour ago. I'm so sorry."

Malachi watched Nyree's face for what seemed like hours. The distant sound of early morning traffic floated up from Fifth Avenue, but the penthouse felt wrapped in a bubble of silence.

She said nothing for the longest time, then pulled her hands away from him. "You're a liar, Malachi. This is not funny. This is low, even for you. You make love to me and then wake me up in the middle of the night and tell me my daddy is dead? You almost had me going with those fake tears. I HATE YOU! Get out! Get away from me!"

She ran into the bathroom, slamming the door behind her. He heard her retching violently. "You make me sick!" she yelled through the door.

The toilet flushed, and he heard her vomit again.

"Nyree, I'm not lying to you. I would never do that to you," Malachi found himself yelling, his voice bouncing off the elegant walls of the penthouse. "Call Kyle if you don't believe me. Why would I do some foul shit like that?"

He was fuming but quickly caught himself. She was lashing out because she didn't know how to process the news. How would he have responded if the roles were reversed? He probably wouldn't have accused her of lying, but then again, he carried a reputation that might never fade—one built on years of deception.

Malachi knew he had told many lies in his life, especially to Nyree, but some things were sacred. He would never lie about someone's father dying.

"Don't cuss at me, MALACHI! Hand me my cell phone and get out!"

"I'll give you your phone," he said, passing it through the cracked bathroom door, "but I'm not going anywhere. We have a six o'clock flight out of here."

She opened the door wider and looked at him, her eyes red and swollen. For the first time, it seemed she might be taking him seriously. The realization was dawning on her face that her father might truly be gone. Malachi pushed the door open further and watched her brush her teeth, her hands trembling as she made circular motions and spat into the sink.

"Kyle! KYLE!" she screamed into the phone on speaker.

"Nyree, Malachi told you?" Kyle's voice was heavy with grief.

"He's lying, Kyle. Tell me Malachi is lying. Tell me Daddy is not gone."

"Sis, I wish I could tell you Daddy's not gone." Kyle's voice cracked with emotion. "You know Malachi wouldn't lie about that. Don't say that again, and if you did, apologize to him now. He loves you, and he wouldn't do that. Where is he? He said he would be there with you until you got home."

"He's right here." Nyree nodded, wiping toothpaste from the corner of her mouth. She turned to Malachi, her eyes now filled with remorse. "Malachi, I'm sorry. You happy now, Kyle, I said it."

Nyree picked up the phone and switched from speaker to regular mode. Pressing it to her ear, she spoke softly, "What happened? Okay. Okay. Okay." Her voice had become small, childlike. "Malachi said we're leaving at six o'clock. I should've been there. I didn't know. I will see you soon."

She hung up and looked at Malachi before collapsing into his arms, her sobs wracking her body. "I'm so sorry, Malachi. I didn't mean it. Please, don't hate me. I'm so sorry. Did you know my father is dead? My father died this morning. I never got to say goodbye."

The morning sun was beginning to rise over Manhattan as she buried her head deeper into his chest. "I didn't tell him I loved him. The last thing I said was 'I'm a grown woman, Daddy.' I didn't want him to worry about me coming to New York. Wow, my daddy died, and I wasn't there for him. He's always been there for me. But where was I? I was being grown..."

"Shhh. Stop it," Malachi consoled her, stroking her hair. "Everybody knows you loved your dad, and he loved you, too. Don't do this to yourself. Come on. Take a shower and let's get out of here. I love you, and I know that doesn't mean anything to you right now, but I'm here for you. Let me get you home."

He kissed her forehead until her breathing began to normalize. "I'm so sorry, Nyree, but don't do this to yourself. I won't let you."

He turned on the shower and watched her walk in, closing the curtain behind her. Sitting on the closed toilet lid, he waited patiently, listening to her cry. The sound of her grief mixed with the rushing water was almost unbearable.

"Nyree, I'm still here," he called softly. "Do you want me to iron something for you?"

She sniffled. "No, thank you. Could you just get me a pair of jeans, hoodie, and underwear?"

"I get to choose your underwear?" he said, attempting to lighten the mood.

Nyree pulled back the shower curtain just enough to give Malachi what he recognized as the "Aunt Esther from Sanford and Son look."

"Alright, dang, you'll kill a brother with that look," Malachi blurted out without thinking, then immediately backpedaled. "I'm sorry. I was just joking. That wasn't funny."

"Hand me that towel," Nyree demanded as she turned off the water and stepped onto the black marble floor. Malachi passed her the towel and started toward the door, giving her privacy.

"Come here," she called after him. "I thought you weren't going to leave me."

"Umm, I... I," For once, Malachi was speechless.

"Look, my daddy died, but that doesn't mean you should stop being your lovable self. I know you didn't mean anything insensitive by it, okay?" She hugged him, the towel wrapped tightly around her body, water still dripping from her hair. "Now, can you bring me some clothes? We got a plane to catch, right?"

"Yes, Miss Lady, we have a plane to catch." He nodded, relieved at her forgiveness. "I'm sorry. I feel bad because I wanted you all to myself and..."

"I wanted you all to myself, too," she interrupted. "I shut the world out, and in the process, my daddy died. I don't blame anyone. Just hold me for a minute. When we get back, you know it's going to be crazy, right? I just want to have one last moment with you."

Malachi held her tightly in the steamy bathroom, their reflection visible in the fogged mirror. It felt like the beginning of the end—a feeling of déjà vu washed over him. They had been here before, but with roles reversed. It had been him crying in her arms when his cousin died from a heart attack a few years earlier. Now, it was the love of his life sobbing against his chest, and all he could do was hold her.

Even though he had written a bestseller, he had no words for her at this moment. He just held her tightly, and for the first time in months, he prayed that he would not lose her. He knew Colin might use this opportunity to step in and take her away. It was a selfish thought, but he couldn't help it—it was how he felt as the morning light filled the penthouse, signaling the end of their brief reunion and the beginning of a journey back to face harsh reality.

Aris

Bam! Bam! Bam! Bam!

Aris pounded on Sean's door at four o'clock in the morning, her slender caramel-complexioned frame silhouetted against the pale glow of the streetlight. The July heat in Gary, Indiana clung to her skin like a second layer, even at this ungodly hour. Her Mercedes-Benz S-Class sat in the driveway of Sean's modest brick ranch house, engine still ticking as it cooled.

"I know you're in there, Sean! Open the fucking door."

Four truly was her favorite number, but this was a bit much, even for her. The Bailey's and Hennessy she'd downed earlier was wearing off, leaving her with nothing but raw nerves and the weight of everything crumbling around her.

First her investors pulling out when they discovered Half Past Eight wasn't just a "gentleman's lounge" but a full-blown strip club. Then Tyler—leaving her forAkim, her own damn hairstylist. And now this custody battle with Sean trying to paint her as some unfit mother.

Sean Parker finally yanked open the door, his six-foot-four frame filling the doorway, butter-colored skin looking golden even in the dim porch light. Those green eyes that had once melted her heart now narrowed in disgust.

"What, Aris? What do you want? Why the hell are you bamming on my door at four o'clock in the morning?" His voice was low, dangerous.

Why the hell am I banging on your door at four o'clock in the morning? It would probably be the same reason you're trying to take my son away from me, you moron, Aris thought, her hand instinctively tightening around her purse where her 9mm rested. The fantasies of putting Sean six feet under had seemed so satisfying when she was buzzed. Now they just scared her.

Instead, she tried to remain calm. She hadn't bothered fixing herself up before speeding across town. Her designer jeans and silk blouse from yesterday were wrinkled, and her normally perfect hair was hastily pulled into a ponytail. She didn't need Sean adding her appearance to his complaint.

"Sean, I want my son," she said evenly, forcing her voice not to shake.

Her thoughts were interrupted when she heard a female's voice call from inside the house, "Sean, who are you talking to? Who is that at the door at this time?"

Through clenched teeth, Sean spoke, "Leave, Aris. Just go home and we can talk about this later."

She laughed, a bitter sound that surprised even her. "Oh, so now you want me to leave without a fuss. Give me my son and I'll leave," she smiled, feeling the last of her high drain away, leaving her dangerously sober.

"Sean, who is it?" the female voice asked again, this time with an edge.

Aris could see that Sean was uncomfortable and annoyed by the woman's questioning. Then, seemingly out of nowhere, she appeared behind him in a lime green silk robe. She was a stunning woman, who had to be every bit of six feet tall, if not taller. Her olive skin was smooth, and her micro braids were pulled loosely into a ponytail. Even this early in the morning, Aris could tell that this woman had it going on. She felt a little intimidated, suddenly conscious of her own disheveled state.

"Um, Ingrid, this is Aris, Matthew's mother." Sean's voice held a note of defeat.

Ingrid pushed Sean to the side and told Aris to come into the house, scolding Sean about having her stand outside in the night air. Sean and Aris exchanged puzzled glances. Aris clutched her purse tightly because this woman was too calm. Aris knew there was no way in the world that a woman could show up at her door at four in the morning to see her man, and she would be this composed.

The inside of Sean's house wasn't flashy, but it was neat and comfortable—hardwood floors, family photos on the wall, and furniture that looked like it came from Rooms To Go. Nothing like the custom Italian leather and glass she had in her Lake Street condo.

Ingrid pointed at the leather sectional for Aris to have a seat, as she sat next to Sean on the love seat across the room. There was silence as everyone sized each other up.

Finally, when Ingrid had enough of the silence she said, "Okay, Aris, what's going on that you came over so early in the morning?" Turning to Sean she demanded, "Is there something you want to tell me? You know I don't have time for foolishness," she said then she looked at Aris.

Sean put his arm around Ingrid and said, "No Baby, Aris is the one who needs to explain this."

I can't believe him. He wants to act like he doesn't know why I'm here. Aris felt her blood pressure climbing, the throbbing in her temples matching the pounding of her heart.

"Sean, I'm here to get my son. You were supposed to bring him home two nights ago and asked if he could stay longer, but then you want to tell DFC I'm an unfit mother and have my parental rights revoked. You're a low down son-of-a—"

"Okay, okay, Aris, I can understand your anger, but really, hurling insults and using such foul language, will that really help your situation?" Ingrid interrupted. "Maybe you and Sean could come to some agreement and keep the courts out of your business. I told you, Baby, I didn't think that was a good idea," she said, facing Sean.

"Well, I don't think that it's appropriate that she runs a strip club, and she's in the street all times of the night while my son is who knows where," Sean whined.

He sounds like a menstruating female. "While my son is who knows where." Really, did he just say that? Oh my goodness. Aris felt her hand twitch toward her purse again, but she steadied herself.

"Listen Sean, you don't know what I do. But you can rest assured Matthew is at home with the nanny when I go out for work related purposes. I have a manager of both of my facilities, so I never have to be out like you're suggesting." Aris leaned forward, her eyes locking with his. "While you're sitting here acting like you're some type of saint, I just viewed footage from the earlier part of the week, and weren't you in Lunar tossing back glasses of L'Or? Yeah," Aris said, shaking her head at Sean.

She pulled out a small DVD case from her purse, dangling it like bait. "You keep talking about me profiting off of the industry, but why don't you tell the world that you're one of my best patrons?"

I didn't come over here for this. It was never my intention to put him out there like that, but his attitude just ain't going to get it. I'm sick of everybody being on their soap boxes; one by one, I'm going to knock them off. Sean is first, then Tyler, and next up, Ms. Nyree Chandler. I always save the best for last. That heifer should've never crossed me. It's more than business with me. It's personal, Aris thought to herself, savoring the look of panic crossing Sean's handsome features.

"Sean, what is she talking about?" Ingrid asked, quickly removing her arm from around him.

"She crazier than that thang. Aris has emotional problems. She takes Zoloft for her depression. I know she did back in the day. Now, you gonna' listen to an alcoholic and pill popper?" Sean asked, his green eyes flashing with anger. "She can't function without a drink."

Aris smoothed her hand over her hair, maintaining her composure despite the jab. "Every now and then, I like to have a glass of wine, but Sean here has two bottles of the Martell Cognac L'Or with his name on them, which we keep locked up in the liquor cabinet," Aris said, her voice steady despite the fury building inside her. Every word was ammunition now.

"So..." Ingrid trailed, trying to keep her composure.

"So, I didn't come over here to talk about my business or

your man tricking off a thousand dollars per bottle of cognac. I just came to get my son. So, Sean, while you're trying to paint a picture of me looking unfit, draw one of your doggone self first..." Aris trailed, letting the implications hang heavy in the air.

"A thousand dollars a bottle and here I am working overtime to help with the mortgage so you don't lose your house? Sean..." Ingrid's voice had dropped dangerously low.

"Ingrid, why you listening to her? You don't even know her. She will say anything to destroy our relationship," Sean said, desperation creeping into his voice.

"Sean, you sound like a fool. I don't want you. I want my son." Aris stood up, straightening to her full height. "That's some ignorant type of mess that a woman scorned would do because she can't have the man. I don't want you. Here, Ingrid, this is the DVD. You can see Sean at the bar and giving money to the ladies in the club. The DVD won't lie." She turned her attention back to Sean. "Now, I'm here to get Matthew."

Sean snatched the DVD from Ingrid and gave it back to Aris. "Take this garbage and go get Matthew and get out of my house. I'll have my lawyer contact you later on today. I'm sure—" Sean was saying when Ingrid interrupted him.

"I'm sure, too. Aris, let me see that DVD."

Aris handed the DVD to Ingrid, a small smile playing at the corner of her lips as she headed toward her son's room. Sometimes justice came in unexpected ways, and at unexpected hours.

Nyree

"Okay. Geez, girl, you act like you were moving to the Big Apple," Malachi told Nyree, as he rolled the last Louis Vuitton luggage into her bedroom and collapsed onto the imported Italian chaise lounge next to the floor-to-ceiling windows overlooking Lake Michigan.

Nyree laughed while watching him fan himself dramatically. The black Versace muscle shirt he wore clung to his chiseled pecs and tattooed biceps, his Evisu jeans fitting his six-foot-two frame in ways that made her remember things she shouldn't. July heat was blazing through the Miller Beach mansion, making it the hottest day of the year in Gary. Beads of sweat rolled down Malachi's caramel skin as Nyree began unpacking her bags, hanging unworn designer outfits back in her walk-in closet that was bigger than most people's apartments.Nyree continued laughing, but something changed. The laughter turned desperate, uncontrollable. It was to the point now that she couldn't breathe, gasping for air as she collapsed to her knees on the custom marble floor, clutching her Fendi top.

"Nyree!" Malachi dropped to his knees beside her, the diamond Rolex on his wrist catching the sunlight. "Come on, baby girl, you gotta breathe. Take it easy. Breathe," he pleaded, the concern in his voice genuine despite their complicated history.

She couldn't catch her breath, her body still processing the shock of losing her father just hours ago. She gestured frantically, mimicking using an inhaler. Malachi immediately knew what she needed and sprinted to her nightstand, yanking open the drawer where she kept her emergency meds. After two puffs, she finally began to breathe normally again. Then, unexpectedly, she laughed—a brittle, hollow sound that had nothing to do with humor.

"What's so damn funny?" he asked, confusion evident in his dark eyes.

Between ragged breaths, she managed, "Your face just now... looking like you couldn't handle two Shaws dying on you in one day." Her laughter dissolved into tears that smeared her MAC makeup. "Two in the morning, Chi. They couldn't even save him. Two a.m. and just like that—the great Edwin Shaw, gone."

Malachi wrapped his strong arms around her, holding her tightly against his chest right there on the closet floor, surrounded by shoes worth more than most people's cars. Finally, he scooped her up like she weighed nothing and carried her to the king-sized bed. With gentle hands that had both counted millions and written platinum verses, he helped her out of her clothes and found her Mickey Mouse nightshirt.

"Remember when we copped this at Disney World?" he asked softly, pulling the shirt over her head.

Nyree nodded weakly as Malachi removed her Prada tennis shoes and slipped on her matching Mickey Mouse socks before tucking her beneath the Egyptian cotton sheets.

Satisfied she was settled, he walked toward the door of the master suite.

"Where you going?" Panic flashed across her tear-stained face.

"You're not gonna leave me here by myself, are you? Not today."

"If you want me to stay, I'm here," he said, voice thick with emotion as the Cartier phone on her nightstand rang, its crystal-clear sound cutting through the silence.

"Who is it? I can't—I can't talk to anybody right now. Don't know what to say to people asking about Daddy when I still can't believe he's gone myself," she admitted.

Malachi checked the caller ID display. "It's your mom."

"Handle that for me? Tell her I'll call back," Nyree instructed, sinking deeper into the pillows.

****

"Okay, I'm leaving now," Malachi announced as he left India's bedroom, his eyes fixed on Colin who was still sitting in the living room. Though he'd done plenty of dirt in their marriage, Malachi blamed Colin for its final collapse.

During their recent trip to New York, he had told Nyree, "There's something I don't trust about Colin. It ain't just that y'all used to fuck with each other. It's something else." He'd watched her flinch at his bluntness. "I see how he plays up to your pops. Don't look at me like that—I ain't jealous of their relationship. I know I'll never have that with your dad after everything we've been through, but dude is a snake. And I know snakes when I see 'em."

"I remember what you said, and I'll handle it soon. I promise," Nyree assured him, walking over to where he stood. "Wait, before you bounce, take this key so you can get back in. I'm going back to bed after Colin leaves, and I want you and India to be able to get in without waking me."

She reached into her desk drawer and handed him a spare key, then explained which one went to each lock and reminded him about the security system code.

"I'll figure it out, Love," he told her, kissing her forehead tenderly. "You need rest, for real, Nyree. Have you called M. Lula yet? I'll hit her up, but promise me you'll get some sleep. It's noon, and you've been up since three this morning. You're gonna have to meet with your family and make funeral arrangements soon. You need your strength."

Nyree nodded, already feeling overwhelmed at the thought of everything ahead. Malachi opened the front door and was immediately blinded by camera flashes. "Dayum! What the fu— fudge?" He caught himself, remembering her house rules. "Sorry, I'm trying to do better with that cursing," he said, quickly shutting the door.

"What is it?" Nyree asked, though she already knew.

"Paparazzi vultures, as usual," he growled. "Go back in there with Colin. You don't need them flashing in your face right now. I'll see what I can do to get them to back off. I'm not bringing India back here with all this. I'll leave her with Kyle and Claudia after I check on them. You want me to bring you something when I come back?"

"A Ginger Ale and some Shrimp Fried Rice and eggrolls from Wing Wah," she said, her appetite finally making an appearance. "By the time you get back, I'll be starving." Her voice cracked. "Malachi, I just can't believe Daddy's gone. And these vultures out here just want to take pictures to sell papers and boost ratings."

"I'm coming back," he promised. "I can't believe your pops is gone either. I'm sorry, Nyree. Really am. I'm here for you, and..." he paused, struggling with words. "Look, I'm out because I don't know what to say and don't wanna say the wrong thing," he admitted before kissing her cheek and heading out the door.

Against Malachi's advice, Nyree joined Colin in the living room, preferring it to the intimacy of her bedroom. They sat together on the Italian leather loveseat, though no one would ever guess they'd once been lovers. Nyree sat with arms crossed defensively, eyes fixed on the imported marble floor as Colin spoke about Edwin's final moments. When Colin finally asked if she and Malachi were back together, she caught the sadness in his eyes.

She didn't want to hurt him. Nyree genuinely loved Colin, and there was no denying it, but what she felt for Malachi defied logic. After all the pain he'd caused—the infidelity, the lies, the drama—he still made her heart race.

Her mind flashed back to two days before their wedding in '95, when he'd stood her up at marriage counseling, claiming he was running errands for his mother.

She remembered asking him point-blank if he'd ever cheated, and how that single tear had rolled down his face as he'd cupped her cheeks and looked into her eyes. "How could you think something like that? No. Of course not. I put that on my soul."

Six months later, she discovered he'd cheated at least twice when two different women claimed to have his child. One baby he acknowledged; the other he denied with, "Ain't no telling who that baby daddy is."

Logic said to stay with Colin, who'd never betrayed her trust, who'd been her father's protégé. But with her world falling apart around her, nothing made sense anymore. So she decided to defy logic and follow her heart—messy, complicated, and bruised as it was.

Solomon

"BOO! Boo, come here," Solomon shouted to Shauna from the living room, as she put the last dish away.

Throwing the dry towel on the table, Shauna wiped her hands on her designer jean capris and sauntered into the living room with an attitude. Nothing could have been that serious for Solomon to be yelling like that. She had just gotten the kids to finally put on their pajamas and get into bed—little Malik, their son, and Taylor, her two-year-old daughter with Mayor Damien Carrington and Madison, Solomon's daughter with Kyra. It was the early part of July, and she was trying to get them into a routine of going to bed early. No more daycare for the toddlers. The girls would be going to preschool in the middle of August, and the principal had made it clear that she expected all children to attend daily and to be on time.

"What is it, Solomon? You gots to holler like that?" Shauna asked, with a southern drawl.

She had been born and raised in Indiana, but when she got agitated she spoke rapidly with a southern dialect that she got from her late father, who was born and raised in Tennessee. The inheritance he'd left her had funded her lavish lifestyle in her beachfront Miller Beach home for years, but that money had dwindled significantly since she'd loaned Damien that damn $75,000 for his mayoral campaign—money he had yet to repay despite their occasional bedroom rendezvous.

Solomon patted a spot on the sofa next to him. She could see that he had paused the news segment he had been watching. As she sat down, she saw Edwin Shaw on one side of the screen, and on the other side Nyree Shaw Chandler and Malachi Chandler—the infamous ex-power couple still making headlines together.

"Okay, rich folk got more scandal going on. That's what you called me in here fo'? Boy, I got to finish putting these dishes away and prepare for my follow-up meeting with First Lady Carrington tomorrow," Shauna said, annoyed.

Tomorrow Shauna would have to tell Beverly Carrington if she would run her senate campaign. It had been a week since their breakfast meeting, which went well. Shauna told Beverly that she would need a week to think it over. Shauna was going to accept the job. It was going to pay a whole lot of money, and Beverly Carrington would help her get things in order so that she could sit for the Indiana Bar and pass the character and fitness portion of the Bar as well. But there was a secret that Shauna and Damien shared that she knew would change Beverly's generosity —their daughter Taylor, the child Beverly knew nothing about. That made her decision even more difficult.

Solomon watched at least four different news segments daily and tuned to CNN periodically throughout the day. Working as the Director of Operations at Tranquil Moments Day Spa—where he'd gotten Shauna a job after her law degree from Valparaiso University hadn't immediately translated into passing the Bar— had made him obsessed with staying current.

Solomon pulled Shauna down to the sofa, as she tried to get up and go back into the kitchen. "No, seriously, you got to see this."

"In local news tonight, rumors have been confirmed that self-made real estate mogul, Edwin Shaw, has died at the age of fifty-seven. Shaw leaves to mourn him: second wife, Amber Shaw, son, Kyle Shaw and daughter, Nyree Shaw-Chandler, Vice President of Acquisitions for Shaw Enterprises. Our own reporter, Rayna Summers, was on the scene when his daughter, Nyree Shaw-Chandler and ex-husband, triple-platinum rapper and bestselling author Malachi Chandler flew into Midway airport this morning."

"Get that camera out of my face. How dare they send you of all people here! You're the one who tried to get me to pay you money so you wouldn't tell the world that you slept with Malachi back in the day," Nyree shouted.

Shauna hit Solomon on the arm playfully and yelled, "Oh my goodness. This is off the chain. Dayum! This is off the chain. The woman comes home because her father has died, and you got news cameras and harlots up in her face. Hell naw, I would have whipped Rayna Summer's ass all up and down the terminals of Midway Airport. Nyree is better than me. Lord forgive me. Umph...Umph...Umph. That just took a lot of nerve. Rayna should've told KBJ news that she wasn't going to be able to do this interview. I don't care if it was an exclusive. Where's the rest, because it looks like she was about to exclusively be put on blast, and Nyree just might throw them hands? Did you see Malachi's face? Dayum, and what were they doing in New York? I wonder if they have a house in New York or something. Weren't they just in New York a couple of months ago? I heard he was shooting a video or something. I wouldn't be surprised if she wasn't out there buying up property. By the way, didn't Malachi write that tell-all book about her family? 'Confessions of a Playa' or something?"

"Okay, look at you with all the scoop for somebody who isn't interested in rich folk and all their drama. Looks like you know all about the Shaws and Chandlers," Solomon teased her, "and what's up with all this cussing you doing, Ms. Lady?"

"Look, I ain't never professed that I was perfect. I'm God's work in progress, and every now and then, I come up short. I don't need you sitting there trying to judge me. You ain't..." Shauna trailed off.

Solomon was getting turned on by her feistiness and grabbed her and kissed her deeply. He let her go and looked in her eyes and then kissed her again. They'd been trying to rekindle what they once had before things fell apart, and Solomon had Shauna just where he wanted her—speechless.

She cleared her throat and looked at him puzzled. "Umm. What was all that?"

"All what?" he asked coyly.

Shaking her head, Shauna attempted to get up, but Solomon gently pushed her back down and kissed her again as he caressed her breast. "Is that what you're talking about?"

"Yes," she whispered, "what is this we're doing here? We got a son together, but that doesn't mean we need to complicate things."

"Let's not put any labels on it. Let's just see what happens and where it takes us." Solomon whispered, thinking about how much he wanted their family back together.

This time Shauna pushed Solomon with force, "I need you to

show yourself out the door now. I got an early morning. Beverly ain't the only one I gotta see tomorrow. Damien's supposed to come by to finally discuss the money he owes me, and Lord knows that man is gonna come with everything but a check." She didn't mention that Damien would probably try to see Taylor too, though his visits as a father were as unreliable as his loan repayments.

Solomon stood up, hurt flashing across his face. "That's how it is? You still entertaining that married politician while I'm trying to rebuild what we had?"

"We can talk about this another time," Shauna said, walking toward the door. "Right now, I got a law career to resurrect and campaign to decide on. And two kids to raise basically by myself."

Shauna

Shauna stood at the door, watching Solomon strap Taylor, Malik, and Madison into their car seats in the back of his new truck. The morning sun highlighted every detail of him, and she had to admit—dude was looking right. That button-down shirt, fitted pants, and leather sandals had him looking like he stepped straight out of a GQ spread. When he brushed past her to usher the kids out, she caught a whiff of his cologne that had her senses spinning.

Damn, is that HIM by Nicole Bradley Candle Co? If that's what they've been going crazy about in the shops, they ain't lying. The scent was unfamiliar territory—she would've remembered something that hit like that. Whatever he was wearing, it did something to her insides that she wasn't ready to face.

Solomon walked to the driver's side and was about to get in when he paused. Taking off his shades, he locked eyes with Shauna, who was still posted up in the doorway, hand firmly planted on her hip, eyes drilling into him.

She'd warned him countless times about approaching any woman standing like that—especially her. *He's really coming back over here? For what? I got Lady Carrington in an hour and ain't got time for whatever drama he's bringing.*

Before she could process it, Solomon was standing so close she could feel the heat radiating off his body. She sucked in a breath and let it out slow, trying to steady herself.

"Can I help you?" she asked, voice sharper than she intended.

"Good morning to you, Ms. Lady," Solomon answered, that smile of his breaking through like sunshine after rain.

Something stirred inside Shauna—something dangerous—but she crushed it down. She wasn't about to let lust cloud her judgment. Not today.

"Good morning to you, Sir," she replied coolly. "That all you came back for?"

"Damn, Shauna, why you always gotta be so hard on a brother?" His eyes softened. "I love you and want you in my life for as long as you wanna be in it. I want you to be Mrs. James. That's what we're doing if it's okay with you."

Then he kissed her lips—not desperate or demanding, just sure and sweet—before climbing into his truck and pulling away.

Shauna remained frozen in the doorway, watching a monarch butterfly drift by, its wings catching the July sun. The symbolism wasn't lost on her. She closed the door, dropped onto the couch, and stared into nothing until her cell phone alert snapped her back.

Wow! Wow! WOW! He loves me. Now what? What the hell am I gonna do about Lady Carrington?

The shrill ring of her home phone cut through her thoughts. *Who in the world is calling this early? Tranquil Moments knows damn well this is my day off. Come on, people.*

"Hello." Her voice was flat with irritation.

"Shauna, this is Aris." The voice on the other end was all

business. "I know it's your off day, but I really need to see you in my office today at noon."

"I have an appointment today," Shauna stalled, mind racing. "But hopefully I'll be finished by then."

Nothing about this call felt right. Aris never bothered staff on their days off unless something was seriously wrong.

"Like I said, I need to see you in my office today at noon. I will be here." The line went dead before Shauna could respond.

An uneasy feeling settled in her stomach, heavy as concrete. With everything else spiraling in her life, this was the last thing she needed. And despite herself, what really had her twisted was that Damien still hadn't called. That silence spoke volumes—and none of it good.

****

Shauna broke into a nervous sweat as she rolled up to Damien's crib. The July heat had her skin glistening under that black BCBG dress that hugged every newly sculpted curve of her body. Six months of grinding at the gym had melted fifty pounds off her frame, transforming her silhouette into something that made heads turn on the regular. Her fresh box braids cascaded down her back, the black and honey-brown pattern catching sunlight as she moved. The buttery complexion that once hid behind layers of makeup now glowed with confidence—this was a Shauna that Damien had never seen before.

This was her first time at his spot, and the irony wasn't lost on her. Her heart dropped thinking about how Taylor—their daughter and Damien's mini-me—had never even stepped foot in her daddy's house. All this time, and the man couldn't be bothered to bring his own flesh and blood home, but had been real comfortable sliding through Shauna's place whenever it suited him.

Just as her finger hovered over the doorbell, the heavy oak door swung open. They both froze, shock registering on their faces.

"What you doing here?" Damien's eyes traveled from her face down to her Jimmy Choo open-toes, taking in every transformed inch of her. For a hot second, he looked shook—like he was seeing a ghost instead of his baby mama.

The black dress accentuated everything the gym had blessed her with—a snatched waist, toned arms, and curves that told stories. Those designer heels made her sculpted calves pop, the result of countless step classes and runs through the neighborhood when everyone else was sleeping. Four months without seeing her had Damien's eyes damn near popping out of his head.

Shauna felt the familiar urge to go off—to let loose all the fury she'd been bottling up about his disappearing act with Taylor. Instead, she kept her voice sweet as pie poison.

"Good morning, Mr. Mayor," she said, emphasizing his title with just enough sarcasm. "I have an appointment to see Mrs. Carrington. May I come in?"

He cleared his throat, suddenly looking like a deer caught in headlights. "You have an appointment to see my wife? Is that what you said?"

"Yes sir, I do." Shauna smiled, savoring the panic flashing across his face.

For the first time, she realized just how much power she held in this situation. Damien was straight shook, and with good reason. His whole political empire—the carefully constructed image of family man and rising star—could come crashing down with just a few choice words from her lips. She was either the glue that would keep his fragile world together or the match that would burn it all down. The realization hit different.

"Follow me to my study. I think you and I need a word," Damien commanded, already turning to walk away, expecting her to fall in line like she always had before.

"Nah, I'm not here to see you," Shauna shot back, her voice ice cold. "And as I see it, you've said more than enough these past months with your silence." She clocked Marisol Waters, Beverly Carrington's assistant, coming their way down the marble hallway.

"Oh Shauna, I didn't know you were here. Good morning, Mr. Mayor, I thought you were gone," Marisol said, eyes darting between them with obvious curiosity.

"Ms. Waters, I was actually heading out when Shauna arrived." Damien's politician smile didn't reach his eyes. "Well Shauna, as always, it was good seeing you. You should contact my secretary for an appointment. I believe you will like to hear the proposal I have for you."

The nerve of this man, acting like they were just casual acquaintances, like he hadn't been MIA from his daughter's life for months.

"Well Damien, I'm quite busy here lately," Shauna replied, enjoying the way his jaw tightened at her casual use of his first name in front of staff. "Perhaps you could just run it past me now."

"Shauna, I would, but I'm really running late for another appointment," he said, already backing away. "So, just schedule some time for tomorrow or the day after. Ladies." With that weak exit, he was gone.

Marisol shook her head, clearly picking up on the tension. Her eyes bounced between Shauna's retreating baby daddy and Shauna herself, trying to connect dots that weren't meant for her to understand. Shauna kept her face neutral, though inside she was both seething and celebrating. The new Shauna—fifty pounds lighter but carrying the weight of her worth—wasn't about to let anyone other than Jeremiah see her sweat.

They walked down the hallway to what Marisol referred to as Lady Carrington's office. The space was massive and plush, decorated in pale blue with clouds painted on the walls. When Shauna looked up, the ceiling was a perfect replica of the sky, complete with an angel floating in the center. A huge fish tank protruded from one wall, exotic fish drifting lazily through crystal water. In the center sat a beautiful glass table surrounded by silk pillows instead of chairs. Behind a cherry wood desk sat Mrs. Carrington herself, looking anything but the terminal patient Damien had described.

"Shauna, I'm glad you're here and hope you have some good news for me," Mrs. Carrington said, her voice honey-coated but eyes sharp as daggers.

Shauna couldn't help noticing that Beverly had to be at least ten years older than Damien. Another lie in his growing collection.

"I'm glad to be here as well," Shauna managed, momentarily thrown by the stark contrast between what Damien had told her and the vibrant woman sitting before her. She settled into a pillow across from Mrs. Carrington and gathered her confidence. "I've had time to think about your offer, and I'd love to work with you on your senate campaign."

"Won-der-ful," Mrs. Carrington replied, drawing out each syllable like she was teaching a kindergarten class.

Ugh, Shauna thought, fighting to keep her expression neutral. If there was one thing she couldn't stand, it was phoniness. *First order of business, we have to work on her image. She's faker than a three-dollar bill. And this woman sure looks good for someone who's supposed to be dying. Damien is a straight-up liar. Told me she was terminally ill and that's why he was staying with her. This woman ain't sick with nothing but maybe a case of believing her husband's lies—just like I used to.*

Malachi

Malachi stood before his bathroom mirror, straightening his black Armani tie. He exhaled deeply, fighting a wave of nausea he knew came from stress. Today was Edwin Shaw's homegoing service, and despite their troubled history, he would be there to show respect. Edwin was his daughter's grandfather, and though he still loved Nyree more than he could admit, he was beginning to accept they might never reconcile.

As he searched his drawer for his platinum cufflinks, his fingers brushed against a folded paper he'd found at Nyree's house. The familiar handwriting took him back, reminding him of everything he'd lost and everything he still hoped to regain.

From the looks of it, she had Poet, Tekesha Martinez create it for him. It was entitled "I Waited On You Malachi".

I waited on you, Malachi
'cause I thought that's what real women do
I waited and waited while you were trying to get your shit right
I waited like I had nowhere else to go or no life
I waited just like I promised I would
even though you never gave me a reason why I should
I waited 'cause you had me believe that you were worth my wait
you threw the hook, I resisted but still took the bait
hey I waited on you,
aren't you gonna do what you said you were gonna do?

Time is up and there is no extension
I fucking waited and while I waited I had no one to relieve my
tension
every man needs a good women right?
one that cooks, cleans, takes care of the kids and don't start no
fights
a man needs a strong women to stand by his side
put up with his bullshit, take it all in stride
are you serious?
I am curious
Why must I take but not give strife?
Why must I act as if everything is alright?
I don't understand how it's okay
for you to do as you want and not as you say
I did everything **you** asked me to do
I did and I waited on you
don't I get some kind of reward
never mind keep it I'd rather move forward
I'll just be waiting again
and then the wait will never end.

The poem made him misty-eyed. Malachi stared at the words, letting them sink deep into his chest. He never truly understood Nyree's pain until seeing it spelled out like this. Damn, Tekesha Martinez had put pen to paper and captured it perfectly—the raw emotion, the betrayal, the heartache he'd caused. If Tekesha had been in his bedroom right then, he would've thrown one of his Mont Blanc pens at her and said, "Pens up." She'd know exactly what that meant between them. Game recognizes game.

He folded the poem neatly, his platinum pinky ring catching the morning light as he placed it back in the drawer of his cherry wood desk. Malachi wondered why Nyree had never given him the poem. Maybe the truth was too raw, too real—like looking in a mirror when you ain't ready to face yourself.

It had been nearly a week since he'd seen Nyree. Seven days of silence after spending every moment by her side in New York. He hadn't called, and neither had she. Today was Edwin Shaw's funeral, and Malachi planned to sit in the back of the church, pay his respects, and bounce before anyone could make a scene. The last thing Nyree needed was more drama.

Malachi pictured what would happen: Nyree entering the church looking flawless despite her grief, little India holding her hand, and Colin Jordan—Mr. Perfect—walking beside them like he belonged there. The thought made his stomach burn. A week ago, it had been him by her side. Now it would be Colin with his investment banker swagger and his connection to Edwin's empire.

"What's this dude got that I don't?" Malachi muttered, adjusting his diamond earring in the mirror. The million-dollar question that kept him up at night. His businesses were thriving —his record label, his books, his investments. But Colin had something he'd lost—Nyree's trust.

The phone's ring jolted him back to reality. He glanced at the caller ID display and felt his heart jump when he saw her name. "Nyree Shaw." Not Chandler anymore. She'd gone back to her maiden name after the divorce, another reminder of what he'd lost.

"I gotta stop doing this," he told himself, watching the phone ring. "Can't jump every time she calls. What am I, her boy toy? There when it's convenient?" He paced across his bedroom's plush carpet. "Damn! She done flipped the script! The way I used to treat females back in the day is exactly how she's playing me now. I'm going out like a straight-up hoe." He shook his head. "Nope. I ain't answering. She can see how it feels to be played."

The answering machine picked up after the fourth ring. "Malachi! Malachi, pick up!" Nyree's voice filled the room, tension evident in every syllable. "I know you're home because I drove by and saw your Escalade in the driveway. Okay, I thought we had something, Malachi. You would do me like this while I'm grieving my father? I should've known you were just out for self, as usual. You didn't even have the decency to tell me yourself —you just leave a message with Colin along with my keys. I thought he was lying, but now I see—"

BEEP. BEEP. BEEP. The machine cut her off.

"What message?" Malachi frowned, confusion spreading across his face. "What the hell is she talking about? I didn't give Colin any message."

It hadn't happened like that at all. Malachi remembered that day crystal clear, like it was playing on a wide-screen in his mind. He'd gone to Kyle's mansion to spend time with India and talk to Claudia about the funeral arrangements. When he returned to Nyree's lakefront estate some three hours later, Colin's pearl white Lexus was still parked in the same spot, untouched.

Malachi grabbed the Wing Wah Chinese food and Ginger Ales

from his customized Navigator's passenger seat before hopping out and jogging up the cobblestone driveway. Anger bubbled under his calm exterior. Nyree wasn't a child, but he'd left her with simple instructions—rest and let Colin bounce. Instead, dude was still there, three hours later.

When Malachi unlocked the door and stepped into the marble foyer, an uneasy feeling washed over him. He wondered if Nyree was okay, then dismissed it. If something was wrong, she would've hit his Motorola StarTAC. He set the paper bag with the Chinese food and the white plastic bag with the Ginger Ales on the antique table in the foyer, along with the key Nyree had given him.

Then the unthinkable happened. Colin emerged from Nyree's bedroom straightening his silk shirt, looking too comfortable for Malachi's liking.

"What the hell?" Malachi growled, his voice echoing off the high ceilings.

"Keep it down," Colin scolded, adjusting his Rolex. "She's finally asleep."

"Oh yeah, bruh?" Malachi's jaw tightened. "Well, let me holla at you outside real quick."

Malachi stood at the door, holding it open. When Colin walked past, Malachi caught the unmistakable scent of Nyree's signature Issey Miyake perfume on him. He swallowed hard, reaching back to grab the keys off the table. No way was he getting locked out.

Once outside, Malachi escorted Colin to his Lexus, making sure they were far enough from the house that Nyree wouldn't hear if things popped off. Colin stood by his driver's side door, looking at Malachi with that smug expression that said, "What do you want?"

"Make this your last time coming around here," Malachi said, his voice low but firm. "Nyree don't need you, okay? I got this, ya dig?"

Colin laughed, that same dismissive laugh he'd been giving Malachi since they first met. He'd always thought Malachi was a joke—the rapper turned businessman who'd fumbled the bag with Nyree.

"Apparently not," Colin shot back, "because she asked me to give her something to help her sleep, and that I did." He smirked. "Now, you might want to bounce because she's going to be asleep for a while. That's how I do, ya dig?"

That sent Malachi over the edge. Less than twenty-four hours ago, Nyree had been in his arms, crying about her father. Now Colin was implying he'd just left her bed? Malachi knew Nyree was vulnerable, but could she have done what Colin was suggesting? The smell of her perfume on Colin's clothes told its own story.

Before he could check himself, Malachi grabbed Colin by his Egyptian cotton shirt and slammed him against the Lexus' polished exterior.

"If you know what's good for you, you'll get the hell out of here," Malachi snarled, his face inches from Colin's.

"You don't want none of this," Colin replied, calmly straightening his shirt after Malachi released him. Then he smiled. "Don't hate the player. Hate the game. Isn't that what you say in your book, 'Confessions of A Playa'?" He chuckled. "Looks like you just got played, playa."

Coming back to reality, Malachi glanced at his platinum Audemars Piguet watch. The funeral would start in forty-five minutes. The Shaw family was probably gathered at Edwin's estate, preparing to leave in their fleet of black Mercedes. It had been months since Malachi had set foot in church. He loved God and believed in Him, but Sunday mornings usually found him recovering from Saturday nights or reviewing contracts for his next business move.

"It's gonna be packed," he muttered, adjusting his black Armani tie. "Press will be everywhere too." The death of Edwin Shaw, real estate mogul and one of the wealthiest Black men in the Midwest, was big news. "Better leave now."

As he drove his Navigator toward Faith Temple Baptist Church, his phone rang it was Nyree.

"Hello?" Malachi answered, keeping his voice neutral.

"Um, hi." Nyree's voice sounded strained. "I got you. We're getting ready to leave my dad's house now. You didn't come to the wake last night." She paused, and he could hear voices in the background. "Look, I can't talk like I want to. There are so many people here, and the cars are waiting for me. I was really hoping that you'd be there, and—"

"I'm on my way to the church," Malachi cut in. "I stopped by the funeral home earlier yesterday. I didn't come to the wake because I didn't think you wanted me there."

"You've been acting funny since New York," she accused, her voice rising. "I don't know why. Just tell me you don't love me and you don't want to be with me, and that'll be that. You told Colin, but I want you to be man enough to say it to my face."

"Nyree, let's not argue," Malachi said, confusion evident in his tone. "Not today. I'm on my way to the church, and maybe we can talk afterward."

Where was she getting these ideas? He'd never told Colin anything of the sort.

"Fine." Her voice softened slightly. "I want you to sit with me. Can you do that?"

"Yeah, I guess. What about Margo and your family?" Malachi asked, knowing her mother had never approved of him, especially after the divorce.

"What about what I asked you?" Nyree challenged. "I didn't say anything about anyone else's wishes. Can you do it for me?"

"Yes, Nyree, I will do it for you and India," Malachi promised.

She let out a sigh that seemed to carry the weight of the world. "Look, I got to go. I'll see you at the church. One." She hung up before he could respond.

Malachi looked at his phone and laughed despite himself. *Did she just say "One"?* That was his signature sign-off—his way of ending every conversation. She'd never said it before, always criticizing him for it. "Nyree Shaw Chandler never ceases to amaze me," he said, shaking his head as he pulled into the church parking lot already filled with luxury cars and news vans.

It was one of the saddest funerals Malachi had ever attended. What broke him most was watching Grandma Lula—a woman who'd built herself up from nothing in the segregated South to become a pillar of the community—collapse in front of Edwin's casket during the viewing. Kyle and Nyree rushed to help her, but she couldn't be moved, her grief too powerful.

Malachi had gone to the casket and gently asked Kyle and Nyree to return to their seats. He stayed with Grandma Lula, whispering words of comfort that no one else could hear. Finally, she stood up like the regal woman she was, adjusting her hat with trembling hands, and Malachi escorted her back to her seat, her tiny frame leaning against his sturdy arm.

A woman in a purple robe sang a gospel song Malachi had never heard before, but it pierced straight through his heart. He could sense Nyree was reaching her breaking point when he noticed her right leg shaking uncontrollably beneath her Donna Karan dress. He thought she was holding it together until she suddenly stood up, black lace handkerchief gripped tightly in her fist, and waved at the singer as if to say, "Sing it, sister."

Her black designer dress made her look fragile, thinner than usual. The wide-brimmed hat sat low on her forehead, and dark Gucci sunglasses hid her swollen eyes. She looked composed until he saw her begin to double over, a primal scream erupting from deep within her soul. Without thinking, Malachi stood beside her, his hand supporting her lower back, steadying her as she swayed.

"Stay strong, man," he told himself. "She needs you right now."

A few seats down, Kyle sat slumped over, face buried in his hands. Malachi had never seen Kyle show much emotion before. In the court of public opinion, Malachi was "Screw Up Number One," and Kyle Shaw came in a very close second. Malachi had broken Nyree's heart, and for that, he carried genuine regret. But

Kyle had stolen half a million from his father's company and never showed an ounce of remorse.

In a notorious BET interview, Kyle had said, "It's money. What's the big deal? He never had any regard for me or my feelings. So the fact that he lost something precious to him should make me feel what? I feel nothing. Yeah, you're all judging me, looking down on me. But ask him how he could treat me like I didn't exist while I was growing up. I love my sister, but she got an elite education while I got educated on the streets of Gary."

"Funny how death changes your mind about things," Malachi thought, returning his attention to Nyree as she dabbed her face with her handkerchief and leaned against his shoulder for the remainder of the service, her Cartier bracelet cool against his wrist.

Standing outside the church after the service, Malachi was convinced the processional walk had to be the longest of his life.

"It felt like the walk of death," he muttered under his breath.

"Excuse me?" Nyree asked, looking up at him through her dark glasses.

"Nothing," he replied quickly.

"No, you said something," she pressed, her voice carrying that familiar stubbornness.

"Nyree, I really don't want to argue with you," he said calmly, forcing a smile as he noticed reporters snapping photos from a respectful distance. "I just don't feel well. I feel like death is all around me." He looked toward his Navigator. "What are we doing? Are you riding with me or what?"

"I'm riding with you," she said, glancing back at Claudia and India, motioning for them to join them.

When they pulled up to Oak Hill Cemetery in the procession of black cars, Nyree finally spoke again. "Well, this is it, Malachi. I bury my father today." Her voice was steady but distant. "We'll leave before they lower the casket. I can't watch that part. Leave the engine running for Claudia and India. I don't want our daughter to see this."

As Malachi exited the Navigator and walked around to open Nyree's door, the sky darkened suddenly. Thick clouds rolled in, and the wind began to pick up, whipping Nyree's dress around her legs as they walked to the burial site where the pastor already stood waiting. Nyree took one of the six chairs placed at the gravesite. Malachi stood protectively behind her, one hand resting lightly on the back of her chair. Her mother sat on one side of her, Kyle on the other, with Amber (Edwin's second wife) next to Kyle, and Grandma Lula completing the family circle.

Malachi barely heard the pastor's words, his mind lost in memories of better days. The only phrase that penetrated his thoughts was "Dust to dust and ashes to ashes." When someone handed Nyree a bouquet of long-stemmed white roses, she stood, placed one delicately on the gleaming casket, then turned and walked away without looking back.

Malachi followed her, his footsteps matching hers, ready to catch her if she fell.

Aris

"Nyree. Nyree!" Aris Smith called out, her Payless pumps sinking into the cemetery grass as she moved toward her former best friend.

Malachi shot Aris a death glare that screamed, "Don't even think about coming over here." For a split second, she caught him subtly shaking his head, warning her off. Too late. She'd already called out to Nyree, and now she'd have to face whatever hurricane of emotions might follow.

Nyree spun around, her black dress whipping against her thighs, nearly losing her balance in the process. Her red-rimmed eyes narrowed as she faced the woman who had once known all her secrets.

"Yes," Nyree said, her voice barely audible over the distant sounds of cars passing on the streets beyond Oak Hill Cemetery.

"I'm so sorry about Edwin," Aris blurted, heat rising to her face. "He was like a dad to me. You know he looked out for me when we were at Indiana University, helping my aunt with tuition when she couldn't make ends meet. I had to be here, and —"

Nyree cut her off, her voice sharp as broken glass. "Daddy loved you. You were like another daughter to him." She paused, the July sun beating down mercilessly on the mourners. "We never understood why you betrayed our friendship and trust with that Half Past Eight mess, but it doesn't matter now."

"I'm so sorry. I'm so sorry," Aris broke down crying and pulled Nyree into a desperate embrace, the scent of White Diamonds perfume mixing with sweat in the humid Indiana air.

Aris clung to Nyree like she was a life raft. Her friend had forgiven her. In this moment, with the Shaw family plot surrounding them, she felt like maybe everything might be okay. There might even be hope with her custody battle with Sean.

Nyree stood rigid, her body unyielding. She allowed her former friend to vent, mechanically patting Aris's back, her gold bangles clinking softly with each movement.

When Aris finally pulled herself together, wiping her eyes with a crumpled Kleenex, Nyree said, "It's okay. Well, it's not okay, but I forgive you." Her eyes hardened. "But there's someone whose heart you broke when you lied about that strip club money—Grandma Lula. You should go talk to her. We'll catch up later," Nyree told Aris, dismissal evident in her tone.

"I love you, girl," Aris said, desperation seeping through her words.

"I love you, too. We'll talk soon, okay? Malachi's taking me home. It's been a long day," Nyree replied, exhaustion etched into every line of her face.

Aris nodded, then froze as she spotted Colin Jordan approaching them. He looked fine as hell in his tailored suit, but something about his walk was off. Something dangerous.

Aris wanted to move but remained rooted to the spot, checking down to make sure she wasn't disrespecting anyone by standing on a grave. The burial had gutted her—like she'd lost her own father. Edwin Shaw was the only father figure she'd ever had, her own daddy being nothing but a ghost and a child support check that rarely came. She regretted never telling Edwin how much he meant to her, especially after betraying the family's trust with that strip club investment. If the Shaws hadn't helped her, she probably would've dropped out of college and ended up dancing at Half Past Eight instead of owning it.

The sky darkened suddenly, and fat raindrops began to fall, bringing no relief from the oppressive heat. Thunder crashed overhead as Colin positioned himself in front of Malachi and Nyree. Aris couldn't hear what they were saying, but Nyree's face told the whole story—she was heated. Malachi was waving his hands, clearly trying to defuse whatever bomb Colin was setting off. He attempted to guide Nyree away, but she was having none of it, jabbing her finger in Colin's face, her mouth moving rapidly.

For crying out loud, Aris thought, *she just buried her father. All this drama can wait. This ain't the time or place. I thought Colin had more class than this. I guess it doesn't matter if these mofos got money or not, the fool in them always shows eventually. And to think I wondered what it would be like to get with him. I know Nyree is my girl and some lines shouldn't be crossed—that's why it was just a thought.*

Colin unbuttoned his suit jacket with deliberate slowness, his movements theatrical. No one seemed bothered by the gesture at first. When the final button was undone, Colin surveyed the cemetery, his Adam's apple bobbing as he swallowed hard. His right hand slid to the small of his back and pulled out a chrome-plated 9mm.

Malachi—all six-foot-four of former wannabe gangster—

instantly pushed Nyree's petite frame toward their truck. Back in junior high and high school, he'd claimed Deuce Block affiliation like most guys in Gary, a necessary survival tactic in their city. He'd known real gangstas, though he wasn't truly one himself, and his Navy training had taught him about weapons. But right now, he was unarmed and vulnerable. Malachi took a step back, raising his hands to show he wasn't looking for trouble.

Nyree, stubborn as ever, pushed past Malachi's protective stance just as Colin's gun fired. The bullet tore into her right shoulder, the impact knocking her to the ground. Her blood soaked into the earth feet from her father had just been laid to rest.

Colin dropped the gun like it had burned him and rushed toward Nyree. Malachi let out a primal scream that echoed across Oak Hill Cemetery. The small crowd of mourners seemed frozen in a tableau of horror, unable to process what had just happened at Edwin Shaw's burial.

Aris wasn't sure where the Gary Police and Lake County Sheriff's deputies had materialized from, but within moments, they were snapping handcuffs on Colin and shoving him into the back of a cruiser, his protestations falling on deaf ears.

Lula Shaw collapsed into a dead faint. Margo, Nyree's mother, and Kyle clung to each other, their sobs adding to the chaos. Malachi gathered Nyree into his arms, tears streaming down his face as he held her until the paramedics arrived and transferred her to a stretcher. He ran to his truck, shouted at Claudia to take the others back to Nyree's house, then climbed into the back of the ambulance, his blood-soaked dress shirt clinging to his chest as the doors slammed shut and the siren wailed into the humid July afternoon.

Solomon

The bitter Gary night clawed at the windows while tension thickened inside Shauna's crib. Six months deep into Senator Beverly Carrington's campaign, and here was Solomon, trying to play moral compass again.

"So, Shauna, all I'm saying is, how can you live with yourself knowing what you're doing? You got your money back, and you're practicing law. How can you continue to defraud this woman..." Solomon trailed off, his judgmental tone hanging in the air.

Shauna's eyes flashed dangerously. "And you're the pillar of the community, right? *Defraud*? Really, is that the term you really want to use?" She leaned forward, perfectly manicured nails tapping against the mahogany table.

"I got my money back, yes. Damien owed me, and his wife happened to pay his debt. So what's your point? His wife made my life really comfortable so I could focus on taking the Indiana Bar and passing. I am in charge of her campaign, and I practice law, which was something I always planned on doing until Damien Carrington entered my life. So the way I see it, that family owes me and my child."

"You want me to go and place my child's birth certificate in that woman's hands? I'm not doing that. Damien has to live with what he's not doing as a father," Shauna snapped, her designer blouse rising and falling with each breath.

"Dress it up how you may, Shauna, you're lying to the woman who has helped turn your life around. That's really low," Solomon countered, his broad shoulders tensed under his sweater as they faced off across her dining room table.

"We all have our things we have to live with, don't we, Solomon?" The coldness in her voice could've frozen Lake Michigan solid.

"You can sit here and act all high and mighty, lecture me on the truth and what-not, but my actions have never been the cause of someone's death. Yeah, I said it." Her words sliced through the room like a switchblade.

The shock on Solomon's face was unmistakable. Pain flashed in his eyes before hardening to stone. Perhaps she had gone too far, but he pushed and pushed and pushed. Everyone has a breaking point, and she was damn near hers.

"Wow, that's really low, Shauna, even for you," Solomon said, his voice thick with hurt he couldn't disguise.

Shauna flipped open her legal brief with practiced nonchalance. "You know what, Solomon, why don't you come by in the morning and get Madison, since she's already asleep, and you can submit your schedule for the month for visitation of Malik. Please, lock the bottom lock on your way out. Thank you." Ice queen mode, activated.

"So, you're putting me out? We have a disagreement, and just like that, it's over?" Disbelief colored his deep voice.

Reading over the legal brief, Shauna marked the end of a sentence with a slight check, looked up and said, "I'll walk you to the door."

"Damn, I bet it's warmer outside than it is in here. That's cold, Shauna." The hurt in his eyes contradicted his attempt at staying hard.

"It's a typical February night in Gary. Five degrees, so I hope you don't melt out there," Shauna responded with razor-edged sarcasm as she handed him his coat and hat from the closet and watched him suit up against the brutal Midwest winter.

"So, are you breaking up with me?" Solomon asked, vulnerability cracking through his facade.

Shauna stood in silence as he buttoned the last button on his coat. The ticking of her expensive wall clock filled the space between them.

"I'm tired of fighting with the world and always feeling like I have to prove myself. No matter what I do, there is always a critic lurking. Solomon, I thought you were going to be different," she finally answered, dancing around his question like she'd dodged subpoenas in her law practice.

"Shauna, I asked you a question," he pressed, hitting the remote to start his truck. Even in the midst of emotional warfare, survival instincts kicked in—nobody with sense would step into the Gary winter night without warming their ride first.

"I don't know, Solomon. I think maybe we need time apart to evaluate this thing," Shauna replied, her expression unreadable beneath perfectly arched brows.

"This *thing*?" The pain in his voice was raw.

"Goodnight, Solomon," Shauna announced with finality as she opened the door. The arctic blast hit her face like a slap, but she didn't flinch.

Solomon said nothing as he walked out on cue, his head lowered, eyes focused on treacherous ice patches gleaming under the streetlights. The silence between them spoke volumes that words never could.

Behind her cold exterior, something twisted in Shauna's chest as she watched him go. But in this game of power and secrets, showing weakness wasn't an option. Not in Gary. Not in '99. Not ever.

Shauna

You know, Shauna," Beverly started, carefully setting down her Caramel Macchiato on the glass-topped desk in her home office, the gold bangles on her wrist clanked together creating a melody of their own. "I've been wanting to talk with you about something."

Shauna's amber eyes narrowed slightly, not feeling the energy behind Beverly's words. She studied the older woman sitting across from her—Beverly's new lacefront wig was laid perfectly, the dark brown strands falling just below her shoulders with a sophistication that matched her cream St. John knit suit. Shauna couldn't understand why a woman with Beverly's natural good grade of hair would rock a wig, but she wasn't about to question the woman signing her checks. That two-carat diamond on Beverly's finger caught the light as she nervously tapped her French-manicured nails against the mug.

Must be nice, Shauna thought, her eyes lingering on the rock. Three months had passed since she kicked Solomon's ass out of her home, and before him, she'd wasted years thinking Damien would put a ring on it. She remembered all those times she had practiced writing "Shauna Carrington" on napkins and in her planner margins, playing herself for a fool while Damien was building his political career with her help—and sleeping in Beverly's bed every night.

The tension in the room was thick enough to cut with a knife.

With voting day for the Indiana Senate race just around the corner, Shauna figured Beverly's nerves were shot.

"Beverly, I believe you have this in the bag," Shauna said, placing her own mug down on a coaster, her box braids swinging forward with the motion. She'd spent an hour that morning making sure each copper-highlighted braid was perfect, her cream Donna Karan pantsuit complementing her butter-colored complexion. In this game, appearance was everything.

"No, no...this isn't about the election. I'm feeling confident about that as well." Beverly shifted in her seat, her brown complexion flushing slightly. "This is something personal. I hope you don't mind me asking you about this." She paused, studying Shauna's face.

Shauna kept her expression neutral, a skill she'd perfected after years in Gary's political scene. *Lord, please don't let this be about Damien*, she prayed silently. *Please don't let her know about Taylor.* She smoothed the fabric of her pants, now her gold bangles clinking softly.

"If it's too personal, I'll tell you," Shauna replied, her voice steady despite the anxiety building in her chest.

"What happened between you and Solomon? He seemed so nice," Beverly said, her voice trailing off.

Relief flooded through Shauna like a cool wave. She allowed herself a small smile. "He is nice, but we're on different paths. That's all."

Beverly leaned forward, clearly not satisfied. "He seems like he has his head on straight, so what gives?"

"It's complicated, Beverly." Shauna took a sip of her coffee. "We just don't see eye to eye on some things."

"Hmmm..." Beverly adjusted her wig slightly. "Well, my husband and I don't see eye to eye on a lot of things, and yet, we're still together. I've seen him with your children, and—"

"Beverly," Shauna cut in, her heart skipping a beat at the mention of her children, "it really is complicated, and if you don't mind, I'd rather not discuss Solomon."

"I didn't mean to pry." Beverly's voice cooled. "Now, let me ask you something else." She paused, smoothing the fabric of her expensive suit. "Why doesn't my husband like you?"

"Damn!" The word slipped out before Shauna could catch it. She straightened her posture, her gold hoop earrings catching the light. "I wasn't aware that Damien didn't like me."

"Yes, you are," said Beverly, her eyes sharp despite her forty-something years. "And you don't like him either."

Shauna crossed her legs, her Manolo Blahnik pumps gleaming. "I like him as much as I like anyone else," she lied smoothly.

The truth was, Mayor Damien Carrington ranked number one on her "I Wish He Was Dead List," but that wasn't something you told your boss—especially when that boss was the wife of the man who had a daughter with you that nobody in Gary knew about.

"Shauna, one reason I like working with you is the fact that you tell it like it is." Beverly leaned back in her chair, exuding the confidence of a woman who had lived in her husband's shadow for too long and was finally stepping into her own light. "So, when did we get to the point that you could not be honest and straightforward? Did you begin to not like him when he did not repay you the money you lent him for his campaign?"

Shauna measured her words carefully. "Okay, Beverly. Yes, when he did not repay my money, that left a sour taste in my mouth. Also, the fact that he ran on a platform and has yet to make good on those promises doesn't sit well with me either." She stopped there, biting her tongue before she could speak the whole truth—that Damien refused to acknowledge their son publicly or provide child support, all while she made him look good to the voters of Gary.

"And that's it?" Beverly pressed, her eyes searching Shauna's face.

"Yeah. That's enough, isn't it?" Shauna asked, catching the unspoken question hanging in the air.

Shauna knew exactly what Beverly wanted to ask: had she ever slept with Damien? The irony was almost too much to bear.

****

One morning, when Shauna had arrived at the house early, she had the privilege of hearing Beverly and Damien arguing through the cracked door of their bedroom.

Damien's voice had been low but intense. "Beverly, go ahead and ask Shauna that...ask her if we ever slept together, and you're going to seem like a paranoid, deranged wife. If that leaks to the media, then what? You don't want people thinking that you won't be able to handle public office, do you?"

"No, I don't want to be viewed as paranoid and insecure," Beverly had replied, her voice steel-edged despite the early hour.

"Damien, make no mistake, I'm no one's fool. Don't play me close because there are some things I'm sure you wouldn't want getting leaked to the media. Your sex toy fetish is just one, for starters."

It had taken all Shauna had not to cackle like a hyena in the hallway. She could just imagine the Mayor of Gary, Indiana with a blow-up doll, his political career in tatters if the public ever found out.

***

"Shauna, are you okay?" Beverly's voice pulled her back to the present.

Shauna blinked rapidly, her long lashes fluttering as she refocused. "Yes ma'am. I'm fine. Thinking about Solomon does that to me." She straightened the papers in front of her, eager to change the subject. "Well, enough about him. We better start mapping out the last few days of your campaign..." She trailed off, thinking about all the lies and deceit and their potentially harmful effects.

She had blown off Aris Smith and never shown up for that meeting about exposing Damien's corruption. There was a gnawing feeling of regret in her spirit, intensified by the knowledge that her son deserved better than a father who denied his existence. For a moment, Shauna wondered if helping Beverly win this Senate seat was really the right thing to do, or if she was just perpetuating a cycle that kept her trapped in Damien's web.

As Beverly began talking about polling numbers, Shauna nodded along, her mind already strategizing her next move in this complicated game of power, politics, and secrets in Gary, Indiana—a game where she had much more to lose than just her job.

Nyree

The late afternoon sun cast golden shadows across the marble floors of Nyree's lakefront mansion. Ten thousand square feet of luxury surrounded her—a testament to her success as CEO of Shaw Enterprises—but in this moment, all that wealth and power meant nothing. She stood with her designer sandals planted firmly on imported Italian tile, hands on hips, designer sundress hugging her curves, staring down the man who'd once been her husband.

Nyree looked Malachi in the eye and awaited an answer to her question. He said nothing as she fixed him with that glare that had intimidated countless business rivals. What he didn't say spoke volumes. She had the answer, but wondered if he would be man enough to look her in the eye and tell the truth. Who was she kidding? This was Malachi Chandler she was dealing with— triple platinum rapper, bestselling author, and business mogul who commanded respect in boardrooms and on the streets. Yet he couldn't give her the simple truth.

I gave his ass too much damn credit again, she thought. What was that saying? "Old dog, new tricks. New dog, still a trick?" It didn't matter how you phrased it—Malachi was still being Malachi, and that was the bottom line.

"So, you're just gonna stand there in your thousand-dollar suit and look at me like I didn't ask you a question?" Nyree asked, her voice carrying the crisp authority that had helped her build

Shaw Enterprises into one of the most successful Black-owned development companies in the Midwest.

Malachi fidgeted as he stood by the mahogany front door, his platinum chain catching the light from the crystal chandelier. He felt uncomfortable with her tone and how close she was standing to him. The scent of her Chanel perfume made it hard to concentrate.

"I didn't drive all the way from The City for all this, Nyree," Malachi said, adjusting his diamond-studded watch. "I've got a studio session in an hour."

"That's not the question, Malachi! Answer the damn question!" Nyree yelled, her voice echoing through the marble foyer of her palatial home.

It had been ten months since she had been shot. Her personality had changed. The woman who had once been the smooth, strategic businesswoman was now hostile, blunt, and straight to the point. The old Nyree would have played chess; this new one flipped the board over. Malachi never knew how to respond to this version of his ex-wife.

"No! Okay! No, I didn't sleep with your stepmother. I don't care what you heard on Hot 97, WGCI or what Page Six is saying. Matter fact, fuck what you heard. I came to get India. She's going to stay with me for a week," Malachi said as he headed toward their daughter's room, his custom Jordans barely making a sound on the polished floor.

He had cursed in her home and did not apologize. She had hurt him with her words, and he retaliated with his. Nyree looked at him and waited for his usual apology for cursing, but it didn't come. In fact, she could have sworn that a small grin graced his lips when the word fell off his tongue. That infuriated her to the point that she smacked his face with the palm of her hand, the impact like a gunshot in the quiet house.

Now she was smiling a sinister grin when his eyes swelled with water. Her diamond tennis bracelet caught the light as she lowered her hand. In her mind, she imagined the sting of her hand making contact with his face caused the reaction. In reality, it was because he had watched her slip away from him twice in his life, and now, this was the third time. The first time she left him, filing for divorce just as his career was exploding, and that had been his fault. The second time, a bullet with his name on it had tried to take her away from him. But now, this was madness. Him wanting her stepmother, Amber Shaw? Where had that come from?

Nyree watched too much television and listened to too many news journalists these days. The May 1999 issue of Vibe had them on the cover under the headline "Hip-Hop's Royal Reunion?" Everybody had something to say about Nyree and Malachi since he'd given her that three-carat yellow diamond ring last month. Once upon a time, Nyree would have laughed at the tabloids, but now, she entertained the madness.

Nyree watched him as he packed India's clothing in their daughter's rose-colored bedroom. She felt a burning sensation in her shoulder where she had been shot. Every time she thought about it, she felt anger and sadness well up inside her like a storm over the lake visible through the floor-to-ceiling windows.

Colin had lost his doggone mind and was really going to kill

Malachi at her father's burial. Wasn't there a better place to do it, she often found herself wondering as she gazed at the lake from her master suite's private balcony. It all happened so quickly, yet, in her mind, it happened in slow motion.

Colin and Malachi had exchanged words. She remembered Malachi telling her to go to the truck in that stern voice he used when shit was about to go down—the same voice he used in the studio when commanding respect. Nyree had been walking in the direction of the Escalade but turned around to intervene. It was her father's burial, and she just wanted Malachi to take her home. Her grandmother had been walking towards Malachi and Colin, too.

Nyree recalled that she had thought her grandmother had been through enough, and these two fools were not going to add to the chaos. Nyree stepped between them in her black mourning dress. Her back had been to Malachi. She looked Colin in the eyes. It had been her intent to plead her case to him, and they would all walk away peacefully. But before her lips could part, she saw the gun and the bullet flying. Deep in her heart, she knew it was going to hit her. Not knowing what to do, she closed her eyes tightly. Even now, almost a year later, seated in her custom-designed mansion that Shaw Enterprises had built along the lakefront, Nyree remembered falling back in slow motion. The thud of connecting with the ground hadn't been felt because she lost consciousness while falling.

"You can go in my master suite and get all your shit, too. I'm done with you, Malachi. I should've known this would never work," Nyree said, her voice carrying through the expansive hallway. "You're the type of dude that will never be able to keep his dick in his pants, no matter how many platinum records you drop or how many millions you make. It doesn't matter how much coochie you get, how good it is, you'll never be able to control yourself. I just thought maybe you had changed. Maybe some people would be off limits, but silly of me to think, she sang perfectly. Deniece Williams would have approved of the sample. Nyree huffed and continued, "that I could've been the one to tame the great Malachi Chandler. I wouldn't be surprised if you're that baby's father."

"You need to go back to seeing your therapist, Nyree, because you're paranoid and crazy as hell," Malachi said sadly, his voice dropping to the quiet tone he used on the emotional tracks of his albums—the ones that always went triple platinum.

"I'm crazy as hell? You're right. I'm crazy for trying to make it work with the man who nearly got me killed," Nyree fired back, her CEO voice in full effect. "The only reason I was going to therapy, you stupid son-of-a-bitch, was so that I wouldn't kill your **ass.** You can't imagine how traumatic it was for me to have to bury my father and fight for my life in the same day and to watch someone whom I thought loved me try to take my life. And truth be told, you should be glad I was going to therapy because if I hadn't been, you might have been the next homicide victim in this city. So, stop talking shit, get your shit, and get the hell out of my house," Nyree told Malachi and shut the door to her daughter's princess-themed room.

It seemed like hours had passed as Nyree sat in the living room's custom leather sectional with India waiting for Malachi to appear. The lake view through the wall of windows usually calmed her, but not today. *Maybe I should go check on him. I hope he's not rummaging through my things,* she thought. *He doesn't have that much stuff up there, so what's taking him so long? Five more minutes and then I'm going in there. I hope he's not in there stealing anything.*

It wasn't too long ago that Nyree used to have to hide her credit cards and money in the bottom of tampon boxes so he wouldn't steal them to buy studio time or cop more product for the streets. And what about when she used to hide her wallet before getting in the shower and then pray that she would remember where she hid it? He had money now—more money than he could spend with his record label, book deals, and clothing line—but shoot, she didn't put anything past him.

Maybe I am being silly about him and Amber. Am I being insecure? The thought nagged at her as she adjusted the diamond tennis bracelet on her wrist.

"Come on India, let's go," Malachi called from the entrance to the sunken living room.

Nyree looked like the perfect angel sitting on the peanut butter leather sofa. Her all-white sundress and sleek genie ponytail made her look so elegant against the backdrop of Lake Michigan visible through the windows. To the naked eye, she was angelic, but Malachi had experienced her wrath one time too many.

"Bye Mommy," India said, her three-year-old voice full of innocence as she blew a kiss and ran to her daddy in her designer toddler outfit.

"Oh, not like you care, Nyree, but for your info anyway, our latest video will be airing tonight on BET," Malachi informed her, unable to resist mentioning the song they'd recorded together before their latest fallout—a track that was already climbing the charts.

"Bye India, Mommy loves you," Nyree responded, her voice softening only for her daughter. She looked at Malachi, her eyes hardening again, and said, "On your way out, leave my keys on the table in the foyer and set the alarm. I don't need MTV Cribs showing up unannounced."

Malachi stood in the same spot with India tugging on his designer shorts. Their daughter was ready to go to his downtown penthouse, but Malachi remained fixated on Nyree. He knew once he walked out that imported mahogany door, that would be it. Malachi wasn't ready for it to be over. Not when Billboard had just named them "Hip-Hop's Power Couple" in their latest issue.

"Can I help you, Malachi?" Nyree asked coolly, crossing her legs, her Jimmy Choo sandal dangling from her perfectly manicured toes.

"Yeah, so, Nyree, this is it? This is how you want it to be?" he asked, his voice taking on that vulnerable tone his fans rarely heard. "You're breaking up with me over something that's not real. You're going to let a rumor kill what we have? After everything we've been through?"

"No, not a rumor. I looked in your eyes, and I saw the truth," Nyree said, glancing briefly at the engagement ring she still wore. "If it's not Amber it's somebody, and I'm not willing to do that dance again. I've built an empire while raising our daughter. I don't need the drama."

"You didn't start acting like this until I gave you that ring a month ago. If you didn't want to remarry me, that's all you had to say. I know you do, but deep down, you're afraid of commitment. Just be real with yourself and don't play games with me," Malachi told her, his voice carrying the authority that commanded respect in both the streets and the boardroom.

The ring was beautiful—a rare yellow diamond that had cost him more than his first record advance. He was right. She was terrified, but she would not admit it. Love hurts, and she had the bullet wound to prove it. A man who supposedly loved her nearly killed her. This was her moment to tell Malachi what she was thinking and feeling. If he really loved her, they could possibly work through it, but pride wouldn't let her open her mouth. She had just had a "fit," as her Grandma Lula would say, and Nyree couldn't bring herself to apologize.

Malachi was right. She needed to go back to therapy. Nyree couldn't bring herself to admitting that either. The last time she had seen her therapist, the woman had recommended that the sessions continue. Nyree insisted that she was fine, but she knew she wasn't. Nyree still had nightmares about being shot. Whenever she traveled for Shaw Enterprises, she stayed in condos. She couldn't stay in a hotel because she was afraid of waking up in the middle of the night and learning that someone she loved was dead.

Nyree walked past Malachi and up the sweeping staircase that dominated the mansion's entryway, the three-carat yellow diamond catching the light as she moved.

When she reached the top she looked down and said, "Leave

the keys on the table and have India call me every day. And tell your A&R that I want my vocals taken off that track before it drops. I don't share credits with men who can't be honest."

As Malachi watched her disappear into the upper level of the mansion they had once dreamed of building together, he wondered if the empire they'd each built separately was worth more than the life they could have rebuilt together.

Malachi

The May sunshine glinted off Lake Michigan's surface as Malachi Omar Chandler slouched in his custom leather "Big Poppa" recliner, watching footage of better days. His spacious Miller Beach home—all 5,500 square feet of hardwood floors, floor-to-ceiling windows, and platinum records hanging on walls—felt emptier than ever. Four days had passed since he'd directly spoken to Nyree, and the silence between them echoed louder than any argument they'd ever had.

When India needed to talk to her mother, Nyree would pick up on the second ring—like clockwork. The conversations were clipped, professional, with Nyree disconnecting the moment India finished her last word. Everything Nyree needed to communicate about their daughter came through Claudia, the nanny, like some corporate memo being routed through an assistant.

On the fifth day, everything changed.

Malachi was replaying the video they'd filmed at the Aquatorium on the lakefront—back when they still smiled in each other's presence—when his phone lit up with her name.

"Hello, Malachi?" Nyree's voice came through breathless, strained.

"Boo—" he caught himself. "Nyree, you okay?" The sound of her labored breathing tightened something in his chest.

"Yes. I mean no. I don't know." Her voice cracked. "I have

something to tell you."

Malachi's stomach dropped. In his experience, those words never preceded anything good. "What is it?" he asked, holding his breath.

"I...I can't do this over the phone. Can you meet at Marquette Park in fifteen minutes? Don't bring India."

"No, tell me now." His tone hardened with concern. "You shouldn't be driving like this. I could come to you—"

"That's not a good idea," she cut in. "I've done something, and you're going to hate me for it, but I wanted you to hear it from me before you hear it elsewhere."

"What is it?" Impatience edged his voice. The suspense was killing him.

"I found out last week that I was six weeks pregnant, and—"

"That's amazing!" Excitement surged through him. "We got so much to plan. I'll be there for you this time, I want—"

"Shut up!" Her voice sliced through his plans. "I just came back from the doctor. I was bleeding badly this morning—worse than I've ever experienced except after having India." Her voice dropped to a whisper. "I lost the baby. I don't know how or why, but that's all I have to say."

The shock hit Malachi like a physical blow. "What the hell you mean that's all you have to say? How could you not tell me? Didn't you think I had the right to know I was going to be a father again?" His volume increased with each question. "How could you do something like this? And you call me irresponsible? You're a selfish, spoiled bitch. I hate—" He caught himself. "I'm hanging up because right now...I hate you, and I don't know if I'll ever forgive you for this."

The silence after ending the call was deafening.

She did it this time, Malachi thought, staring at the ceiling's custom crown molding. *If she was trying to cut me deep—mission accomplished.* He'd never thought of Nyree as typical. She was CEO of Shaw Enterprises, her father's real estate empire. She moved differently. Spoke differently. She was supposed to be his queen—his goddess—elevated above the drama that characterized his previous relationships.

This must be karma, he realized, *for all the women I made have abortions.* The thought twisted in his gut like a knife. How many times had he handed over cash with a casual "handle it" before Nyree? Before India? Before he understood what it meant to want your own flesh and blood walking this earth?

Malachi was known for his rap verses, but suddenly, a different rhythm flowed through him—a heartbroken melody rather than hard-hitting bars. Words poured from someplace deeper than his usual creative well, a love song titled "Love Gone Wrong." The lyrics captured his raw pain, the betrayal of seeing their "little creation" lost while being kept in the dark.

As night fell over Lake Michigan, Malachi remained in his theater room, surrounded by state-of-the-art equipment that couldn't drown out his thoughts. Claudia moved quietly through the house, managing India and fielding calls while giving him space. He was grateful for her discretion—one of the reasons he'd hired her when he and Nyree first separated. She knew when to disappear.

Absently, he flipped from ESPN to the local news. The

world's problems scrolled by without registration until the final segment jerked him to attention. There on the screen was Nyree—*his* Nyree—leaving an office building with a man's arm wrapped protectively around her shoulder.

The cognac bottle nearly slipped from his fingers. The man wasn't a relative. Wasn't a bodyguard. The familiarity between them was unmistakable—the slight lean of her body toward his, the practiced way he guided her through the crowd of reporters.

Recognition hit Malachi like a bucket of ice water. Solomon James. The "accountability partner" from Nyree's grief support group. The man she'd mentioned so casually that Malachi hadn't given him a second thought.

Rising unsteadily, Malachi stalked to his custom bar and grabbed his finest Hennessy. Back in his chair, he drank straight from the bottle, something that would have sent Nyree into a lecture about "respecting quality spirits." But she wasn't here to see him spiraling, was she? She was leaning on Solomon James.

When the bottle was nearly empty, he called her.

"Nyree... Nyree," he slurred, the words thick on his tongue.

"What?" The snap in her voice could have cut glass.

"I'm about to come over there. That's what." Even as he said it, he wondered how he'd make the drive with the walls swimming around him and the 60-inch flat screen seemingly floating toward him in 3-D.

"Stay your drunk, tired ass where you are," she hissed. "Where is my daughter? Malachi, you're a clown."

The insult stung worse than he wanted to admit. "Seems like we have something in common then. I'm a clown, and you're a trick. We are the whole damn circus." His voice rose. "I'll be over there, and then you can talk all that big talk to my face."

Fury radiated through him. He ran a hand over his head, feeling the stubble that had grown too long. As a former barber who prided himself on immaculate grooming, the neglect was telling. Only one woman had ever knocked him off his game like this—Nyree Shaw-Chandler. For all his success as a businessman, author, and rapper, she remained his blind spot.

"Chi, whatever," she sighed. "You really don't want to see me. After the day I've had, I'm liable to leave your ass slumped in the dirt, and that's on my daddy."

The threat sobered him slightly. In all their years together— dating, marriage, divorce, co-parenting—he'd never heard Nyree speak like that. Putting something "on her daddy" was street language he didn't associate with the sophisticated leader of Shaw Enterprises. Was she actually threatening to shoot him? Had they fallen this far?

A humorless laugh escaped him. Malachi didn't believe in putting hands on women, nor did he tolerate them getting physical with him. His technique had always been to defuse, to redirect—pick a woman up and spin her around until she got dizzy before he'd take a hit.

But Nyree was talking about ending him. About bullets.

Is this what we've come to? he thought, the realization settling like a weight on his chest. *When a relationship becomes life-threatening, it's time to walk away.*

Then, an epiphany hit him with unexpected clarity. *Wow. Nyree should have left me a long time ago. I put her and my baby in danger with that Colin Jordan situation. I love her enough to let her go... and stay gone this time.*

The tears that had been building for years—tears he'd held back through childhood trauma, fallen friends, failed relationships, and fatherhood struggles—finally broke free. They cascaded down his face unchecked as the cognac bottle slipped from his fingers to the imported carpet.

Despite the heartache, something else emerged: freedom. For the first time in his life, Malachi was facing reality without a crutch. No one was there to hold his hand, to criticize his choices, to distinguish right from wrong for him. In that moment of complete desolation, Malachi Omar Chandler —Gary's golden child, Miller Beach's most famous resident— finally grew up.

He and Solomon James would meet eventually. He wasn't sure how or when, but when they did, it would be on Malachi's terms —the terms of a man who had finally learned the cost of love and loss in the shadows of the steel mills of Gary, Indiana.

Aris

All the boxes had finally been removed from her office. Aris exhaled slowly as her eyes drank in the magnificent beach view from her floor-to-ceiling windows. The glistening Lake Michigan shoreline stretched out before her—a view she'd been too stressed to appreciate until now, when it was no longer hers.

She ran her manicured fingers across the empty mahogany desk, her caramel skin glowing in the afternoon sunlight. This Indiana University business degree on her wall meant nothing now. All her education, all her hustle, all her sleepless nights—gone because Nyree's family decided she wasn't worth backing anymore.

"Funny how you never miss what's right in front of you until it's gone," Aris whispered to the four walls of her now-barren office, her voice echoing slightly in the emptiness.

The sudden knock at the door made her pulse quicken. The moment she'd been dreading—and needing—had arrived. The heavy door swung open slowly, and there he stood.

Malachi Chandler filled the doorframe with his six-foot-four frame, dressed in a custom tailored charcoal suit that hugged his broad shoulders just right. His dark chocolate complexion was flawless, and that smile—damn, that smile could melt steel. When he flashed those perfect white teeth, Aris felt something stir deep inside her that she had no business feeling for her former best friend's ex.

"You ready to do this?" His deep voice carried across the room, commanding attention like he did on his platinum-selling albums.

Aris straightened her fitted cream silk blouse and smoothed her pencil skirt before stepping toward the conference table. Her stilettos clicked rhythmically against the hardwood floor, and she caught him watching her hips sway with each step.

"Yeah, I'm ready as I'll ever be," she replied, her voice steadier than she felt inside.

Malachi lowered himself into a chair, his muscular frame making the executive chair seem small. "Ai'ght then, let's do this." His eyes locked with hers, and for a moment, the air between them crackled with electricity.

"Where's your lawyer?" Aris asked, crossing her long, toned legs as she sat opposite him.

Malachi waved his well-manicured hand and laughed—a sound that vibrated through her body like bass from a car speaker. For the first time, he was seeing Aris as more than his ex-wife's bestie. He took in her high cheekbones, pouty lips, and the way her caramel skin seemed to glow from within. For a brief moment, he undressed her in his mind, imagining how that skin would feel beneath his fingertips.

Forcing himself back to business, he cleared his throat. "Aris, I have a simple agreement my lawyer put together. Nothing fancy —straight to the point. I ain't on no bullshit. You got something I want. I'm willing to pay for it, and that's that." His Gary accent thickened when he spoke passionately, a trait she found unexpectedly sexy.

She leaned forward slightly, giving him just a hint of cleavage. "Why are you so willing to help me? You're probably one of the few friends I have left in this city."

"Look, I've been where you are—or where you were," he corrected himself. "I know what it's like to be down and out with the world shitting on you." His eyes darkened as he continued, "Real talk, what Tyler did to you was foul as hell. Sean used to be my boy, but when I got stabbed outside The Cave Club, he left me bleeding on the ground. I don't like what he's doing to you now. Trying to take your son because you're a businesswoman putting food on the table? That's some straight bullshit."

His passion made his cologne—something expensive and masculine—drift across the table to her.

"It ain't like you out there selling ass or shaking it for dollars. Your company was in trouble, you were in trouble, and I wanted to help a sister out. Now you can get a fresh start and hopefully keep your son where he belongs—with his mama."

"Thank you," she whispered, emotion threatening to close her throat as she placed her slender hands on top of his larger ones. The contact sent electricity shooting up her arm. "Thank you."

"Now, there is something I'll need you to do," Malachi told her, not moving his hands from under hers.

"What?" Aris asked, bracing herself for the catch.

"I'd like you to hold a press conference letting people know you sold your company to me."

"And?" Aris waited for the other shoe to drop, for Malachi to reveal his true intentions.

"And sign this contract. Take your check. That's it," Malachi said with a shrug of his broad shoulders.

"Really?" Suspicion colored her voice.

"Yes. Read the contract and let's chop this up. I've got a cashier's check for two million dollars in my hand made out to you." He pulled an envelope from his inside jacket pocket. "I think that's fair, don't you?"

Aris gasped, her full lips parting in shock. She'd been hoping for maybe $500,000 for the property—enough to pay off her $300,000 business debt and survive for a while. Two million would change her life completely. Malachi had already purchased her struggling gentlemen's club in a separate deal. When she was drowning, he'd shown up with not just a life preserver but a luxury yacht.

"Yes, it's a fair deal," she managed to say, regaining her composure while her heart hammered in her chest. "I'm just wondering what you have up your sleeve, Malachi." She gave him a smile that had made many men weak before him.

A hearty laugh erupted from deep in his chest. "A lot of people wonder that about me. I told you why I'm doing it, and it just so happens that the people who've tried to make your life hell—" his eyes narrowed dangerously "—well, let's just say I'm feeling a need to settle some scores. Don't worry, Sweetness, we're on the same team." The affectionate nickname rolled off his tongue like honey.

Something electric shot through her body when he called her "Sweetness." She couldn't help herself. Aris knew she shouldn't be checking out Nyree's ex like this, but damn—she was a woman with needs that hadn't been met in far too long. The way his intense gaze connected with hers sent heat cascading down her spine and pooling low in her belly. She quickly snapped herself back to reality and focused on the document.

With trembling fingers, Aris read through the pages, initialing in five different places before signing her name at the bottom. A tear escaped and rolled down her cheek as she dotted the "i" in Smith.

"Look, Aris, if you don't want to do this, I completely understand," Malachi said softly, his voice gentler than she'd ever heard it.

"No, no, it's time I moved on." She sighed, wiping away the tear. "I don't even know how I got myself into this mess in the first place. I'll have time to spend with Matthew now. It's fine." She sniffled and turned away from Malachi as she composed herself.

She excused herself and hurried to the ladies' room to get herself together.

You weren't going to cry. What happened to that? Some businesswoman you are.

When she returned to what used to be her office, she found Malachi standing at the window, his powerful silhouette framed against the sunlight.

"I'd like to apologize for that. I'm usually not an emotional person. This has just been so draining," she told him, her voice stronger now.

He turned and crossed the room in three long strides, pulling her into an embrace that enveloped her completely. His strong arms wrapped around her, and she caught the scent of his cologne mingled with something uniquely him. "It'll be okay," he murmured, his deep voice rumbling against her ear.

She held onto him tightly, pressing herself against his solid chest. "Really? Do you think so?" she asked, looking up at him through wet lashes.

"Hell, if two million dollars can't get you straight, I don't know what will," he laughed, the sound vibrating through her as he gently backed away just enough to look into her eyes. His hands remained on her arms, his touch burning through the silk of her blouse.

She smiled and laughed with him, "You're right, I guess. But it's not about the money, Malachi." Her smile faded slightly. "What hurts is the people I trusted left me out in the cold when I needed them most."

"I know exactly what you mean, Aris." His eyes darkened with understanding. "I promise you I will set the record straight for both of us. I got you." He reached into his jacket and pulled out the check. "Here, put this in your purse and don't spend it all in one place."

She took the check, her fingers brushing against his.

"I hope this doesn't sound wrong," he continued, "and I don't want to offend you, but I would love it if I could run some business ideas past you over dinner tonight. I want to talk about my company, Casual Boi Entertainment."

Aris blushed, the warmth spreading across her cheeks. Going home to an empty house held no appeal. It would have been nice to have someone to share her good news with. "Single momma" was her reality, and for the first time in a long time, it didn't seem so bad—not when a man like Malachi was looking at her like that.

"Umm, I don't think so," she surprised herself by saying, her natural caution kicking in.

"Okay," he said, disappointment flashing across his face. "Aris, I didn't mean to be out of line. I just didn't want to eat alone tonight. Nyree has taken India on vacation. I found out that my son isn't even mine, and well—" he stopped himself. "I'm rambling. You better get to your bank and handle your business." His voice had lost its confidence.

"Damn, looks like you're going through some heavy stuff too. I'm so sorry," Aris said, feeling genuine compassion. "Could we maybe get together for breakfast in the morning instead?" she suggested, thinking breakfast seemed more innocent than dinner.

But even as she said it, her mind had already undressed him, put him in her bed, his dark, powerful body moving over hers. His cologne still filled her nostrils, and the memory of his gentle touch lingered on her skin.

"What time?" Malachi's voice broke through her fantasy.

"Huh?" Aris blinked rapidly.

"What time?" he repeated, concern crossing his features. "Are you okay? Don't go having a stroke on me. Your eyes just rolled back in your head. Why don't you have a seat?"

Malachi grabbed her firmly by the arm and guided her to a chair. His touch was strong yet gentle, and her skin tingled where his fingers made contact.

She gripped his forearms as she sat, feeling the hard muscle beneath his suit jacket. "I'm fine, really," she whispered. "I better get going."

"You're going to sit here for a while, and then we'll see if you're well enough to leave. I'd feel terrible if something happened to you." His eyes roamed her face with genuine concern.

"There's nothing wrong with me," she insisted. "For a minute, I got lost in a thought, that's all."

"Mmm, I'm not buying that, Aris." His voice lowered an octave. "Sometimes your body reacts strangely to stress. I could drive you home, and after our breakfast meeting tomorrow, bring you back here for your car."

"No, no. Look, I'm fine." She tried to regain her composure. "Thank you for caring, but if you knew what I was thinking, you'd laugh."

"I need a laugh," he said, his lips curving into a smile. "Tell me. You weren't thinking I deserve what I'm getting because of the ass I've been in the past, were you?"

"Wow, Malachi. You're way too hard on yourself." She shook her head. "No, I was having a..." she paused, "...a naughty thought about you."

"Do share," he flirted, raising one eyebrow in that way that made women across the country swoon when he did it on BET.

"I can't," Aris blushed again, the heat rising to her face.

"You have to," he insisted, moving closer. "It's about me."

"I undressed you in my mind," she confessed in a rush, "and we made mad passionate love, and that is all." She jumped up and headed for the door, embarrassment washing over her.

Malachi caught her by the arm and gently pushed the door shut with his other hand, trapping her between his body and the door. The heat from his chest radiated through her back.

"So what was so funny about that?" he asked, his breath warm against her ear.

"It wasn't necessarily funny," she admitted, her voice barely audible. "I was just embarrassed. It was a stupid thought."

Malachi turned her to face him and leaned in slowly, giving her time to pull away if she wanted. When she didn't, his full lips captured hers in a kiss that started gentle but quickly intensified. He parted her lips with his tongue, exploring her mouth with a confidence that made her knees weak. She followed his lead, kissing him back with a hunger that surprised her. The kiss was pure magic—Aris swore she saw fireworks exploding behind her closed eyelids.

When they finally broke apart, they were both breathing hard.

"I should go," Aris announced, steadying herself against the door, her lips still tingling.

"Can I take you to dinner tonight and breakfast in the morning?" Malachi asked, his eyes dark with desire.

"Let's see how dinner works out tonight," she replied, finding her confidence again. "I'll see you at seven o'clock when you pick me up." She gave him her most seductive smile.

"Seven o'clock it is," he confirmed, leaning in to brush his lips against her cheek, sending shivers down her spine.

Aris practically floated to her car, her body humming with

excitement. In less than an hour, she'd gone from broke to millionaire—dramatic enough on its own. But now she'd crossed a line she never thought she would. She felt something powerful for her former best friend's ex-husband, something that terrified and thrilled her all at once.

As she slid behind the wheel of her car, she caught her reflection in the rearview mirror. Her eyes were bright, her cheeks flushed, her lips slightly swollen from Malachi's kiss. For the first time in months, she looked alive.

"What are you getting yourself into, girl?" she whispered to herself, but she couldn't stop the smile that spread across her face as she started the engine.

Whatever it was, she couldn't wait for seven o'clock.

Solomon

"So, you really did it, Aris? I'm telling you this wasn't smart. Trust me when I say this is gonna come back and bite you in the ass something serious," Solomon said, pacing his living room while cradling his cordless phone between his ear and shoulder. The summer heat in Gary was already brutal, and his AC unit struggled to keep up.

"Look, Solomon, I couldn't let the deal of a lifetime pass me by. Two million dollars! This gonna have me sitting pretty in the new millennium, and you know damn well I needed that money. What was I supposed to do?" Aris shot back, her voice betraying the confidence her words tried to project.

She couldn't bring herself to admit Solomon was right. After cashing Malachi's check at Tech Federal and following Solomon's financial blueprint—the same one he'd carefully mapped out for her months ago—her stomach had been in knots. When Solomon broke down how to make two million work, neither of them imagined Malachi "Cash Money" Chandler would be behind it all.

"Damn, Aris!" Solomon's deep voice boomed through the phone. "I know your situation better than anybody, but all money ain't good money. You just sold your soul to the devil in gator boots and a platinum chain. I just started handling his accounts. You really think dude just handed you two million dollars out of the kindness of his heart? The properties you sold him on 5th Avenue and the spa are barely worth half that. Come on now, Aris, use your head!"

Solomon wiped sweat from his brow, his gold watch—the only luxury he allowed himself—catching the afternoon light. In the past year he'd worked as Aris's money man, he'd never seen her make such a reckless move. Sure, two million would change anybody's life. Hell, it would change his too—pay off his mother's mortgage in Glen Park, set up college funds for his kids, maybe finally open that accounting firm he'd been dreaming about. But Solomon knew street economics better than most CPAs with fancy degrees. His grandmother's words echoed in his mind: "The love of money is the root of all evil."

"Aris, you still there?" Solomon asked after the extended silence.

"Yeah," she replied, attitude dripping from that single word. "Can't you just be happy for me? I ain't got nobody to share my good news with, and I thought at least you might be in my corner."

"Aris, exactly! There's a reason you ain't got nobody to celebrate with!" Solomon's voice softened but remained firm. "The love of money done already cost you everything. Everyone who should be in your life right now, you've done wrong. Nyree, your ride-or-die since Kennedy- King Middle School— you can't exactly ring her up and tell her this news, can you? Sean, well, that fool don't count. Tyler partly the reason you in this mess. What about your aunt who raised you when your mama abandoned? Your Zeta sisters? Aris, this whole situation is messier than Broadway after the steel mill shift change."

"Wow, so you Mr. Perfect now, right? Like you never done nothing wrong in your life?" Aris snapped, her voice rising.

"I'm not saying I'm perfect. Lord knows I'm the last one to judge somebody else's choices. I just don't want to see you get hurt. I'm a man first, and something about dude's motives don't sit right with me. Hope I'm wrong, but I'm looking out for a friend, that's all," Solomon said, his tone genuinely concerned.

"Thank you, Solomon, but I don't need looking after. Save that Captain Save a Hoe energy for Shauna." Aris's words turned sharp as blades. "Remember when I tried to make something happen between us? It was Shauna this and Shauna that, how perfect she was—and how did that work out? Oh yeah, she got cozy with the Carringtons and left your ass on the curb like yesterday's trash. Everybody ain't like your baby mama."

"Damn, tell me how you really feel," Solomon replied, the sting evident in his voice. "I kept it one hundred with you about my situation with Shauna. I didn't play games with your heart, Aris. I'm just a brother who cares about you."

"Give me a minute and I'll be right with you," Solomon heard Aris say away from the receiver, her voice suddenly honeyed and sweet.

A man's voice rumbled in the background: "Always late for everything. Time is money, baby girl." The voice carried that distinctive Gary-by-way-of-East Chicago accent that Solomon immediately recognized as Malachi Chandler's.

Solomon had recently balanced the books for Malachi's rapidly expanding Casual Boi Entertainment. The label was blowing up after signing that hot new R&B group from Chicago last winter. There was something unmistakable about Malachi's voice—that smooth operator tone that had talked many into bad decisions. Solomon shook his head, feeling a mix of anger and jealousy he had no right to feel. Aris had never been more than his boss, yet hearing Malachi in her condo set something off in him.

The urge for a drink hit Solomon like a freight train. The last time he'd gotten twisted was back in February when Shauna put him out, the same night snow had buried Gary under sixteen inches of heartbreak.

"Aris, call me if you need me. You know this ain't right," Solomon said, his knuckles bulging around the phone.

"Yes, I hear your concerns, and you've heard my position on the matter. Thank you for your input, and I will be in touch," Aris replied with that professional tone she used when someone important was listening.

"I'm gonna let you go, but the game you playing is dangerous. Don't get involved with him," Solomon warned, his final attempt.

"Thank you again for your concern. No need to worry about Matthew, he and I will be just fine. Talk to you later, bye." The line went dead.

Solomon stared at the cordless phone as he placed it back on its cradle. By no means was Solomon a hater, but he couldn't understand what women saw in Malachi Chandler. The man's personality was dark as his skin with a blinding smile and fresh gear now that he had money, but nothing about him should have women losing their minds.

Solomon regretted ever mentioning to Malachi about the attraction he once had for Aris during a late-night studio session. Even though it would be petty, Solomon couldn't help wondering if Malachi's sudden interest in Aris was connected to Solomon's admission. Malachi struck him as the type who'd go after a woman just to prove he could.

Solomon met Nyree at Methodist Hospital's Grief and Loss group shortly after she had been shot by her ex, Colin. They'd had several conversations after group sessions ended, even hitting the cafeteria for coffee a few times. Once, they stayed so long that workers had to flash the lights to let them know it was closing time. He found Nyree captivating—smart and vulnerable in all the right ways. Though they didn't discuss her relationship with Malachi in detail, Solomon believed the smartest thing she ever did was walk away from that man, even if she briefly went back to him.

Solomon knew Malachi's history—how he lied, cheated, and hustled his way through life, yet somehow came out on top every time. Life just wasn't fair. *When I lied and cheated and tried to make it right, I lost everything. When I thought Shauna and I would make it work, she chose the Carringtons' money and power over what we had. None of my kids want anything to do with me except through child support checks. Their mamas have no problem cashing those, but my children barely know my face.*

A thunderous pounding at his front door jarred Solomon from his thoughts. *Who the hell banging on my door like the police? I hate when people show up unannounced.*

Solomon opened the door to find Shauna standing there,

soaked to the bone. He'd been so consumed by his thoughts he hadn't noticed the summer storm raging outside, rain coming down in sheets across Miller Beach.

"Come on in," he told her as she brushed past him, leaving puddles on his hardwood floor. "Everything alright?"

"No, no, you were right. Everything's falling apart," Shauna said, her voice trembling. Her eyes darted around his condo. "Why you walking around in your boxers? You got company? I'm sorry. I shouldn't have come here. This is the last place I should've shown up." She turned toward the door.

"I don't have company. You did right coming here," Solomon said, blocking her path. "If something's wrong, I want to help. But first things first, I need to get you out of those clothes." His voice carried a hint of flirtation.

"Excuse me?" Shauna asked, taken aback.

"You're soaking wet, and that's not good. Some of your clothes are still upstairs in my closet. Go take a hot shower, get changed. I'll make some of that spicy chicken soup you like, hot tea with lemon and honey—just how you want it. Then we can talk about whatever's got you running through thunderstorms."

"For real?" Shauna asked, vulnerability replacing her earlier defensiveness.

"Now you got me all wet with that hug, so maybe I'll have to join you," Solomon joked, though not entirely. "I'm playing... well, not really. Go get changed before you catch pneumonia." He noticed she was wearing her natural curls now, no more expensive braids from that salon on Broadway. "How are the kids? Been wanting to call, but figured you wouldn't want to hear from me."

"They're good. They're with your mama right now. They miss you," she paused, looking directly at him, "and I do too. I'll be down in a minute." Shauna slipped off her rain-soaked Nike Air Max sneakers and left them by the door.

Shauna seemed nervous, jumpy. Something deeper than the storm had driven her here. Solomon sensed it immediately. He had an uneasy feeling that a decision he'd made months ago was coming back to haunt him. Silently, he prayed it wasn't the case, but when you dance with the devil, eventually he comes to collect. Solomon could almost hear the cash register sound in his head. *Damn! Next to me, Malachi Chandler looking like a saint.*

"You might as well strip right here and let me throw those wet clothes in the washer," Solomon suggested.

"How about you come get them once I'm in the tub?" Shauna countered.

"Why? You don't need to play hard to get with me."

"I'm not playing—" Shauna's words cut off as Solomon lifted her shirt over her head, revealing dark purple bruises covering her ribs, chest, and back. She quickly tried pulling her shirt down. Too late.

"Shauna, what the hell happened to you? Who did this?" Solomon demanded, his voice tight with rage.

Though he'd asked the question, he already suspected the answer. His fury was instant, and his tone made Shauna flinch. He knew she'd never heard him speak like that.

"I really could use that warm bath," she said, batting her eyes to hold back tears.

"Yeah, sure. I'll run it with some Epsom salt. You need to see a doctor, call the police. Have you reported this? Shauna, say something."

"Solomon, I don't know what to say." Her voice cracked. "If I report this, everything falls apart. Shit'll hit the fan, and my kids will suffer. I should've listened to you. I ended up behind the eight ball is all I can say. If I talk, I fear for my life." Her eyes pleaded with him. "Can you come upstairs and sit with me once I'm in the tub? Just don't say 'I told you so.' Please."

When Solomon heard the bathroom door close upstairs, fear rippled through his body. He wasn't a doctor, but he knew those bruises were recent—not from today, but something even more frightening had driven her through a storm to his doorstep. His instincts told him this was somehow his fault.

Solomon prepared Shauna's tea exactly how she liked it—green with lemon and two dashes of honey. The woman upstairs seemed vastly different from the confident assistant who'd walked out of his life just months ago. *"What a difference a day makes,"* his mother always said. That was it—he needed to call his mother. She'd claim she didn't want to get involved in more of his drama, as always, but Mrs. James never hesitated when her grandchildren might be at risk.

When Solomon opened the bathroom door with tea in hand, he heard Shauna crying.

"Shauna," he whispered. "You okay? Brought your tea."

She sniffled, "Yes, I'm gonna be fine. Can you hand it to me?"

Solomon slid the shower curtain back just enough to pass her the mug. He tried not to look, but he was still a man. Her body looked beautiful surrounded by bubbles, though he couldn't help noticing more bruises on her legs. Shauna had lost weight since he'd last seen her—maybe fifteen pounds. If she lost any more, it would be concerning, but Solomon knew better than to mention it. Shauna had always been sensitive about her size. When she was thicker, it was a sore point; if he told her she looked too thin now, that wouldn't go over well either. Better to keep quiet.

Solomon sat on the closed toilet lid. Taking a deep breath, he asked, "You want to tell me what's happening?"

He stared at the mint green and chocolate swirls on the shower curtain—the one she'd picked out last year when she redecorated his bathroom.

Shauna winced as if in pain. "This is the first time in days I've felt safe. I didn't know where to go or who to talk to. Couldn't go to my mama—you know how she is. The rest of my family ain't speaking to me. 'Course, when they heard I was working for the Carringtons, everybody and their mama was blowing up my phone. I got let go last week."

"For real? Right after Beverly took office? Damn, that's how the Carringtons do you, huh?" Solomon joked, still not understanding the connection to her bruises.

He'd let Shauna tell the story her way. His cell phone rang— the caller ID showed UNKNOWN.

"Who calling me private like this?" Solomon wondered aloud.

"Don't answer!" Shauna warned, panic in her voice as she peeked around the shower curtain.

Solomon frowned but picked up anyway. "Hello? Hello?"

A distorted voice on the other end said, "Your baby mama is marked for death. If I was you, I'd make sure her insurance policy paid up."

"Who is this? Who the hell is this?" Solomon demanded, but the line had already gone dead. "I'm calling the police, but first, Shauna, you need to tell me what's really going on."

"I'm sorry," she whispered. "That was about me, wasn't it?"

"Said you're marked for death and to check your insurance. Talk fast. I need to call the cops."

"The reason I got fired is because Beverly confronted Damien about Taylor, and Damien thought I told her, so he confessed everything. I was handed a severance package and told to leave Indiana. I told Beverly she could take her money and shove it up her Senator ass.

"Two days later, when I was taking trash out, a black Chevy Caprice tried to run me down in the alley behind my place. I've been getting threatening calls every night. Last week someone left a dirty diaper at my door. This morning..." her voice faltered, "there was a dead black cat on my welcome mat."

"Wait, you think Damien's behind this? Or Beverly?" Solomon asked, his mind racing through possibilities.

Shauna didn't answer. She rubbed her temples like her head was pounding. All she could do was shrug helplessly. "My life is spiraling, Solomon. Nothing makes sense anymore. I'm in danger, my babies are in danger, and now I've dragged you into this mess too. Coming here was a mistake. I thought it would be safe, but I was wrong. You just got your life back together, and here I come with all my drama."

"Solomon," she continued, her voice breaking, "am I bad luck? A drama magnet? Why does everything go wrong for me? Can't keep a man—every one I've ever loved has either died, cheated, or left me for someone else. What's wrong with me?"

"Ain't nothing wrong with you," Solomon said firmly. "I'm tired of seeing women tie their worth to a man."

"Solomon, please. I don't need a sermon right now. Can I just lie down? My head's killing me."

"Sure. There's soup downstairs. I gotta handle some business, but Mama will be here later to check on you. She'll have my cousin come sit with the kids while she comes over. Get some rest," Solomon told her as he closed the bathroom door.

As the door shut, Shauna sank deeper into the bubbles, trying to ease her troubled mind the only way she knew how—through poetry. It had been months since she'd written anything, but the words started flowing:

A Fool For You

Blinded by love, lies, soul ties A day late, a dollar short, now I realize I was a fool for you...

As she composed in her head, Shauna didn't know that Solomon was already making calls—not just to his mother, but to people who could help protect them both from what was coming. Because in Gary, Indiana in the summer of '99, when money, power, and betrayal collided, nobody was safe—not even the Money Man himself.

Nyree

"Malachi. Malachi!" Nyree called out, her Louboutin heels clicking against the Italian marble floors as she moved through his sprawling 5,500 square foot lakefront mansion.

The gleaming black Range Rover Sport sitting in the circular driveway had confirmed he was home, but the silence mocking her calls sent a chill down her spine. Normally, Nyree Shaw—CEO of Shaw Enterprises and queen of Midwest real estate—wouldn't dream of letting herself into anyone's home uninvited. But the key she'd never returned after their umpteen split a few months ago felt heavy in her hand. Funny how Nyree had demanded her key back to her 10,000 square foot estate the moment they'd separated, yet here she was, still able to walk into his sanctuary whenever she pleased.

The warm June air drifted through the expansive windows overlooking Lake Michigan. Miller Beach stretched out beyond the manicured lawn, the prime Lake Shore Drive address a testament to how far the boy from Gary's various neighborhoods had risen.

When she reached the gourmet kitchen, Nyree froze. The Dom Pérignon chilling in a crystal ice bucket. Two champagne flutes—not one, but two. Fresh strawberries arranged artfully beside a bowl of melted Belgian chocolate and a canister of whipped cream on the black granite countertops. The aroma of something delicious wafting from the professional-grade

Viking oven reminded her of those intimate nights when Malachi would cook for her, displaying the culinary skills he'd picked up during his world tours.

Nyree's heart plummeted to her stomach as she imagined those same skilled hands working their magic elsewhere. In the bedroom. On another woman's body.

She spun around, her designer dress swirling at her knees, and headed for the door. Then she heard it—a feminine laugh floating through the corridor. A laugh that stirred something familiar in her memory but that she couldn't immediately place. Nyree's perfectly manicured nails dug into her palms.

He told me if I ever needed him, he would be there for me. What a damn lie. The thought crashed against her mind as tears threatened to form. *I need to get the hell out of here.*

The voices grew louder, emanating from his studio—that state-of-the-art recording space where Malachi Chandler, three-time Grammy winner and platinum-selling artist, created the music that had built his empire alongside his bestselling books and business ventures. The space where he'd made magic happen before her eyes countless times.

A female artist? Nyree wondered. Malachi had always scoffed at female rappers, claiming none had the unique style or voice he was looking for on his label. "Must be someone real special for Mr. High Standards to pop bottles with," she muttered bitterly, eyeing the champagne setup again.

She moved down the hallway toward the studio, anger and curiosity propelling her forward. The door stood slightly ajar. The recording light above it was dark—no session in progress.

That laugh again. Deeper this time, more intimate. The sound twisted Nyree's insides like a knife.

"Malachi?" she called out, pushing the door open slightly.

"What?" A woman's voice responded, startled.

"You didn't just call me? I could swear—hold on." Heavy footsteps approached, and suddenly Malachi filled the doorframe, his 6'4" muscular frame effectively blocking her view. The diamond studs in his ears caught the light as his expression shifted from surprise to annoyance.

"Nyree, what you doing here?" he asked, voice dropping an octave as he positioned himself firmly in the doorway.

"What *you* doing?" Nyree demanded, trying to peer around his broad shoulders.

"Nothing much, why? What's up? I didn't know you were coming by." His tone was casual, but his eyes darted nervously behind him.

"Well, I'm here now, so let me come in and record something," she flirted, falling back on the charm that had once made him weak.

"Umm, naw, not today. Why don't I come by your place in about an hour?" Malachi suggested, his hand gripping the doorframe.

"I'm here now. So why don't I just come in," Nyree insisted, attempting to push past him.

The daily workouts with his personal trainer had sculpted Malachi's frame to perfection. He towered over her, immovable as a brick wall despite her efforts.

"Nyree, look," he said, lowering his voice, "you don't want to come in here. I'm finishing up a session with a client, so if I can stop by in a few, that would be great. I never interfere with your business." He closed the studio door completely, guiding her back down the corridor toward the main house.

Just as they were walking away, a woman's voice called out, "Malachi!"

He quickened their pace without acknowledging the call. Nyree planted her feet and turned to face him, her expression hardening.

"Who is that?"

"Nyree, it's business."

"Malachi, who is that?" She demanded more forcefully, the diamond tennis bracelet on her wrist catching the light as she crossed her arms.

No answer was necessary when Aris appeared in the hallway, wrapped in what appeared to be one of Malachi's shirts, her hair slightly disheveled. The same Aris Smith who had once been Nyree's confidante. The same woman whose failing businesses —the luxury spa and Half Past Eight Strip Club—had been bailed out by Malachi to the tune of two million dollars after the Shaw family pulled their investments.

"I see," Nyree said, the pieces clicking into place as her gaze shifted between Malachi's frustrated expression and Aris's defiant stance.

"Nyree, you don't see shit. I really hope you're not about to start tripping," Malachi warned, his jaw clenching.

In a tone so calm it was frightening, she replied, "No, I'm not going to trip. I mean, why would I trip about my ex-husband and ex-best friend screwing each other behind my back? Everybody in Gary has been talking about it for months, but now I see for myself."

"Whatever, Nyree. You really don't know what you're talking about," Aris responded, arms crossed defensively over her chest.

"Aris, please, I got this," Malachi interjected. "Nyree, stop it. I told you I was handling business."

"Yes…you…did," Nyree nodded slowly. "Aris, you were always good about handling my leftovers. It's all good. Malachi, I would expect nothing less from you."

With that, she stormed out, the front door slamming behind her with enough force to rattle the windows. The summer heat hit her like a wall as she marched to her custom midnight blue BMW M5, the engine roaring to life with a vengeful growl.

Nyree peeled out of the circular driveway, tires screeching against the pavement as she accelerated down Lake Shore Drive. The speedometer climbed—40, 50, 60 mph in a 20 zone—as tears blurred her vision. Through the haze of pain, a small figure appeared in her path. A child on a bicycle, eyes wide with terror.

She swerved, but too late. The sickening thud and the sight of the bicycle twisted beneath her wheels would haunt her forever. When the car finally skidded to a stop, Nyree stumbled out, her legs barely supporting her weight as she rushed to the small, motionless body.

She gathered the child—no older than her own three-year-old daughter India—into her arms. Blood stained her designer dress as she screamed for help, her cries echoing unanswered down the normally bustling street. *Where was everyone? Where was the notorious Ghetto Paparazzi that usually documented every move of Gary's elite?*

With trembling hands, she pulled her phone from her Chanel crossbody and dialed 911, the operator's calm voice a stark contrast to her hysteria as she was assured an ambulance was on its way. The minutes stretched like hours as she cradled the limp child.

Finally, she called the one person she knew would come, despite everything.

"Look, I know you hate me, and I hate you too," she choked into the phone, "but could you come down the street and get my car? I'm probably going to be arrested and taken to jail. I just hit this boy, and I think he's dead."

"What the hell are you talking about?" Malachi responded, confusion and irritation evident in his voice.

"Just hurry and come get my keys and stuff, please."

Within minutes, Malachi appeared, sprinting down the street, his face falling as he took in the scene—the damaged car, the child, and Nyree's blood-soaked clothing.

"Damn, Sweetheart, this shit is a mess," were the only words he could manage.

"Yeah, I know. I called Kyle, but I keep getting his voicemail. I told him that I want Nicole Rouse to represent me. Take care of India. I can bail myself out, hopefully," she said, hearing the approaching sirens and noticing the first of the Ghetto Paparazzi arriving with cameras ready.

"Nyree, don't worry, I got you."

She laughed bitterly. "Whatever. Looks like you got Aris. This is the climax to a messed-up day. My doctor thinks that I may have cervical cancer, and now I might die in prison," she blurted, as paramedics rushed toward them.

"What did you say?" Malachi asked, stunned.

"You heard me. I don't want to talk about it," she replied, fighting back tears that threatened to ruin her perfectly applied makeup. She couldn't tell if she was crying over her potential diagnosis, the innocent child she might have killed, or the sight of her ex-husband's shocked face as he finally heard the news she'd come to tell him before discovering his betrayal.

"Ma'am, tell us what happened?" a paramedic asked, kneeling beside her.

"I don't know," Nyree whispered, her voice breaking. "I don't know what happened. I don't know when life got this screwed up. I was driving, and he wasn't there, and then he was, and... I don't know." She handed over the child to the female paramedic with braided hair, unable to hold back her sobs any longer.

A terrible thought crossed her mind: this could have been India. Her precious baby girl, the one good thing that had come from her relationship with Malachi. How would she feel if some emotionally wrecked woman had hit her child? Where were this little one's parents? She'd been holding him for at least ten minutes, and no one had appeared looking for him.

"Nyree, what happened here? Can we talk over here?" A familiar voice cut through her thoughts. Officer Brad Carrington approached, his gaze hardening when it landed on Malachi.

Malachi squinted, recognition slowly dawning despite not wearing his contacts.He wanted to know where he had seen this dude. "Who is this, Nyree?" Malachi demanded, jealousy adding fuel to his already simmering anger.

"Officer Brad Carrington, meet Malachi Chandler," Nyree introduced them shakily.

Malachi refused to let it go. "No, I read that much. Who is HE?" he asked loudly, drawing the attention of the growing crowd and the flashing cameras of the Ghetto Paparazzi.

Brad stepped forward. "Sir, I don't know what your problem is, but you need to stand right there and get out of the lady's face. I need to ask her some questions, and—"

"And so do I," Malachi interrupted, moving closer.

"Mr. Chandler, I'm warning you. If you continue, you will be arrested for obstruction of justice," Brad cautioned, one hand moving to his belt.

"Brad, can you give me one second with Malachi? Just one second," Nyree pleaded. Brad nodded reluctantly, keeping his eyes locked on Malachi.

"Malachi," Nyree whispered, stepping closer to him, "please, do not make a scene. I'm not sure what the problem is, but India needs one parent to be there for her and not in the slammer, so keep your cool." She grabbed his hand and squeezed it. "You act like you think me and him are together. Brad and I went to school together, and he does security for me sometimes. You know he's the mayor's brother, but other than that, nothing. So, stop it."

She hugged him desperately, the familiar scent of his cologne momentarily taking her back to better days. "You're mad at me, but please, stop this. My life is hanging in the balance here. Please, if I ever needed you, I need you now."

"Nyree, I need a statement from you," Brad called firmly.

She wiped away her tears and looked deeply into Malachi's eyes. No words were needed; her gaze silently begged him to behave, to be the man she once knew.

He nodded slightly, feeling her pain despite his anger. "Infinity... you know," he said softly—their old code, their secret way of saying what they couldn't express in front of others.

Nyree looked back as she walked toward Brad. "I know. I love you infinity squared."

"Infinity times infinity," he called after her.

She blew him a kiss before turning to give Brad her statement, cameras flashing around them, documenting every moment of the Shaw Enterprises CEO's fall from grace.

"This doesn't look good," Brad told her quietly. "I need your driver's license, and you're going to have to come down to the station and answer some questions. You're my girl, and I don't want to put you in the back of this squad car. So, we're going to have your car towed." He glanced at Malachi with undisguised dislike. "Now, because I like you and don't want you publicly humiliated, I'm going to let you see if 'What's-His-Face' over there can drive you to the station. Why do you continue to waste your time with him? Never mind. Be at the station in the next twenty minutes. Don't make me regret this."

"Thank you, Brad. It was an accident. You know I wouldn't hurt a child intentionally." Nyree's voice was barely audible.

"I know that. But just so you know, your license is probably going to be suspended. You had to be going at least 60 miles per hour in this 20-mile-per-hour zone. What were you thinking?"

"I wasn't thinking, Brad. I went to the doctor and got my results back. It wasn't a good visit. I came to talk to Malachi, and we had a fight before I could even tell him the news, and well, you know the rest."

"Twenty minutes. We'll talk. You better call your lawyers."

"Where are the parents?" Nyree asked, suddenly remembering the child's family must be frantic.

"I have an officer looking for them. This is messed up—parents just let their kids wander the streets like this." Brad's phone buzzed. "Wait a minute, this is the hospital calling. Twenty minutes, Nyree. Twenty minutes."

As Brad stepped away to take the call, Nyree walked back to where Malachi stood waiting impatiently. Despite everything—the betrayal, Aris, their complicated history—he was still there. For now, that would have to be enough.

"Let's go to your house," she said quietly. "I need you to drive me to the police station, please."

They walked silently up the block toward his mansion, each step heavy with unspoken words, as the summer sun beat down mercilessly on Lake Shore Drive.

Malachi

Three hours.

One hundred and eighty excruciating minutes of pure psychological torture.

Malachi's platinum Audemars Piguet watch mocked him with each passing second as he sat alone in the sterile police station waiting room. His diamond-encrusted pinky ring tapped an anxious rhythm against the metal table—the only sound besides the occasional radio chatter and ringing phones from the officers' bullpen beyond the frosted glass partition.

His mind raced like a Ferrari on the Indianapolis Speedway, images of Nyree's tear-stained face haunting him with each blink. *Where was she? What were they doing to her in that interrogation room?* The thought of her—Shaw Enterprises' iron-fisted CEO, reduced to a criminal suspect—made his stomach twist into a painful knot.

"They found some irregular cells and want to biopsy them. They want to make sure it's not cancer."

Her words had sliced through him like a switchblade to the gut. *Cancer.* The same disease that had taken too many people he loved. What if Nyree—fierce, unstoppable Nyree—suffered the same fate? What if the mother of his child, the only woman who'd ever truly understood the broken boy beneath his multi-platinum facade, was snatched away by death? Or worse yet, locked away in some hellhole prison for years over a tragic accident?

The thought sent a shudder through his 6'4" frame. Malachi lowered his head to the cold table, using his muscular arm to shield the tears that threatened to fall. A Grammy-winning rapper crying in a police station—the Ghetto Paparazzi would kill for that shot.

The pain radiating through his chest mirrored what he'd felt a few months ago, when Nyree had called him from her home, voice breaking as she told him she'd been six weeks pregnant but had just miscarried. A child he never even knew existed until it was already gone—a possibility snatched away before he'd had time to process it.

Had that miscarriage been connected to this? Had cancer been silently growing inside her even then? The thought made bile rise in his throat.

His Motorola StarTAC vibrated against the table. The limited-edition platinum case—a gift from Nyree on his last birthday—displayed a name that made his jaw clench: *Aris*.

"Damn," he muttered, considering letting it go to voicemail. Against his better judgment, he swiped to answer. "This is Malachi Chandler."

"Oooh, so formal," came the syrupy voice on the other end. "This is Aris Smith."

"Yeah, I know. What's up?" He kept his voice low, glancing around to ensure no one was listening.

"I see they got your girl all on the news for hitting a little boy. He's in critical condition." Her laugh—the same one that had drawn Nyree's attention in his studio earlier—slithered through the phone like something venomous.

Malachi's free hand clenched into a fist. "You know what, you're not right. How could you think something like that is funny?" He took a deep breath, remembering where he was. "Never mind. Maybe I wasn't clear, so let me be crystal clear now. Stop calling me, don't come by my house, leave me alone. Am I clear?"

"Wow, it's like that?" Aris's voice dropped an octave, that dangerous edge Malachi had glimpsed earlier returning full force.

Movement caught his eye—Nyree emerging from the interrogation room, flanked by Attorney Nicole Rouse in her trademark red-bottomed stilettos and thousand-dollar pantsuit. Even from across the room, Malachi could see the hollow emptiness in Nyree's eyes.

"Yeah, it's like that, and I would appreciate you respecting my request," he snapped before ending the call and pocketing the phone.

He rushed toward Nyree, his heart sinking further with each step. Gone was the commanding presence that could make real estate moguls tremble with a single glance. Gone was the confident swagger that had first caught his eye at that neighborhood fish fry six years ago, where Aris had played matchmaker, introducing them with a knowing smile that now seemed sinister in retrospect. The woman before him looked like a stranger—skin ashen against her designer clothes, shoulders slumped in defeat, eyes vacant as if her soul had checked out, leaving only an empty vessel behind.

Malachi had seen this look only once before—when he'd had to tell her that her father died. But this was worse somehow. This was Nyree defeated by her own actions, her own emotions, her own body betraying her from within.

Nicole's blood-red lips moved efficiently, her voice low but commanding. "Malachi, her bond is $100,000. There is someone over there at the desk who can take care of the matter." She nodded toward a bored-looking clerk in the corner. "You will be responsible for knowing where Nyree is at all times."

Her eyes narrowed as she leaned closer, designer perfume wafting between them. "I do not want either one of you saying anything to the media about this case or any other matter. I don't care if they ask you how your dog died when you were five. You say nothing." The Harvard-educated attorney's gaze could have frozen Lake Michigan in July. "I suggest for the next few weeks you try to be incognito, Nyree. If you need me, call me."

She pulled Nyree into a tight embrace—an unusual gesture from the notoriously cold "Barracuda of the Midwest Courtrooms." Something in that hug sent a chill down Malachi's spine. It was too final, too much like goodbye.

Nicole's red-soled heels clicked ominously against the linoleum as she guided Malachi toward the bail desk. "I'll win her case," she whispered, just for his ears. "But you need to prepare yourself."

"For what?" Malachi asked, dread pooling in his stomach.

"For whatever happens with her health. That child might recover, but the possibility of cancer..." Her voice trailed off meaningfully. "Enjoy your family, Malachi. Never take another moment in life for granted. The universe doesn't give warnings before it snatches away what matters most."

As Nicole spoke with the clerk about bail procedures, Malachi glanced back at Nyree. She stood exactly where they'd left her, unmoving, unseeing—a statue in designer clothes. For a terrifying moment, he couldn't tell if she was breathing.

Outside, camera flashes illuminated the night through the station windows. The Ghetto Paparazzi had assembled en masse, hungry vultures waiting to document the fall of Gary's power couple. Somewhere among them, he knew Aris would be watching, waiting for her moment to strike again.

And beyond all that—somewhere in Methodist Hospital North Lake on 5th & Grant—a three-year-old child clung to life because of what had happened between them today.

Malachi felt the weight of it all pressing down on him like a concrete slab. He'd seen enough of the streets to know when someone was trapped with no good way out. For the first time since he'd clawed his way from poverty to the penthouse, that someone was him.

And worse—it was Nyree too.

ONE YEAR LATER

Rayna Summers sank into the director's chair, her crimson stilettos clicking against the metal frame as she crossed her legs. The set lights of "The Real Tea with Rayna" still burned hot overhead, casting harsh shadows across her face that even her MAC foundation couldn't soften. She ran a perfectly manicured nail along the rim of her champagne flute, savoring the aftermath of chaos she'd orchestrated on today's show.

"So, what did you think of today's episode?" Rayna asked, her voice dripping with false innocence as she eyed her assistant Mario Adams. The year 2000 was proving to be her breakthrough moment in Gary's cutthroat media landscape, and she wasn't about to let anyone—not even her right-hand man— rain on her parade.

Mario adjusted his wire-rimmed glasses, his caramel complexion darkening with discomfort. "Well, Rayna, you were looking for a show to increase your ratings, and I believe you definitely did that. That's all I can say." The disgust in his voice couldn't be more apparent if he'd painted it on a billboard outside the studio.

It was the most ghetto spectacle he'd witnessed since joining the industry—hood drama packaged as entertainment. Mario felt the weight of his journalism degree grow heavier by the minute. Being associated with "The Real Tea with Rayna" was starting to feel like a stain on his résumé rather than a stepping stone.

"When the episode with Nyree Chandler went down, the camera man stopped filming, didn't he?" Rayna asked, pretending concern while mentally calculating the publicity value of today's on-air assault.

Mario's jaw tightened. "Rayna, you gave everyone specific instructions to tape and tape everything. So, I'm sure the camera guys got that. They're probably selling that footage to all media outlets as we speak." He hesitated before continuing, "Honestly, what you did today was beneath you, and it backfired. You went too far, Rayna."

He leaned forward, lowering his voice though they were alone. "How could you bring Shauna Buchanan, your LAWYER, on here and ask her those questions about her fiancé? I didn't know she had a child by former Mayor Damien Carrington. I sure as hell didn't know that Damien was paying Solomon to keep Shauna occupied." His eyes widened. "Who knew that the mayor's wife had put a hit out on her husband's ex-mistress? I mean, Rayna, that was awful, and again, not to sound redundant, but this is your LAWYER."

Rayna flashed a smile that didn't reach her eyes. "That was a hot mess, but I bet my ratings are through the roof." She inspected her French manicure, diamond bracelet catching the studio lights. "Nyree Chandler is going to pay for attacking me. I am going to have my lawyer press charges..." Her voice trailed off as she realized the irony.

Mario snorted. "I hope you have another lawyer besides Shauna Buchanan because the way you humiliated her on the show today, you'll be lucky if she doesn't conjure up a lawsuit against you. Damn, with friends like you, folks don't need enemies."

"Business is business." Rayna's eyes narrowed. "That's where young bucks like you get it twisted. Friendship and business should never be mentioned in the same sentence." She reached for her Louis Vuitton purse, extracting a compact to check her red lipstick, still perfect despite the day's drama.

"I mean, if anyone knows this to be true, it's Nyree Shaw Chandler," she continued, emphasizing the full name of Gary's most prominent businesswoman with a hint of jealousy. "She helped her 'best friend' Aris, who then helped herself to Malachi." A flash of hunger crossed Rayna's face at the mention of Malachi's name.

"Now, Malachi never did answer my question about why he found it necessary to bail Aris out. And did you see how he skated around the question about his sexual encounters with Aris?" Rayna's voice grew animated. "Yeah, I know they denied it, but they had sex. That's why Nyree slapped me—because I asked Malachi which woman was better in the sheets."

She laughed, a brittle sound that echoed in the empty studio. "I mean, it was a good ending for Aris. She came up financially and remained custodial parent of her son."

"Yeah, I guess," Mario said, his expression making it clear he wasn't buying Rayna's justifications.

Rayna rolled her eyes. "Are you still upset about the Shauna and Solomon debacle? Don't be. Shauna put herself in that situation." She snapped her compact shut. "Actually, I don't even know how you did not know about that drama. I think everyone knows Solomon's history with women, and I just wondered if Shauna might fear for her life. Loving a man like Solomon can be deadly." She noticed Mario's disapproving headshake. "Mario, stop shaking your head at me like that."

She was getting increasingly annoyed with Mario, but she couldn't deny his talent. All this commentary from him was unnecessary. If she didn't need him so badly, she'd fire him on the spot. Anyone could be replaced, but they were the dynamic duo of Midwest gossip media, and she wasn't ready to rock the boat—not when she was five minutes away from making it to the national stage. Once she arrived, she'd ditch him like she did most people in her life.

Rayna had finally carved out her niche in Gary, Indiana. The industrial city with its share of urban decay had become fertile ground for her brand of exploitation journalism. She'd used all the chaos amongst some of the major stakeholders in the city —especially the Shaw family drama—to elevate her platform. In this business, you had to roll with the punches, and sometimes throw them first. Rayna had learned that a long time ago.

While the slap across the face she received from Nyree Shaw Chandler—CEO of Shaw Enterprises and one of the wealthiest women in the Midwest—still stung, Rayna was certain it would be the catalyst that launched her career to the next level. She touched her cheek, feeling the lingering heat. Worth it for the headlines tomorrow.

Malachi had escorted his ex-wife off the stage after that. Rayna's mind drifted to memories of him—six-foot-three of pure chocolate temptation, muscles flexing under his tailored Armani suit. The bestselling author of "Confessions of a

Playa'" had given Rayna her first big break when he granted The Midwest Vein an exclusive interview. She'd parlayed that connection into countless scoops about his tumultuous relationship with Nyree, but she wanted more—much more—from Malachi Chandler.

Rayna had one regret about today's show. She had dug up dirt on Aris Smith, Shauna Buchanan, and Solomon James but hadn't gotten the opportunity to ask Nyree about allegedly eloping with Malachi in Las Vegas. She also wanted to know why the State of Indiana had allowed Nyree to adopt the boy she injured in that car accident last year.

The day was still young. Rayna contemplated taking a camera crew to the palatial lakefront mansion where Nyree and Malachi were living. She could ambush them there, forcing answers to her questions while the cameras rolled. Her producer would love it—more footage for tomorrow's show.

Her cell phone rang, the Nokia's distinctive tone cutting through her plotting. The incoming call displayed "Margo Shaw"—Nyree Shaw Chandler's mother.

A slow, predatory smile spread across Rayna's glossy lips. Maybe she wouldn't need to ambush anyone after all. Margo Shaw had never approved of her daughter's relationship with the notorious rapper-turned-businessman. Rayna still remembered how Margo had slipped her an envelope full of cash last year, begging for dirt on Malachi to break up the couple.

"This day just keeps getting better and better," Rayna purred as she pressed the green button on her phone, already imagining the secrets—and the check—Margo might offer this time. One way or another, she'd get what she needed to destroy Nyree and claim Malachi for herself.

"Margo, darling," she cooed into the receiver, "what an unexpected pleasure..."

Excerpt From My Love Won't Last Forever: His Wife
Rayna Summers

I'm always running late for something. One day, I'm going to be on time for something. It's just not going to be today. My Granny used to joke that I would be late for my own funeral. Rayna Summers snickered at the joke. The smile quickly faded when her eyes met Malachi Chandler's eyes. Just for the mere second their eyes were in sync, Rayna knew her man was fuming. She knew him well. Even from across the crowded room, he looked pissed off.

Malachi looks hot as a pepper. Rayna brushed past people in the busy tavern to make her way to the table where Malachi was sitting. For a Thursday afternoon, Sheffield's was packed. The crowd gave credence to Thirsty Thursday. Meeting at Sheffield's had been Malachi's idea. Rayna would have much preferred spending a quiet evening at home, hers or his, it didn't matter. They hadn't seen each other much lately. Her schedule had not changed. It was always hectic, and they managed to see one another. *How had his schedule been? What had him so occupied that he couldn't see her?*

When they had first started seeing each other, Malachi would rotate his schedule to see her. There were times when he'd arrange meetings with individuals via Skype. He would even "Skype" at her place just so he could be in her presence.

Usually, she would receive a text in the morning from him

saying, "Good morning, Sunshine." In the last two months, a lot of their traditional activities had ceased. She was making more money than she had ever made in her life, and that preoccupied her thoughts.

"Hey," Rayna said, as she scooted into a bar chair and tossed her oversized Michael Kors purse into the empty seat next to her.

Malachi had given the designer handbag to her a couple of months ago and said, "Only the best will do for my lady."

"Ummm, hey," Malachi said annoyed, as he looked at his Rado R-One and continued, "What happened to three o'clock? You know I hate to wait."

She rolled her eyes at the comment. If anyone knew that Malachi Chandler hated to wait, it was her. She was really hoping not to hear his spiel on being punctual. By now, he should have known that three o'clock always meant three-fifteen. Her eyes glanced at her Rado Jubile and saw it was three-thirty. She could understand him being annoyed. Usually, she would have a good excuse for being tardy, like a meeting ran over or traffic, but not today. The train stopping on the tracks in the Miller section of Gary, Indiana was always a legitimate excuse for being late.

It was something about his tone when he called her earlier she found disturbing, and meeting at Sheffield's had not set right with her either. They frequented Sheffield's, but it just didn't feel right today.

"You want something?" He asked dryly, after looking at her for some time.

"I'll have a glass of Moscato. After the day I've had today, I could probably use something stronger, but Moscato will be fine," Rayna said, tossing her long curly locks.

His attitude was starting to wear on her nerves. He could be temperamental. Most times, she would cater to his ego, but today, she just was not feeling him or his attitude. If he was going to be in one of his funky moods, she did not want to deal with it. For certain, she did not want to hear about Nyree or the kids. They had been together for two years, and during the course of the conversation, he always seemed to bring up his ex-wife and their children. Rayna resented them.

When she had told Malachi she was pregnant, his response had been, "Umph. You know I told you when we first got together that I didn't want any more children. When Nyree lost my baby I was devastated. I can't go through that again."

Those had been his words, and all he had spoken regarding the situation.

With tear-filled eyes, Rayna asked, "So what am I supposed to do?"

Smugly, he replied, "I dunno what you're looking for me to say, but do whatever you gotta do."

A former guest on Rayna's talk show had commented on the topic of *"Keeping Your Man"* and said, "By any means necessary, do what you got to do to keep him."

So, Rayna did what she thought was necessary to keep Malachi. Daily, her body ached from her actions. She often wondered what it would be like to have a child. She had been deprived of motherhood, and for that, she hated Nyree Chandler.

Every time he mentioned his ex wife, Rayna felt like puking her brains out. Nobody was as perfect as he made Nyree sound.

Hell, if she was that damn perfect they'd be together, wouldn't they?

Malachi beckoned for their waitress and placed Rayna's order.

When the waitress left he started,

"How was your day? Everything good at the studio?" Malachi inquired.

Squinting and adjusting the contact that felt like it was folded in half in her right eye, Rayna exhaled. She made a mental note to ditch these contacts tonight and start on a brand new box tomorrow morning. For a moment, she considered wearing her eye glasses again, but that was a brief moment.

"Dammit, this contact has been irritating me all day. My day was okay, why what's up?"

"Here's your Moscato," the waitress said, placing the glass in front of Rayna, then turning to Malachi she asked, "Can I get you another Corona, Mr. Chandler?"

Flashing his million dollar smile, he said, "No, I'm good."

"Okay, just holler if you need something," she said flirtingly, as she sauntered off.

Rayna rolled her eyes. She could not even hide her feelings. Everyone knew who Malachi was, and it seemed like every woman in Lake County, Indiana, regardless of race, was trying to throw their panties at him. He just seemed to eat it up, too. *He is so disrespectful. Now, he'd think I was wrong if I reached across this table and smacked that grin off his face.*

"Look, we have fun right? We've had fun together right..." Malachi was saying, and Rayna was feeling a little queasy.

Oh snap. Where is this conversation going? I gotta do something but what? I don't even like this, and he hasn't really said anything. This whole conversation was making her feel uncomfortable. Hot bile was rising up in her throat. One more second, and she would be puking all over their table.

She gulped some of her Moscato. It was not lady like, but at this point, she was not feeling much like a lady.

"Uh-huh," is all she could manage to utter.

"You know I like to give it to you straight, no chaser. I've been spending a lot of time with Nyree and the kids lately, and I've decided that I want my family back. You know, I've invested in the television studio, but that's yours to do as you please. I hope we can still be friends..."

Whoa! Damn! I didn't see this coming. Did he just say he hopes we can still be friends?

"Wow. That's all I can say. I umm, wow. I thought we had something..." she trailed off, not really knowing what to say.

She wondered where all of this was coming from. For years, well over a decade, Rayna had wanted Malachi Chandler. Now, she had him, and just like that, she was losing him. This was unreal.

"Rayna, it was fun, but we both know that you never wanted me for **me.** You wanted what you could get. You're an opportunist, and I gave you an opportunity. Now, the ride is over. You get to walk away with more than you've ever had."

"What?" Rayna fumed.

She was appalled that Malachi had spoken to her in that manner. She wanted to say something to change his mind. Being a talk show host and owner of one of the busiest television stations in Lake County Indiana, one would think she would never be at a loss for words, but she was.

"So, let me get this right, Malachi, you're leaving me for your ex wife?"

She took another sip of her drink and gave him a look that said, "I dare you to say I'm right," and then threw the drink at him. She missed her intended target, which had been his face. Half of the contents in the glass splattered on his Ralph Lauren shirt. Although it was not his face, she was pleased the drink landed on his shirt. He prided himself on his Ralph Lauren collection, and she had just ruined one of his prized possessions. True, he could get another shirt, but she took pleasure in knowing she would be the cause of him having to replace this particular shirt. This shirt had been ordered off line and not purchased in a department store, so getting it might be impossible.

Malachi gasped as he looked down at his shirt. Shaking his head in disgust, he drew his lips in tightly, released them, raised his hand and hit the table hard.

Finally, he responded, "You know what, Rayna, that was real childish. You only did that shit because you know I won't hit a woman. Just know, if we weren't in this bar I would choke the shit out of you, real talk. I really don't know how I've tolerated you this long. Yep, that's what I'm saying. I'm going back to my family. Like I said, the studio and all that is yours to keep. Look, I gotta run, but here's a couple hundred dollars. Feel free to continue to drink, have dinner or whatever. It's on me and be sure to tip the waitress nicely."

He got up and walked out of Sheffield's and never looked back.

Rayna looked at the four one hundred dollar bills on the table and whispered, "Malachi, you're definitely going to pay in more ways than one."

A tear dropped from her right eye as she raised her near empty wine glass to her lips and contemplated ordering another drink.

Books By This Author

My Love Won't Last Forever: Matrimony Book 1

My Love Won't Last Forever: Chaotic Bliss Book 2

My Love Won't Last Forever: His Wife Book 3

Contradictions

Love of My Life

The Diva's Dating Assessment Guide: Girl, Please

Typical Hood Story: 2 Raw and Uncut Stories-
Ivan Marrick and Nyree Chandler

Crazy Faith Journal- Nicole Bradley

Crazy Faith Anthology- Nicole Bradley

Never Would Have Made It: A Testimony of What
God Has Done In My Life- Nicole Bradley